AN ELEPHANT NEVER FORGETS

Amelia Lionheart

2nd Edition – 2014

Amelia Lionheart
An Elephant Never Forgets
softcover 978-0-9937493-9-1
ebook (mobi) 978-0-9937740-3-4
ebook (epub) 978-0-9937740-4-1

Printing
Minuteman Press (Calgary North), Alberta
Information and Sales: info@mmpresscgy.com
Printed & bound in Canada

The paper used in the publication of this book is from responsible forest
management sources.

Other titles in this series:
Peacock Feathers
The Dolphin Heptad
Can Snow Leopards Roar?
The Humming Grizzly Bear Cubs

To,
Michelle + David,
I hope you enjoy the
Sri Lankan fun!
In conservation,
Lionheart
11 May, 2019

Website: http://www.jeacs.com

Dedicated to my Sri Lankan
family and friends – worldwide

You know who you are!

ACKNOWLEDGEMENTS

Just like the *elephants who never forget*, I, too, want to remember those wonderful friends who continue to take an interest in my books. The community grows! I would first like to thank those who assisted me with the first edition of this book:

Joanne Bennett; Chesalon LLC – Vinodh Gunasekera, Malik Perera, Gihan Liyanage and Emmanuel Timothy; Mary Anna and Warren Harbeck; Alya and Alina Malik; Brayden, Joshua and Amanda Paul; Robin Phillips; Nihal Phillips, Lushanthi Perera and Varini Perera; and Benita Ridout.

An additional thanks to all of you and have helped with the second edition of this book:

Glenn Boyd, for handling the printing of the books and production of all marketing materials in his consistently exceptional and efficient manner;
Michael Hartnett, who continues to provide unfailing know-how, encouragement and marketing ideas;
Sarah Lawrence, for her advice, support and dedication in bringing these new editions, and the new book, to publication;
Elaine Phillips, my cheerful editor, who proofread the pre-print publications, yet again, with joy and enthusiasm;
and last, but not least, **my family and many friends**, for their encouragement and support.

Once more, a simple but heartfelt thank you!

YOU
CAN MAKE A DIFFERENCE

You are UNIQUE! This means YOU have special gifts to help change the world. Talk to your parents about ways in which you can recycle or conserve at home. Ask the wonderful folk at zoos and conservations close to you how you can get involved in all kinds of fun and educational activities. Get your friends and neighbours involved. Look up websites for zoos and wildlife conservations, and check out what's going on around the world!

THEME SONG

Jun-ior Environ-menta-lists and Con-ser-vation-ists!

When we think about our world, all the animals and birds
Who are losing their homes day by day
If each person does their part, it will cheer up every heart
So let's take a stand and act without delay!

We've decided we will strive to keep birds and beasts alive
And to make CONSER-VA-TION our theme
We will talk to all our friends, try to help them understand
That our world must come awake and not just dream!

All the creatures that we love, from the ele-phant to dove,
Must be cared for and well protected, too
So all humans, young and old, have to speak up and be **bold**
Or we'll end up with an 'only human' zoo!

Where environment's concerned, in our studies we have learned
That composting at home can be a start
And recycling's very good, each and every person should
Be aware of how we all can do our part.

To the JEACs we belong, and we hope it won't be long
Till our peers and our friends all will say
They believe that con-ser-vation and environ-menta-lism
Is the only way to save our world today!

Will you come and join our band? Will you lend a helping hand?
Though it's serious, it can be great fun!
Tell your friends about it all, let them join up, big and small
And our fight against destruction will be won!

Jun-ior Environ-menta-lists and Con-ser-vation-ists!

ABOUT THE JEACs

The JEACs (*Junior Environmentalists and Conservationists*), a group created by *Amelia Lionheart* in the first book of her series, attempts to enlighten children – through the means of adventure stories – about conservation and environmental issues. The author is delighted that the JEACs, once only a figment of her imagination, have become a reality in recent years.

The JEACs firmly believe that some of the key factors in **saving our planet** are:

- **P**articipation
- **A**wareness
- **C**o-operation
- **E**ducation

****

JEACs' MISSION STATEMENT AND GOALS

We are an international group of Junior Environmentalists and Conservationists who long to **save our planet** from destruction. We will work towards this by:

- educating ourselves on the importance and necessity:

  o of protecting *all wildlife* – especially endangered species – and the techniques used by conservation groups all over the world to reach this goal;

  o of preventing our *global environment* from further damage, and finding out how we can participate in this endeavour;

- creating awareness of these issues among our peers and by sharing knowledge with them, encouraging more volunteers to join our group;

- becoming members of zoos, conservations and environmental groups in our region, actively participating in events organized by them and, through donations and fundraising efforts, contributing towards their work.

Table of Contents

CHAPTER 1

Travellers from the West

'There it is – look!' cried Gina excitedly, pressing her nose against a window in the airport lounge as she watched the Boeing 747 land gracefully on the runway, slow down, and taxi to its gate. 'I can see the maple leaf on its tail – that has to be the flight from Canada – right, Rohan?'

'Sure is, kiddo,' said her older brother with a smile. 'Okay, folks, let's get to the exit.'

Nimal winked slyly at Anu and said, 'It'll take at least 45 minutes, yaar. They have to collect their baggage and clear customs. After all, it's a jumbo jet and has millions of passengers. What's the hurry?'

'The hurry, old boy,' said Anu, pinching him admonishingly, 'is because we don't want our guests to get there before we do. So move!'

'Is it called a jumbo because it's so humongous?' asked Gina.

'Probably,' said Nimal. 'It's one of the largest planes.'

They made their way to the lounge. The Binjara International Airport, beautifully laid out, was not too crowded on a Thursday morning.

The Patels were eager to meet their friends, Amy and Michelle (known as *Mich* by family and friends) Larkin, again. They had first met in Australia. Jack Larkin, Mich and Amy's uncle, was a close friend of the Patel family and had invited the Patels and his Canadian nieces to Brisbane for their Christmas holidays. He was in the process of setting up a new conservation for sea creatures, with a special focus on dolphins, and wanted to involve the youngsters in the project. The six children hit it off immediately. They spent a wonderful time using their talents, had a superb adventure and, since then, corresponded regularly via email. Now, six months later, they were going to spend another holiday together, on a conservation in Sri Lanka.

The Patels lived on the Patiyak Wildlife Conservation Centre in North India, located a fair distance away from the city of Binjara where the boys, Rohan and Nimal, went to boarding school. Anu and Gina went to a boarding school for girls, in a town called Minar, which was a two-hour train journey from Binjara. Rohan, Anu and Gina's father, Jim Patel, was the manager of the Conservation.

Nimal, their cousin, had lived with them from the age of three since his father, Greg Patel – Jim's brother – was a renowned computer consultant and travelled internationally on business, accompanied by his wife. Their home base was also on the Conservation.

The Larkin girls lived in Canada, on the Manipau Wildlife Conservation Centre, where their father was the manager. The girls went to a boarding school in the city of Wasanda – about 600 kilometres away from their home.

'When will they come out?' moaned Gina, climbing down from a chair. 'I'm *sure* they've been in there for hours. And I can't see a thing, even when I stand on a chair.' She was nine years old, four foot seven inches tall, and impatient to meet her friends.

'Patience, kiddo,' grinned Rohan, rising hurriedly to rescue the little girl from being run over by a train of trolleys. He picked her up and put her on his shoulders. 'Now can you see?'

'Oh, yes, thanks, Rohan,' crowed Gina happily. 'I'm taller than everyone else now!'

'Yeah, you're a giantess,' said Anu, smiling at her. 'What can you see?'

'Nobody's coming out yet.'

'Give them a few more minutes,' said Nimal, 'and then, I'm sure, they'll be the first ones out.'

After ten minutes had dragged by, Rohan said, 'I think people are coming out now.'

Anu and Nimal rose quickly as Gina squealed, 'There they are!'

'Where?' said Nimal.

'Look – oh – they're hidden behind that big lady in the pink sari.'

'Okay, I see them, too,' said Rohan.

'They're here! They're here!' chanted Gina happily, as they all waved madly.

Amy and Mich saw the group and waved back; a few minutes later, there was a joyous reunion.

'Oh! It's superfab to see you all again,' cried Amy, as she hugged and kissed each of them exuberantly.

'Mich, you've grown so tall and fat,' grunted Nimal, picking up the little girl who was the same age as Gina, and giving her a big hug.

'I'm *not* fat! I've only grown taller,' said Mich with a giggle, hugging him back. She was as skinny and wiry as Gina was, though an inch and a half taller.

'Gee whizz! You guys have certainly shot up since we saw you in December. What *have* you been eating?' teased Amy, standing arm in arm with Anu and looking at the boys in mock admiration. 'Or have you been on the rack again?'

'You know teenage boys grow like weeds,' said Nimal. 'But you and Anu are the same height now.'

'Nimal's five foot eight and a half inches, while Rohan's a couple of inches taller,' said Anu with a grin. 'I haven't grown at all, still the same old five foot four inches, so maybe I've stopped.'

'Well, you're only fourteen, Anu; you still have time to grow a bit taller,' said Amy, who was a year older. 'As for you, Rohan, your voice has changed and you look about nineteen even though we're the same age.'

'He's still a kid at heart though,' said Nimal cheekily, before his cousin could say a word. 'Yearns for his fluffy toys, crayons, bucket and spade.'

He ducked out of reach as Rohan swung a mock karate punch at him.

'Luckily *my* voice broke during school term,' retaliated Rohan, whose voice was now a deep bass. 'Most of my classmates were at the same stage, so I didn't get ragged too much. However, dear Nimal has started becoming a bit falsetto now and then. He's got a wide range – can sing soprano, alto or baritone.'

'Yeah, I take the high road and he takes the low road, for now,' said Nimal, not a whit abashed. 'But, I doubt I'll take as low a road as he does.'

'Rohan's voice seems to come up from his boots,' laughed Anu. 'And, since school only broke up yesterday, we haven't had a chance to see if he can still sing in harmony. Plus, we were too excited at the prospect of meeting you to do anything but reminisce about our holiday together.'

'Where's Hunter?' asked Mich.

'At the hotel,' said Nimal. 'We weren't allowed to bring him here to meet you.'

'Right, let's get back to the hotel,' suggested Rohan. 'You girls look pale – you must be exhausted.'

'I guess it'll catch up with us,' confessed Amy, 'but at the moment, I'm so thrilled that I don't feel tired at all.'

'Let's go, folks,' said Nimal, taking over the luggage trolley, and in a short time they were driving out of the airport, seated comfortably in the mini van belonging to the hotel.

'Whereabouts is your school, guys?' asked Amy.

'A short drive from the hotel, and if you're not too tired this evening, we'll take you there,' said Rohan.

'Great,' said Amy. 'I'm sure we'll be okay. The flight wasn't full so we stretched out on the seats and got lots of sleep. What's the programme for today?'

'We've been invited out to dinner,' said Anu.

'By whom?' asked Amy.

'Mr. and Mrs. Ghosh, Umedh's parents,' said Rohan. 'He's my best friend and is in my class – nice chap.'

'Is he the same guy you mention in your emails?' asked Amy.

'Yeah,' said Rohan.

'Will they g-g-give us Indian food?' asked Mich, trying to stifle a yawn. 'We've been longing to have some *real* curries.'

'Yeah, they will, Mich,' said Gina. 'They asked Rohan and he told them you loved Indian food.'

'I think,' said Anu, 'we should grab a quick lunch and then let the two of you rest. After all, we don't want you burnt out at the beginning of our hols – do we?'

'Great idea, Anu,' said Rohan. 'We'll wake you around 4 p.m. It's nearly 11:30 now, and we'll be at the hotel shortly.'

Upon reaching the Shah Jehan Hotel, they thanked the driver, got out of the van, and collected their room keys from the reception desk.

'Where's Hunter?' asked Mich.

'He should be back any minute,' said the receptionist. 'One of our staff took him for a walk. What a well-behaved dog he is.'

Just then, Gina squealed, 'I can hear his bark. He must be close.'

She and Mich ran to the door and, sure enough, there was Hunter – a sleek, jet-black Alsatian dog, his long tail wagging crazily. He barked joyfully and bounded up to the girls who fell on their knees, hugging and kissing him, Mich getting her face well-licked as Hunter, recognizing a friend, welcomed her boisterously.

The others surrounded the dog, and Hunter fawned over Amy, too.

'Together again. The infamous gang,' said Rohan with a laugh. 'Okay, you licky, sticky crowd, let's go to our rooms.'

They took the lift to the ninth floor, put the suitcases in the girls' room – which was large enough to hold all four of them – and went through the connecting door, to the boys' room.

After quick calls to the Larkin and Patel parents, informing them that the girls had arrived safely, Rohan looked around the group with a grin and said, 'Well, JEACs – what's next on the agenda?'

'Food! Glori-ous food!' croaked Nimal, as his voice cracked right in the middle of his chant. 'What a question. I'm simply . . .'

'STARVING!' yelled the others.

'True, mes amis – I'm a growing boy, I am,' he said with a chuckle. He grabbed Gina, who was so excited that she was bouncing on Rohan's bed, seated her on the carpet next to Mich, and continued, 'Now, Mich and Amy – what would you like to eat?'

'We're easy,' said Amy. 'Why don't you order something while Mich and I have a quick wash.'

'How about Chinese food, since we'll be having Indian tonight?' said Anu.

'Scrumptious,' said Amy. 'We love Chinese food, too.'

'Okay, aunties,' said Nimal, bowing low. Mich and Gina promptly jumped on his back. 'Now,' he continued, standing up and carrying them into the girls' room and tumbling them on to a bed, 'if you will be kind enough to keep these two little hooligans in here, we *men* will order the meal.'

He stalked out haughtily, followed by shrieks of laughter from the girls who found his cracking voice hilarious.

'And,' he added, poking his head into their room for a moment, and speaking in a high falsetto, 'if the two li'l chidums not be'ave, I make big, black dog eat 'em.'

He closed the door and the boys ordered a feast, not forgetting Hunter who was listening hungrily. Half an hour later, they were tucking into a delicious meal.

'What are the plans for tomorrow?' asked Amy.

'We have to be at the airport by 11 a.m., which means we leave here at 10:30. Our flight takes off at 1 o'clock and we should reach Sri Lanka around 6 p.m.,' said Rohan.

'That's only a five-hour flight then,' said Amy.

'Four hours, 45 minutes of flying time,' said Nimal. 'Lalith and Priyani Vijaydasa will pick us up at the airport and take us to some relative's place for the night. We leave for Alighasa Wildlife Conservation Centre the next morning.'

'Wasn't it super that the Vijaydasas, when we met them in Australia last year, invited us to spend our summer hols in Sri Lanka – at their Conservation?' said Anu. 'I really liked them. Also, Sanjay Almeida, who used to work at our Conservation, is now working at Alighasa. His mom's Sri Lankan and he's Priyani's second cousin, and he wanted to live in Sri Lanka for a few years and get to know that side of his family.'

'Yeah, it'll be great to see him again,' said Nimal.

'We're going to have a blast,' said Rohan. 'I don't know the details, but while we're there, they're going to relocate some animals. There's also a big fundraiser.'

'Such luck,' said Nimal. 'And guess what I discovered? In one of the languages of Sri Lanka, which is Sinhala, *aliya* means elephant, and the Conservation is named *Alighasa* because it has many elephants. It should be *tons* of fun.'

'Will there be baby *ephalunts*?' asked Mich, using the JEACs' favourite mispronunciation of the word elephant. 'I would love to play with some.'

'Me, too,' said Gina.

'I'm sure there'll be a few infants,' said Nimal.

By the time the meal was finished, Mich was yawning widely and trying to cover it up.

'Time for bed, I think,' said Amy, looking at her sister. 'Gina, honey, are you going to have a nap, too?'

'Yes, a short one,' said Gina.

'But, what about the things we g-got them?' asked Mich sleepily.

'We'll do that when we're wide awake, chicken,' said Amy.

'That's sweet of you girls,' said Anu. 'Actually, we've got some things for you, too. They're not only from us, but also from some of the others at the Conservation.'

'Oh, that's so kind,' said Amy, touched by the generosity of people she had never met. 'We have some things for all your parents, too, and, of course, for people in Sri Lanka. We'll fish them out later.'

The two younger girls went to bed and fell asleep quickly.

'It's grand to have both of you here,' said Rohan to Amy. 'I just wish we could have taken you to our Conservation this time.'

'I guess it'll have to be next time around, but it is *super* to be together again. I miss all of you very much,' said Amy. 'It's nice to be in touch with you and Anu, Rohan, and the occasional, *very rare*, note from you, Nimal. Thank goodness for email.'

'Sorry, Amy,' began Nimal apologetically. 'I confess, I don't write a lot of letters . . .'

'*Lot* of letters?' queried Anu.

'Well, I mean, not very often . . .'

'*Often*?' interrupted Rohan.

'Okay, so I guess I rarely write,' said Nimal, grimacing at Amy. 'But, I figured that since you, Anu and Rohan were in touch almost daily, and Mich and Gina wrote once a week, there would be nothing left for me to say – given your verbosity. And you know me, strong, silent chap that I am.'

'Not *that* silent,' chuckled Rohan. 'He can carry on for an hour or more when he has the floor.'

'Hmmm, yeah,' said Amy, smiling wickedly at Nimal. 'A little bird told me about the last meeting when you tried to convince some chaps to join the JEACs. If I remember correctly, two went to sleep and the other five agreed to join up if you would just shut up talking.'

'Yeah, that was a good one,' said Nimal with a chuckle. 'I'll never forget how Arvind's snore suddenly turned into a loud snort and everybody jumped in fright. They had slumped into torpor. Who told you about it? Rohan?'

'No – Anu. She made such a good story of it that we nearly died laughing,' said Amy. 'I repeated the story to some of my school friends and they're all dying to meet you. Shall I give them your email address?'

'Hey, no way,' said Nimal hastily, his voice rising squeakily. 'You know *my* letter writing skills.'

'Okay. Gee, I'm tired now,' said Amy, yawning suddenly. 'Sorry, folks, but I guess I'd better have a rest. What will the three of you do?'

'I'm going downstairs to do some writing,' said Anu. 'They have a computer which guests can use.'

'Editing *Peacock Feathers*?'

Anu nodded. Her story related the adventure the four Patels and Hunter had had, the previous summer, on the Patiyak Wildlife Conservation.

'That's fantastic, Anu,' said Amy who was very proud of her friend's writing. 'And what are you boys going to do?'

'Play some tennis, work out at the gym and then dress for the evening,' said Rohan. 'We knew you'd be tired, so we decided to be nice, and leave you alone this afternoon.'

'But *only* this afternoon, mind,' said Nimal. 'After that you'll have to tolerate us constantly. We won't let you out of our sight.'

'No problemo, amigo mio. See you in a bit.'

Soon there was total silence in the bedrooms. Amy, Mich and Gina were fast asleep; the boys took Hunter with them and dropped Anu off at the hotel office for guests, where she was soon in another world.

CHAPTER 2

Growing Up Is Hard To Do

Some hours later Rohan heard a soft knock on their door. 'Come in,' he said.

Gina poked her head into their room, looking owlish. She had just woken up.

'Hey, kiddo,' said Rohan, 'Come on in. Are the other two still asleep?'

'Like logs,' said Gina shutting the connecting door. 'You're already dressed. Where's Nimal?'

'Giving his hair the finishing touches,' whispered Rohan, nodding towards the bathroom. 'I think one bottle of gel was insufficient.'

As they were chuckling, the bathroom door opened, and they turned to stare at Nimal who was looking very natty in a light blue T-shirt and navy trousers, his hair lying flat on his head and not standing up as it usually did.

'Wow, Nimal!' exclaimed Gina. 'You look really, er, really, um, *cool.*'

'Thank you, mon enfant,' said Nimal, with a grin. 'I'm glad you approve.'

'I'm not sure the others will *recognize* you,' continued Gina cheekily. 'I've *never* seen you like this before.'

'And perhaps you never will again,' said Nimal loftily. 'So feast your eyes on this thing of beauty. But, for this evening, if you will strive to look gorgeous, I may deign to take some notice of you.'

'Oh, blow! He's got verbal diarrhoea, Gina,' said Rohan. 'It's the hairdo. Quick, let's destroy it.'

They advanced threateningly on Nimal. 'I'll shut up. No rough-housing. You'll make a noise and wake the two sleeping beauties,' he pleaded, backing towards the door.

Gina giggled and promised to desist. 'Where's Anu?' she asked, cuddling Hunter.

'Lost in her world of words,' said Rohan, looking at his watch. 'We'd better fish her out.'

'Yeah. Gina, you can use our bathroom, and I'll help you iron your clothes before I fetch Anu,' said Nimal.

'*I'll* get Anu,' said Rohan. 'If you go on your own, Nimal, the hotel staff will die of fright.'

He ducked Nimal's karate punch, and left the room.

'Anu? It's 3:30,' he said, entering the room where Anu was busy at the computer. 'Sorry, sis, I didn't mean to make you jump.'

Anu looked around and grinned. 'No problemo.'

'How's it going?' asked Rohan.

'I've edited four chapters so far. Boy, editing a book is time-consuming, though absolutely critical,' said Anu. 'Let me just save this draft. You look spiffy – that green T-shirt suits you.'

'Thanks,' said Rohan with a grin.

Anu packed reference books, papers, discs and pencils into her writing case, while Rohan tidied the room. She had a tendency to spread her things all over the place when she was in the throes of writing, and her room generally looked as if a cyclone had hit it.

They went upstairs to find Gina already dressed.

'Good grief, Nimal!' exclaimed Anu, spotting him. 'I mean, er you . . . you . . . er . . . you *do* look nice,' she concluded lamely.

'Nimal blushed in embarrassment,' said Rohan mischievously, pretending to read from a book, 'Look,' he mumbled, 'it's only my hair after all. The gel didn't work so I was compelled to use *glue*. But it was only one bottle!' Rohan trailed off as the others collapsed with laughter.

'Perhaps *you* should be writing books, too, Rohan,' said Nimal, slightly pink in the face, but taking their ragging in his usual good-humoured way. 'I just thought I should try and look a bit decent for a change.'

'You *always* look nice, Nimal,' said Gina earnestly. 'I feel very proud when I go out with you and Rohan, because you're both so handsome.'

'I'm touched, Gina,' said Nimal, giving the little girl an affectionate hug.

'I agree, and I must say your slightly longer hair, compared to your usual crew cut, suits you,' said Anu, smiling at him. She turned to

Rohan and continued, 'By the way, bro, is Darini going to be at Umedh's this evening?'

Rohan winked slyly. 'I hope so, sis, otherwise – *what* a waste of glue!' He ducked as Nimal threw another punch at him, and continued, 'Do you want to use our bathroom, too?'

Anu dressed quickly and they had just laid out their gifts when Amy and Mich joined them.

'Oooh, Nimal,' said Mich staring at him, 'you . . . er . . . look . . . um . . . v-very d-different.'

'And extremely handsome,' added Amy hastily, trying to keep a straight face.

'Gee whizz, as you girls would say,' said Nimal. 'I hope all this stammering and stuttering means something good, Mich. I was just trying to tame my hair – for *your* sakes – and, since the rest of you always look stunning, I figured I should try not to look like something Hunter had dragged in backwards through a hedge.'

Amy smiled knowingly at Anu. Personally, she thought Rohan and Nimal were two of the handsomest boys she knew – with their sharp features, dark brown eyes, light brown skin and athletic builds. No, she certainly had no objection to hanging out with *them*. And to add to that, they were decent guys.

The Larkin girls looked refreshed. They brought out their gifts for the Patels, including Hunter, and there were exclamations of delight, hugs and thank yous. Hunter enjoyed tearing open his gift from Canada – a humongous bone – and immediately started chewing on it.

'Now, what would you like to do?' asked Rohan, after Nimal's parents had called to welcome the Larkins. 'We don't have to be at Umedh's till 7 o'clock, so we've got a couple of hours.'

'I'd love to catch up on news,' said Amy.

'Sounds great,' said Anu. 'We'll order something to drink and have a good old chin wag.'

Gina and Mich went to the other room to examine their gifts, chattering nineteen to the dozen. They loved being together and, although they did most things with their siblings and never felt left out, being nine years old, they had their own interests.

Both girls had short curly hair, Mich's ash-blonde and Gina's jet-black. They were excellent gymnasts, and although neither excelled at academic studies, Gina was in a fair way to being a musical genius with a talent for writing verse and music, while Mich's art, especially in the form of cartoons, was developed far beyond her age.

The teens, meantime, caught up on more detailed news than emails allowed for during term.

'After meeting you folks last winter, I realized that if I wanted to specialize in Dolphin and Human Therapy, I would have to study really hard,' said Amy. 'So I haven't had much free time – kept my nose to the grindstone.'

'Me, too – did it pay off?' asked Nimal.

'Sure did. I actually managed to get 80s for a change. What about you?'

'I was okay, too.' Nimal had a good brain – when he chose to use it.

'Gee, that's swell,' said Amy. 'Maybe, one day, we'll reach the academic levels that these two attain so easily.'

'Yup, and, needless to say, they got top marks,' said Nimal.

Anu chuckled and said, a naughty gleam in her eyes, 'There's no doubt we're a brilliant bunch, and far too good to be true.'

'Oh, definitely,' agreed Rohan and Amy.

'My head's so swollen with pride that I won't be able to get through the door,' added Rohan.

'Mine, too,' grinned Amy. 'Don't you agree we're perfect, Nimal?'

'Nope. Not as long as we remember our zillions of faults,' said Nimal, gloomily. 'I may have done well *academically*, but I got a *C* for conduct.'

'What happened?' asked Amy eagerly, since Nimal's tales of woe inevitably stemmed from humorous incidents.

'It was all the fault of that dratted mouse . . .' began Nimal. A knock on the door, heralding the arrival of a waiter with juice and biscuits, interrupted him.

Gina and Mich joined the teens, and once everyone was served, Amy said, 'Please continue, Nimal – he was just going to explain why he got a C for conduct,' she continued, turning to the younger girls.

'What happened, Nimal?' asked Mich, who loved hearing about the crazy things he did.

'Anu, you tell the tale – you're our storyteller,' said Nimal.

'No problemo,' said Anu with a grin. 'Let's start with Nimal's complaint that "It was all the fault of that dratted mouse." It was a Saturday and the karate students were finishing a class. Suddenly, there was a loud scream from upstairs, something fell with a tremendous crash, and then there was the unmistakable sound of a maid having hysterics.

'Naturally, the whole class charged upstairs. Umedh, Nimal and Rohan, among the first to reach the scene, found water flooding the area, the cleaning cart overturned, and the maid drumming her heels and screeching fit to wake the dead.

'The karate instructor dealt with the maid first and sent one of the boys to summon the matron, while others sorted out the cart. Then Nimal spotted the cause of all the trouble. Cowering fearfully in the furthermost corner of the room was a *tiny dormouse*. It had, somehow, got into the cleaning cart, and the maid, seeing it suddenly poke its little head out from among her mops and brooms, had taken fright – to say the least.

'The dormouse, mimicking her, decided to have its own brand of hysterics, and was chittering in fear. Some of the boys tried to catch it, but it scampered all over the place – poor thing – it was terrified! Nimal yelled to the others to back off. By then the maid had been escorted out of the room by the matron, and our hero sat down a little distance away from the dormouse and started charming it out of its fear. Well, you know what animals are like with him. In a few minutes the dormouse crept into his hands, and Nimal was able to pet and soothe it into calmness.'

'Oh, I wish I had seen it,' said Mich, who, like the others, loved watching the way animals responded to Nimal.

'So what happened then?' asked Amy. 'I should have thought you'd get an A for conduct, as a reward for your act of . . . er . . . *heroism*.'

Anu chuckled and continued. 'It would have been fine if Nimal had just let the dormouse out into the garden. But, you know the lad, he fell in love with it and they formed an MAS – sorry, a *Mutual Admiration Society*. It lived in his pocket for two days and became very tame, losing all fear of the boys since they spoilt it, too.

'On Monday evening, during prep, the dormouse decided to become *The Brave Exploring Mouse* and ventured out of Nimal's pocket. Unfortunately, Miss Grouchy – that's what they call one of their teachers – was taking prep that night, and was busy marking exam papers at the same time. She happened to be wearing a long, heavy skirt, which swept the floor.

'The BEM reached the skirt, found it was an easy climb and scooted up – undoubtedly seeking adventure. He reached Miss Grouchy's lap safely, and from there to the table was a small leap, which the BEM made with ease. Miss Grouchy, engrossed in her exam papers, did not even see him till the mouse, by now used to lots of attention and food, wondered if her pen was edible and crept right on to the paper she was correcting.

'That was the beginning of the end. The BEM and Miss Grouchy stared at each other for a split second before pandemonium broke out. Miss Grouchy knew exactly whom the mouse belonged to, and once she had finished her diatribe at Nimal, she ordered him to get rid of it *immediately*, informing him that she would deal with him later.'

'And, as a direct result of the BEM's behaviour, *I* was given a C for conduct unbecoming in a student, and all that hogwash,' concluded Nimal woefully. 'Plus, I had to put poor old BEM out into the garden.'

The others howled with laughter.

'Yeah,' gasped Rohan, 'and now the BEM has his own little family, and the whole lot come out to greet Nimal with joy, whenever he visits them.'

'What fun you guys have,' said Amy enviously, wiping away tears of mirth.

'Gosh, time to go,' said Rohan, looking at his watch. 'We want to take you via our school.'

Soon they were driving through the city towards the school, Hunter sticking his head out of a window and enjoying the breeze in his face.

'Gee, there's a lot of poverty here – in the midst of these huge homes,' said Amy, looking stunned. 'It's . . . quite a shock. How do you handle it?'

'Not easily,' said Anu, compassionately. 'In our own neighbourhood, our parents work with our church and community centres, and we're encouraged to share as much as possible. Unfortunately, it's more complex than just giving money, and the government has put some programmes in place. I know it's rather a shock seeing it for the first time.'

'I guess, despite TV programmes which give us glimpses of the reality in other parts of the world, until you actually *visit* a developing country, your mind doesn't quite take it in,' said Amy.

'We'll discuss it, in detail, after our trip to Sri Lanka,' suggested Rohan, seeing that she was very disturbed. 'From what we've heard, they have a great deal of poverty, too.'

'Yeah, we try to be extremely grateful for what we have and lend a hand as much as possible,' said Nimal, seriously.

The car moved on and they soon turned in at the gates of the school.

'Here we are! The seat of learning honoured by the presence of two brilliant chaps like us,' said Nimal, attempting to lighten the atmosphere.

'Wow! It's huge,' said Mich, looking with awe at the number of buildings and the acres of grounds.

'We have 1,200 boarders and there are over 3,000 students in total,' said Rohan. 'There are lots of buildings and, of course, the various games fields and stadiums take up tons of space.'

'Which is something India, like Canada, has in abundance – space,' said Anu.

'Impressive,' said the Larkin girls.

'Is it very expensive to attend?' asked Amy thoughtfully.

'Actually, our parents chose this school, above others, for some important reasons,' explained Rohan. 'It was founded by an English Christian missionary about 100 years ago, and we have scholarships which enable some of the poorer families to send their sons to a good school; each family who can afford to do so – like ours – contributes towards those scholarships. Our school is also very involved in church and community programmes and each student is required to contribute both time and money. There's no snobbery allowed here.'

'I *really* like that,' said Amy, and Mich agreed.

They drove around the school and then headed back towards the city. Turning off into a residential area, they stopped outside a red brick house with a beautifully tended garden.

'What do we call Umedh's parents?' asked Amy. 'People are more formal here compared to Canada, aren't they?'

'That's right – Mr. and Mrs. Ghosh will be appropriate,' said Anu. She carried a bouquet of flowers and gave Amy the basket of fruit they had brought for their hosts.

They walked up the path to the house, but before they could ring the bell, the door opened and a cheery voice greeted them.

'Rohan! Nimal! Good to see you. Come on in. Yes, you as well, Hunter.'

Introductions were made and Umedh said, 'Great meeting you ladies at last. I've heard so much about you.'

Gina and Mich gazed up at Umedh and, in the forthright, honest way most young children have, exclaimed together, 'What happened to your right eye, Umedh?'

'I was born like this,' said Umedh, quite unembarrassed by the question.

'Oh! Does it hurt?' asked Gina, sympathetically.

'Not at all, Gina.'

'Doesn't it open?' asked Mich.

'No, it stays closed.'

'But can you see okay?' asked Gina.

'No problemo, kiddo,' said Umedh. 'I can see, very clearly, that you two are the most beautiful young ladies I have *ever* met. Now, come with me. Mum, Dad – they're here.'

They giggled and hung on his arms as he led everyone into a cosy living room/library, where Mr. and Mrs. Ghosh welcomed them warmly.

Umedh, the same age as Rohan, was brilliant at inventing all kinds of things, both electronic and otherwise, and his ambition was to be a computer engineer. He was five foot nine and a half inches tall, had an athletic build and was very sophisticated for his age since he had travelled widely in both the United Kingdom and the United States, visiting relatives. Like his friends, he was an eager conservationist and had been the first in their school to join the JEACs.

Mr. and Mrs. Ghosh had planned a pleasant evening: Gina and Mich were soon involved in a board game; the cook spoilt Hunter; and the teens chatted together. After listening to the others for a few minutes, Anu wandered over to check out the books, which crammed the floor-to-ceiling shelves.

Umedh, at Amy's request, pulled out a photograph album.

'Hey, isn't that Helen MacDonald, whom we met in Australia?' said Amy, pointing at a picture of a wedding party.

'Yes, it is,' said Umedh. 'How do . . . oh, of course! You met her at the conservation in Australia. She's my aunt by marriage now.'

'But when we met her, she didn't mention you, yaar,' said Nimal.

'And you didn't say anything to me, either,' said Rohan.

'Helen only became my aunt in March this year,' said Umedh.

'Right. I remember you mentioned a family wedding during our midterm hols,' said Rohan, 'but I didn't realize . . .'

'It was sudden – one of those super-speedy romances,' explained Umedh, grinning widely. 'I meant to mention that Helen was now my aunt, but it completely slipped my mind, yaar.'

'No problemo, man,' said Rohan with a chuckle.

'How *could* you forget something like that?' began Amy and then laughed. 'I guess it's a typically *male thing*. Girls would never forget to tell each other news of that kind. So, what's the story?'

'Jay, Mum's youngest sister, is my favourite aunt. She's not much older than I am, so when I reached my teens, and grew taller than her, she asked me to drop the "aunty". You chaps met her once.' The boys nodded and Umedh continued, 'Jay's always been crazy about fundraising for animal conservations. In February of this year, she attended a conference, met Dan MacDonald from Scotland, and they fell in love at first sight. They got married a month later. Mum, Dad and I attended the wedding; and Helen, Dan's only sibling, came, too.'

'Wow! How romantic,' sighed Amy. 'Where do they live now?'

'Scotland – Dan manages a conservation in the Cairngorm mountain range,' said Umedh, 'and Jay's in charge of the fundraising.'

'Small world,' said Rohan.

As Rohan and Amy continued to pore over the pictures, Umedh said to Nimal, in a low voice, 'Your cousin's really pretty. Does she have a boyfriend?'

'*What*? Hey, back off, man – she's like my sister,' began Nimal protectively. Seeing that Umedh was smiling understandingly, he calmed down and grinned back, saying, 'Anyway . . . what's with *you*, yaar? You're usually attracted to computers and gadgets, not girls.'

'She's quite – er – unusual – no offence,' said Umedh, looking at Anu admiringly. 'You *know* I wouldn't do anything to hurt her.'

'Sorry, yaar. Of course I know you wouldn't mess around – you just took me by surprise,' said Nimal. 'But she's far too young for things like that and, in any case, she's like you and your inventions – not yet interested in the opposite sex and totally into her writing and books.'

'You know I'm a confirmed book-a-holic, too, yaar, and I thought she was the same age as you – fourteen,' said Umedh.

'Oh, yeah, you're right – though she's a few months younger,' said Nimal.

'Would you and Rohan object to my becoming her friend?' asked Umedh.

'Guess not,' said Nimal slowly. 'Rohan would be thrilled if she liked you, and naturally, I'd be glad, too. No offence, yaar.'

'None taken – thanks, yaar,' said Umedh, and immediately strolled over to where Anu was looking at a book on conservation.

Nimal joined Rohan and Amy on the sofa, muttering under his breath, 'Guess who's fallen flat on his face?' He nodded over towards the bookshelves and they saw Umedh and Anu deep in conversation about the book.

'Another one bites the dust,' said Rohan with a grin. 'At least we won't have to frighten this one off, whether anything comes of it or not. He's a decent chap.'

'We can have some fun . . .' began Nimal with a mischievous chuckle.

'Now, boys, promise you won't rag her just yet, okay?' said Amy hastily. 'You know she's pretty naive about things like that, and Umedh seems like the perfect guy for her. Good thing he's your buddy – I know how protective you get when guys hover around your sisters.'

'We promise,' said Nimal, and Rohan nodded. 'And, don't forget, you and Mich are part of our family, too, and we'll get *protective* in a hurry if we see any no-gooders around you.'

Amy smiled, but before she could retaliate, the doorbell rang and Mrs. Ghosh ushered in a beautiful girl. She was five foot six inches tall, with a good figure, and her jet-black hair was twisted up into a sophisticated hairstyle. Her sparkling, doe-shaped eyes, set in an oval face, took in the room at a glance, lingering on Rohan and Nimal, who stood up politely. Anu and Umedh joined the others, and Mrs. Ghosh made the introductions.

'This is my niece, Darini,' said Mrs. Ghosh. 'You boys have met her a couple of times, but the girls have not.

Amy, Anu, Rohan and Umedh glanced at Nimal and hid their grins. He was smoothing down his hair and had turned pale. Darini walked across the room, and Nimal, moving quickly to offer her his seat, tripped over a small stool and turned red with embarrassment.

'Darini,' said Amy quickly, coming to his rescue, 'I hear that you want to work with orphans.'

'Oh, that was months ago,' said Darini, tossing her hair. 'I'm going to be an actress. *Everyone* tells me that with my looks and figure, I should start with modelling and then move on to Bollywood.'

'B-but, y-you s-seemed so eager to work with the o-orphanages,' stammered Nimal.

'That was *before* I spoke to this guy who's in films,' said Darini. 'I met him recently, and he's going to put me in touch with an agent who represents models.'

She carried on in this vein until Mrs. Ghosh announced dinner, and they all moved into the dining room.

'Wow! She has a mighty high opinion of herself. Get a load of that *vitamin I*,' whispered Amy. 'What *does* Nimal see in her?'

'He looks rather stunned, and I think his crush is fading fast – poor chap,' said Anu.

In the dining room, Darini, smiling sweetly, prevented Amy from sitting between Rohan and Nimal and did so herself, talking ceaselessly about her aspirations, and how beautiful everybody told her she was – she was clearly not interested in anything, or anyone, else.

They had a delicious meal and, since Mr. and Mrs. Ghosh knew that the Larkin girls had only arrived that morning and that the group was leaving for Sri Lanka the next day, they did not press them to stay late, although Umedh was reluctant to let them go. Darini was staying over. Nimal found Hunter and put him in the car.

'Can I keep in touch with you via email, Anu?' asked Umedh.

'Sure,' said Anu. 'Rohan will give you my address. I enjoyed our discussion, and your stories about the Durrell Wildlife Conservation Trust were fascinating. I would love to hear more.'

Rohan bit back a smile – his friend was going to rave about this. He suddenly had an idea. 'By the way, yaar,' he said, 'why don't you join us in Sri Lanka? I know you're starting a computer course tomorrow, but what about later? You could come in time for the relocation of the animals and the fundraiser – take the same flight as Dad and Uncle Jack.'

'*You have to come! You have to come!*' shrieked Gina and Mich, hanging on the boy's arms and dancing around him.

Umedh's eyes lit up and he looked at his parents eagerly – they nodded approval.

'Yippee!' yelled Mich and Gina, exuberantly.

'Guess I have no choice,' laughed Umedh. 'That would be superfab. But won't your hosts mind?'

'I doubt it – they said they had lots of room. We'll work something out and let you know,' said Rohan.

'It would be great if you came, Umedh,' said Amy.

'Yes, and, after all, you're a JEAC, too,' said Anu.

'I owe you big time, yaar,' muttered Umedh, as he shook hands with Rohan.

They thanked Mr. and Mrs. Ghosh for the delightful evening, said goodbye to Darini, and drove off. It was past 10 o'clock, and the younger girls fell asleep in the car, so the boys carried them to their rooms where Anu and Amy put them to bed.

'Feel like a drink before you turn in?' asked Rohan, as Amy and Anu came into their room.

'Sounds good,' said Anu, curling up on one of the beds. 'How about hot chocolate?'

'I'll order some with marshmallows,' said Nimal, picking up the telephone and placing the order.

'Aren't *we* confident and grown-up over the phone these days,' said Rohan teasingly, trying to get a rise out of Nimal who had been unusually quiet.

'I guess we all have to grow up at some stage, yaar,' said Nimal, sighing deeply as he sank into a chair beside Amy.

'You're okay, buddy,' said Amy. 'What do you say, Anu? Wouldn't you say he was the nicest of guys?'

'Of course, I would, naturally – Nimal and Rohan are the best,' said Anu warmly.

'Whoa! I think she's fading, Amy,' said Rohan. 'She'd *never* admit that unless she was under the strong influence of sleep. Ah, here's the hot chocolate. Perhaps that'll wake her.'

'Guess people change,' said Nimal thoughtfully. 'But I thought she was different – my crush is crushed, yaar,' he continued, turning to Rohan. 'You won't have to listen to me singing Darini's praises any more.'

Rohan gave him an affectionate punch on the arm.

'We all go through it, Nimal,' said Amy. 'Nice girl, absolutely gorgeous, but definitely not your type.'

Nimal grinned sheepishly, shook himself like a dog, tousled his hair, and said, 'Growing up is okay, but it's a painful process – I'm putting it off for now. Back to my crew cut tomorrow. Making friends with animals is safer by far.'

The others laughed, and Anu said thoughtfully, 'I think it's great to have good friends, of both sexes. Like this evening – I had a super time.'

'I like Umedh a lot,' said Amy, 'and admire the way he's so comfortable talking about his eye.'

'Yeah. Although we've known him for years, and he's visited Patiyak, the boys usually hung out together, and I've never really talked to him. I enjoyed talking with him today, and I'm glad we're going to be email buddies – I've never had a male buddy before,' said Anu. 'It'll be fun when he joins us in Sri Lanka.'

The others were silent for a moment, knowing that Anu, while sensitive to other people's emotions, was surprisingly naive when it came to boys who were interested in her. Amy, streets ahead of her, was beginning to chat with Anu about things like that.

Rohan said, carefully, 'Yeah, sis, I agree. He's a *super* chap. After all, he's my best friend – what else could you expect?'

The serious discussion ended in laughter. They sipped their hot chocolate and the conversation turned to their Australian friends.

'Wasn't it super to hear about Mike and Monique's engagement?' said Amy, sighing romantically. 'They make such a perfect couple.'

'Thrilling – November wedding,' said Anu. 'And, for their honeymoon, they'll go to Canada, France, Scotland, the Channel Islands, and end up here. Peter's going over to be best man.'

'I can't wait to see them,' agreed Amy, stifling a yawn. 'Oooh – time for beddie-byes, folks. What time do we need to be up tomorrow?'

'Eight or 8:30 will do,' said Rohan. 'We have to leave at 10:30.'

'Okay, goodnight, boys,' chorused the girls, giving Hunter a final kiss; and soon there was nothing to be heard in either room except for deep breathing and Hunter's occasional snorts in his dreams.

CHAPTER 3

Aliyas

Anu knocked on the door of the boys' room and Nimal opened it.

'Gosh, since when have you been awake?' she said. 'It's only 7 a.m. You're both dressed *and* you've had a haircut, Nimal. Oh, good morning, Hunter,' she added, hugging the dog who jumped up at her.

'Since five,' said Nimal. 'We've been to the gym, taken Hunter for a run, and have even had a first brekker. Are the others still asleep?'

'Yeah,' said Anu. 'But I'm wide awake and dying for some juice. Is it okay to get room service this early?'

'No problemo, sis,' said Rohan cheerfully. 'I'll order some. The Larkins must have been pretty zonked – we'll give them till 8:30.'

'Yeah – and I'll dress in here.'

'Good idea,' said Nimal. 'Do you want us to vamoose so you can use the bedroom?'

'No, thanks, the bathroom's fine.'

She dressed, and the three of them were enjoying fresh juice when there was another knock on the door.

'We're decent, come on in,' said Nimal, opening the door and grinning down at Gina and Mich, who looked wide awake but were still in their pyjamas. 'You could pass for twins, except for the colour of your hair and skin, and, at the moment, you look like a couple of urchins with your new hairdos.'

'They're not hairdos, Nimal,' said Gina, as she and Mich hugged Hunter who bounced happily at them. 'We haven't had time to comb our hair since Amy's in the bathroom, so we thought we'd come and see what you were up to.'

'Oh? Did you think we were getting into trouble?' asked Anu, smiling at the duo. 'Did you both sleep okay?'

'Yeah,' said Gina, climbing on to Rohan's bed and bouncing on the mattress – it was one of her favourite pastimes, and Mich watched her with a grin.

'Now, kiddo, you know this isn't a trampoline,' said Rohan, grabbing his bouncing sister, giving her a hug and then putting her on the floor.

'I feel so . . . so . . . exe-cu-berant today,' said Gina, hugging him back. 'It's a feeling of . . . er . . . *utopia*, and Mich feels the same. You have to give her a hug, too.'

'Sure thing,' said Rohan, picking up Mich and giving her a big hug, which she returned enthusiastically. 'But, my darling sis, I think you mean to say *exuberant* and *euphoria* – don't you?'

'Hmmm, yeah, probably,' said Gina thoughtfully, while the teens tried not to laugh. 'I heard the four of you using those words yesterday, but I guess I didn't get them quite right.'

'Well, now you know,' said Anu with a smile. 'Come on, Mich, I'll help you pack. Gina, you can shower and dress in the boys' bathroom. In the meantime, boys, why don't you call the Ghoshes and thank them for a lovely evening?'

'Will do,' said Rohan. 'I'll also brief Dad about Umedh joining us.'

After a hearty breakfast, the JEACs were ready for their trip.

'Not only are we together again,' said Anu dreamily, 'but we're on our way to another adventure: a new country, another conservation, meeting interesting folks, and learning lots. I think we're a pretty lucky bunch.'

'Yes,' said Gina, and broke into song, singing to a tune similar to that of the 'Dream Song' from the musical *Joseph and the Amazing Technicolour Dreamcoat*.

'We're going away, to a new country
We're gonna meet with some friends we know
And we will play there, with baby ali-yas
They're cute and cuddly, we'll love them so.

Rohan and Amy, Nimal and Anu,
Mich and old Hunter, and silly me
Sri Lanka's calling us all to visit
We'll be there shortly, just wait and see.

A trumpet sound, a roar or two
Watch out, dear creatures,
Nimal's here, too!
You do not need to worry 'cause
He'll charm you every time.

So let's be off, come on, please hurry
The plane is waiting for you and me
We're gonna have some brand-new adventures
And we're together, in harmony!
Yes, we're all together . . .
In har-mo-ny!'

The others gaped at her and then broke into applause. It never failed to astonish them when Gina ad-libbed – making up verse and setting it to a well-known tune or to her own original tune – and then sang her composition on the spot.

'When did you make that up, Gina?' asked Nimal.

'Oh, just now,' said Gina, embarrassed by the attention. She took her talent entirely for granted. 'Do join in, come on,' she begged.

'But . . . but . . . we don't know the words,' said Mich, who loved singing Gina's songs.

'Let's write them down,' said Amy.

Anu fished out paper and pens, and Gina dictated the words. The 'Dream Song' was a favourite of theirs and they had no problem with the tune.

Everyone sang it through, twice, including Nimal, despite the fact that his voice cracked every now and then. Hunter joined in with occasional barks.

'Here's the bellboy,' said Rohan, hearing a knock on the door. 'We'll sing it again on the way to the airport. Let's go, JEACs!'

They were soon bowling along to the airport, singing Gina's song – in great harmony.

'*Shukhriar*,' said Rohan to the driver, tipping him handsomely after he had helped load their baggage and Hunter's kennel on to two trolleys. 'Right, let's get ourselves and Hunter checked in.'

The airline officer dealt with their tickets and baggage efficiently and then asked for Hunter's documents.

'Excellent,' said the officer, going through the papers and picking up the telephone. 'Everything's in order and I'll call our CSA – sorry, Customer Service Agent – to meet Hunter and take him on board.'

'You're *sure* he'll be okay?' asked Mich anxiously.

'Don't worry, Mich,' said Nimal. 'Pets are placed in special pressurized, temperature-controlled compartments on the plane and looked after very carefully. Their carriers are securely strapped in the cabin so that they aren't jolted, in case of air pockets, or during take-off and landing.'

'You've certainly done your homework, young man,' said the officer, smiling at Nimal. He turned to Mich and Gina, 'Hunter will be quite safe, young ladies – here's our agent.'

The children said goodbye to Hunter, giving him loving pats and hugs, and when Nimal opened the door of the kennel, Hunter walked in immediately, sat down, and even put out a paw to close the door.

The officer was impressed, as was the CSA, who reassured the children that their pet would be well looked after. Then he said, 'I have to take Hunter away, now – but he'll be ready for collection shortly after your plane lands. There aren't too many people disembarking at Sri Lanka, so you shouldn't have any problems.'

'Thank you very much,' chorused the children, waving goodbye to Hunter and the CSA as they moved away. Hunter barked his farewell and then settled down.

Rohan thanked the airline officer, collected their boarding passes, checked the number of their gate and then, noting their gloomy faces, looked at his watch and said, 'We've got time for an ice cream – any takers?'

'YES!' exclaimed the others.

'Good idea,' said Anu. 'I was feeling horrible about Hunter, though I'm sure he'll be fine, won't he, Nimal?'

'Yes, of course,' said Nimal cheerfully.

After their ice creams they made their way to the boarding lounge; a little later, they boarded the plane and quickly found their seats.

'What time's lunch?' asked Gina.

'I'm hungry, too,' said Mich.

A passing flight attendant heard them, and smiled, saying 'We'll serve lunch shortly after take-off. Can you wait till then?'

'Sure,' said Gina and Mich, just as the pilot's announcement came over the air.

A few minutes later, the plane rose smoothly. The children drew down the window shades since the afternoon sun was glaring in, and were soon enjoying a delicious meal. By the time they had played a few word games, the flight was over. They disembarked and were soon reunited with a very happy Hunter.

The CSA said goodbye to Hunter and commented, 'That is one contented, well-trained, obedient dog. We enjoyed having him on the flight.'

'Thanks very much for looking after him,' said the JEACs, gratefully.

They collected their luggage and moved to the exit.

'I don't see the Vijaydasas. Can you boys spot them?' said Anu.

'Nope,' said Rohan, looking easily over the heads of the other passengers. 'But there are three people waving at us. Come on!'

At the exit gate, two tall women and a shorter man came up to them.

'You *must* be the JEACs – the Patels and Larkins – correct?' stated the man.

'That's right,' said Rohan, smiling politely.

'Welcome to Sri Lanka!' said all three, beaming at them.

'Unfortunately, Lalith, Priyani and Sanjay couldn't meet you tonight, so we offered to come instead. We'll explain later,' said one of the women.

'And my darling cousins were actually on time because they took *only half a day* to get dressed,' boomed the man. He had such an infectious laugh that the youngsters began laughing, too.

The women smiled at his teasing and introduced themselves, as they greeted each child with a hug.

'I'm Chandini – Priyani's cousin,' said the older woman. She was tall for a Sri Lankan woman, slim and pretty.

'And I'm Renuka,' said the other woman, who was even taller, also very pretty and had long curly hair. 'Chandini's sister, and,' she continued, before the man could introduce himself, 'this vertically challenged man is our cousin – Priyani's brother. We had earth tremors the last time he roared with laughter.'

'I'm David,' said the man. 'My giantess cousins quite outstrip me. We're all *very* pleased to meet you.'

Hunter, who was on a leash and had been standing behind the children, now pushed his way forward.

'Hunter, sit! Shake with friends,' said Rohan.

The dog sat down and waved a paw in the air, and the three adults shook it solemnly before fussing over him. Hunter, recognizing kindred spirits, licked them thoroughly.

'I nearly forgot. I have food for you, Hunter,' said David, offering him some dog treats. Hunter licked him gratefully, got his *okay* from Rohan, and gobbled up the goodies.

'Good boy,' said David, patting him. 'We thought he might be hungry after the flight because he wouldn't have been given much food to eat, right?'

'Yes, sir,' said Nimal, 'and thanks a ton.'

'You only call me *sir* if you attend my school – I'm principal of a school close to the Conservation – please call me David. Also, if you like, you can call Chandini *Akka*, and Renuka *Akki*. They're my older cousins and *Akka* means big sister – since we couldn't call both of them Akka, we rechristened one of them *Akki* and the names stuck.'

'We'd love to call you Akka and Akki,' said Amy promptly, 'if you don't mind,' she finished, looking at the smiling women.

'If our verbose cousin had given us half a chance, we'd have suggested it ourselves,' said Akki.

They were a merry, friendly trio and the JEACS felt as if they had known them for years.

'Let's find our van,' said David, leading the way out of the terminal. 'Girls, let me take your knapsacks. What *do* you have inside, Gina?' he continued, pretending to stagger as she handed it over. 'A baby elephant?'

Giggling, Gina said, 'No, just some books and my flute. I couldn't possibly fit a baby elephant, or rather, *aliya*, into it.'

'Clever girl,' said David, as they loaded the van, climbed in and drove out of the airport. 'You even know the Sinhala name for elephant. Now, what do *you* know about Sri Lanka, Mich?'

Mich, a little shy, had not said a word so far, but she remembered something she had learned from a Sri Lankan friend. 'Every year they have a festival, in August, and there are lots of elephants all decorated beautifully. They go in a procession, taking the tooth of the Buddha from one temple to another. And there are dancers, fire-eaters, and acrobats. I think it's a religious festival but it's also a big tourist attraction, isn't it? It's called *The Perahera*.'

'Excellent,' said David. 'It's the annual *Esala Perahera* which is held in Kandy – a city in the middle of Sri Lanka. The elephant is considered the only animal worthy of carrying the reliquary which houses the tooth.'

'What's a reliquary?' asked Gina.

'A container for holy relics,' explained Anu.

'Good! Take ten marks for the right answer, Anu,' said David. 'Oh, sorry. I keep forgetting I'm not in school. Akka's a teacher, too, but she teaches physical education – and beware – she may suddenly order you to start marching or to touch your toes.'

As the youngsters burst out laughing, Akka said, in her droll way, 'I would tell David to touch *his* toes but, unfortunately, his stomach is the camouflage behind which his toes hide, and he'd fall over if he attempted to get a glimpse of them.'

David roared with laughter, and the JEACs joined in. There was obviously a great deal of affectionate bantering amongst the cousins.

'Don't worry about Akki trying to *teach* you,' said David. 'She just tries to *control* everybody.'

'Really?' said Mich and Gina.

'Don't listen to him,' said Akki, with a smile. 'I'm the *Financial Controller* for the Centre, which means that I deal with their accounts.'

When they reached the main road to Colombo, the driver accelerated and the van sped along. Amy and Mich were petrified since he appeared to narrowly miss hitting the other vehicles on the road.

'Oooh,' squealed Mich. 'Are you *sure* he's a good driver?' she whispered to Akki.

'Oh, yes, dear,' said Akki comfortingly.

'Whoa, we just missed another car,' said Amy, clutching Rohan's arm as the van swerved to avoid oncoming traffic.

'Don't worry, ladies,' said David. 'In most western countries the driving is relatively tame, but if we aren't aggressive here, it'll take us all night to get to Colombo – which is only 25 kilometres away. The driver's good – we missed all the cars on the way out, and I'm sure we'll miss them on the way home, too.'

'Er . . . okay,' said Amy. She added, apologetically, 'In Canada we drive on the other side of the road and they . . . er . . . drive rather *differently* here, don't they?'

'That's what I would call the understatement of the century,' teased David.

'Let's tell you why the others couldn't meet you,' said Akka, hoping to distract the Larkin girls.

'Yeah, what happened?' asked Anu. 'Are they okay?'

'They're fine,' said Akki, 'but a wholly unexpected situation arose on the Conservation. Perhaps David would like to explain, since he has the gift of the gab.'

'Sure, Akki, abuse me every time,' grinned David. 'Right! But first, how much do you know about elephants?'

'A fair amount,' said Nimal.

'Tell me what you know and then my beloved cousins won't accuse me of being a "teach".'

'Okay, I'll start,' said Anu. 'They're the largest land mammals and, like *homo sapiens*, live in social communities. They also care for their young. Gina, please continue.'

'Ephalunts cry when they're sad; they try and help each other and sometimes other creatures – and they have a great sense of humour.'

'Mich?' said Anu.

'The babies are adorable and their trunks often get in their way until they get used to them. They get jealous, angry, throw tantrums and are very competitive.'

Amy continued, 'In wild herds, the older elephants maintain discipline and ensure that the smaller elephants aren't bullied. I read an article, which mentioned that babies, in particular, needed discipline – they're extremely mischievous and will *push* their caregivers to see how far they can go. They don't realize their own strength and it takes them a while to understand the word "no". In a baby elephant orphanage, caregivers use a wagging finger while saying *no*, and when the infant is obedient, a treat is forthcoming. If it misbehaves, the treat is withheld – apparently, they learn very quickly with treats. Your turn, Rohan.'

'I read the same article, and the infants are only reprimanded *as soon as the incident occurs*,' continued Rohan, 'never retrospectively, and once a baby has been punished, shortly afterwards the caregiver will comfort it, so that it knows it's forgiven for doing something wrong. A baby ephalunt needs to feel secure and loved.

'It's also fascinating that they often live in matriarchal societies. Female units stay together for life, led by the oldest member – called the matriarch – who makes all decisions for the family. Young males, when they grow up, join a herd of bulls, who have their own codes for living. They're awesome – you next, Nimal,' said Rohan.

'I adore them, too,' said Nimal. 'They have the same average lifespan as *homo sapiens* – three score and ten – and a similar rate of development. They're the only creatures, other than humans, who mourn their dead and even bury them – often covering the body of a loved one with sticks and leaves to ensure no predators have access – and they return to the "burial" spot, now and then, for many years. They make friends, are extremely loyal, and remember both animals and people who have been kind to them. I guess that's where the saying *an elephant never forgets* comes from. They also remember those who have hurt them, or their family, and if they come across them again, will definitely attempt to seek revenge.

'They communicate telepathically, and over long distances they communicate via a medium called *infrasound* which humans can't hear. They rely mainly on their senses of hearing and smell, which are extremely acute.'

'And so,' concluded Anu, smiling, albeit a little sheepishly, 'you can see that we have a fair knowledge of ephalunts and love them dearly. Sorry for the long saga.'

'Not at all,' said the three adults.

'I'm impressed at your knowledge,' said Akka. 'Even I didn't know that much about elephants.'

'Or *ephalunts* as you youngsters like to say,' said David. 'I'm thrilled at the extent of your knowledge. However, unfortunately, there's always a problem in humans and animals living peacefully together, and that's the cause of the current situation.'

'What happened?' said Nimal.

'If it's okay with you, I'll tell you after dinner,' said David. 'We'll be reaching Neeka's house soon.'

'No problemo,' said Nimal.

CHAPTER 4

Mr. CADD

Five minutes later, they turned into the gateway of a large house, where a hefty young man greeted them.

'Hello, folks! A hearty welcome to Sri Lanka. I'm Kithum Handunge, Neeka's brother, and this,' he added, introducing the petite young woman who joined him, 'is Deepthi – my wife.'

'*Ayubowan*,' said Deepthi, greeting them in the traditional Sri Lankan manner by joining her hands together and bowing her head.

'*Namaste*,' said the Patels, following suit in the Indian tradition, while the Larkin girls imitated them.

'Kithum's another cousin,' explained David, as they unloaded the suitcases from the van, and everyone introduced themselves. Hunter sat down and held up a paw to shake.

'Gosh,' whispered Gina to Anu, 'is *everyone* a cousin in Sri Lanka?'

'Of course,' laughed David, overhearing her. 'Actually, if you go back far enough, we're *all* related somewhere along the line.' Seeing Gina and Mich's confused looks, he stopped teasing them. 'My mother is one of eleven brothers and sisters, each of whom married and had two or three children – so there are 27 of us first cousins.'

'And at our annual extended family picnic,' added Kithum, 'we have close to 500 people – even though many of the cousins are abroad.'

'Golly,' said Mich in awe.

'Now, I'm sure you're all hungry, but would you like to freshen up first?' asked Deepthi.

'Yes, please,' said Anu.

'Follow me,' said Deepthi, leading the way. 'It's a large, rambling house, and three of us couples, along with our children – and yes, we're all cousins – share it.'

'Where are all the others?' asked Nimal.

'Actually, since it's a long weekend, they've gone upcountry where it is cooler,' explained Kithum. 'You'll meet Neeka later and she'll return to the Conservation with you tomorrow. The kids wanted to stay and meet you, but we told them they could do so at the fundraiser.'

'We've put you in here,' said Deepthi, showing them into two large rooms. 'I hope you'll be comfortable.'

'Oh, thank you so much,' said Anu gratefully. 'You shouldn't have bothered – we could have kipped out in sleeping bags in one room.'

'Of course not,' said Deepthi, looking shocked at the idea. 'When we have all this space? The bathroom's over there. When you're ready, join us in the living room. Will Hunter come with us? We'll give him something to eat and then someone will take him for a walk.'

'Yes, please,' said Nimal, 'and thank you.'

The others chorused their thanks as well.

They freshened up quickly, unpacked the little gifts Mrs. Patel and Mrs. Larkin had packed for their hosts, and went into the living room. The adults were very appreciative of the little Indian and Canadian souvenirs.

'We have a few things for you folks, too,' said Akki, 'but they're back at the Conservation.'

'Calls to parents first and then dinner, I think,' said Akka, looking at her watch. 'It's 8:30 and I'm sure they're hungry.' She looked at the JEACs inquiringly.

'Yes, please,' said Nimal politely. 'Something smells very good.'

'Are you always this polite?' teased David. 'I would have thought you'd be *starving* by now and hollering for food.'

Everyone laughed, and Rohan said slyly, 'I think Nimal and the girls are rather tired, David, which is why they haven't told you they're starving. It's usually their theme song.'

'Thus says the chap who eats twice as much as us,' ragged Nimal, punching him lightly.

After quick calls to their parents, they followed Kithum into the dining room where the table was groaning under the weight of all the food.

'Wow!' exclaimed Nimal, 'I haven't seen many of these dishes before.'

'We thought you might like a Sri Lankan meal on your first night here,' said Deepthi. 'I hope you won't have upset stomachs because we use coconut milk and coconut oil in our cooking,' she added anxiously.

'Don't worry. We've all got cast-iron stomachs,' said Anu cheerfully, 'and everything looks simply delish.'

'Well, do sit down and serve yourselves,' said Akki.

'These,' said Akka, handing a plate of what looked like vermicelli string cakes to Amy, 'are called *stringhoppers*, a traditional Sri Lankan dish, made out of flour and then steamed. Those other dishes are coconut *sambol*, *kiri hodi* – a gravy made out of coconut milk and some spices – chicken curry, prawns and various pickles and chutneys,' she added, pointing out each dish. 'I hope you won't find anything too hot.'

'Tuck in, folks,' said Akki, 'and I'm going to put on some music.' She turned on the stereo system and lively, toe-tapping music filled the room.

'That's great music!' exclaimed Gina. 'Are they singing in your language?'

'It's our famous *baila* music,' said David. 'They're singing in Sinhala, one of the languages of our country.'

'What's the song playing at the moment?' asked Amy.

'One of the most popular songs of all time, although it's very old,' said Akki. 'It's called "Chuda Maani Key" and, although it's sung mainly in Sinhala with some standard verses, people add English or Tamil verses as they sing.'

'Will you teach us some baila songs, Akki?' asked Anu.

'Sure. We'll have a sing-song after dinner.'

'Superfantabulous!' chorused the youngsters.

'Whew! That was a scrumptious meal,' said Nimal, a little later, and the others agreed with him.

'Now, for dessert, we have *wattalapan* pudding,' said Kithum, as the ladies brought in large bowls of what looked like a dark brown custard pudding, but much thicker and richer.

'It's made with coconut milk, eggs, jaggery, cashew nuts and a few spices,' explained Akka, serving large helpings into each bowl.

'Mmmm, this is absolutely delish,' said Mich, cleaning up her bowl rapidly.

'Would you like some more?' said Deepthi, smiling at her. 'And what about you, Gina? Nimal?'

'Yes, please,' chorused the girls.

'Er . . . I hate to see food go to waste,' said Nimal, 'so I wouldn't mind a little more, too, please.'

The bowls were soon empty, and everyone moved into the living room. The children had just settled comfortably on the rugs when a very pretty woman walked into the room. She was about David's height, had short, thick hair, and a charming smile.

'Hello, folks! I'm Neeka Handunge,' she said.

The JEACs rose to greet her, and she gave each of them a hug and a kiss, including Hunter, who had returned from his walk.

After some general conversation, Neeka said to David, 'Aiya, when will my speech be ready? I need to practise it soon.'

'Next week,' said David.

'Oh, thanks, Aiya,' said Neeka gratefully. She turned to the youngsters and said, 'We're hosting a large fundraising event at the Conservation, in about three weeks, and hundreds of people will be attending. I have to make a speech, but since my first language is Sinhala and not English, David Aiya is writing it for me.'

'I felt I *had* to,' said David, grinning at his cousin teasingly, 'because, otherwise, Neeka is sure to confuse people. By the way, her middle name's *Mrs. Malaprop*.'

'Now, Aiya, be quiet,' said Neeka, punching him good-naturedly.

'What does *Aiya* mean?' asked Gina.

'It means older brother,' explained Akka, 'and quite often we address older cousins, or even friends, in this way.'

'Who's Mrs. Malaprop?' asked Mich, looking instinctively at Anu who was a voracious reader.

'She was a lady in a comic play written by Sheridan,' explained Anu. 'She loved using big, impressive words and phrases but, unfortunately, she invariably got them muddled up. So now, when anyone makes a mistake of that nature, they're often called *Mrs. Malaprop* or people say they have used a *malapropism*.'

'Right on, Anu,' said David. 'Let me give you an example. I know Neeka won't mind; she'll just beat me up afterwards. Some years ago she, Priyani and I were discussing a problem I was facing in my school, and we concluded that I would have to take a firm stand on the issue. Neeka got so excited that she said passionately, "Aiya, you have to be firm. Just lift up your foot and say it has to be done." Once Priyani and I had finished laughing our heads off, while Neeka looked at us in astonishment, we explained to her that the correct saying was *put your foot down*.' He gave Neeka a big hug and continued, 'Neeka, as you will discover, has the endearing quality of being able to laugh at herself, and doesn't mind if others laugh *with* her, as long as she knows they're not being nasty.'

'Get away with you, Aiya,' said Neeka, cheerfully. 'Don't try to butter me up now. One day I'll tell you about all the terrible things *he* did when he was young.'

The children thought Neeka was super.

'Now, I've heard that you started a group called the JEACs, and we'd love to hear about it,' said Neeka.

The JEACs gave a brief description of their group, its vision and goals.

'That's fascinating,' said Neeka. 'Gina, I also understand that you wrote a theme song, and Mich drew matching cartoons – would you sing it for us, please?'

'Okay,' said Gina, shyly. 'But we need a DVD player, projector and the piano.'

'I'm on it,' said Kithum, setting up the equipment while the girls ran to get the CD with the cartoons.

Akki sat down at the piano and said, 'Is it set to a tune we know?'

'Do you know the song about the "Railway Cat" from the musical *Cats*? It's a fairly similar tune,' said Mich. 'Gina composes lots of songs – this morning she composed one about coming here to a tune similar to that of the "Dream Song" from *Joseph*.'

'We'll have to hear that, too, and yes, I do know the "Railway Cat"' song,' said Akki.

The JEACs sang, while the cartoons on the screen changed appropriately. Akki accompanied them on the piano.

The JEACs
Jun-ior Environ-menta-lists and Con-ser-vation-ists!

When we think about our world, all the animals and birds
Who are losing their homes day by day
If each person does their part, it will cheer up every heart
So let's take a stand and act without delay!

We've decided we will strive to keep birds and beasts alive
And to make CONSER-VA-TION our theme
We will talk to all our friends, try to help them understand
That our world must come awake and not just dream!

All the creatures that we love, from the ele-phant to dove,
Must be cared for and well protected, too
So all humans, young and old, have to speak up and be **bold**
Or we'll end up with an "only human" zoo!

Where environment's concerned, in our studies we have learned
That composting at home can be a start
And recycling's very good, each and every person should
Be aware of how we all can do our part.

To the JEACs we belong, and we hope it won't be long
Till our peers and our friends all will say
They believe that con-ser-vation and environ-menta-lism
Is the only way to save our world today!

Will you come and join our band? Will you lend a helping hand?
Though it's serious, it can be great fun!
Tell your friends about it all, let them join up, big and small
And our fight against destruction will be won!

Jun-ior Environ-menta-lists and Con-ser-vation-ists!

The adults applauded in delight.

'That's some performance, JEACs. The song and cartoons are perfect,' said David. 'You folks must come to my school to talk to the kids and also sing your song. I'll have a projector ready for the cartoons and do the slide show for you.'

'My school would love it, too,' said Akka, 'and, I think, the youngsters in the nearby church groups would be thrilled to hear about the JEACs as well.'

'We'd be glad to,' said Anu, and the others nodded in agreement.

'Now can we learn at least one baila song, please?' asked Gina.

'Sure thing,' said Akki.

Kithum brought out a guitar and they taught the JEACs a couple of simple Sinhala baila songs. They particularly enjoyed learning *Chuda Maani Key* and Gina made up a verse in Hindi.

At the end of the session, Neeka asked them more questions about their group and said, 'It's a perfect group for all youngsters. Perhaps you would talk about it and sing your theme song at our fundraising event. It would be fantastic, especially given the current situation.'

'Sure thing,' said Rohan, speaking for everyone. 'Now, could you tell us about the problem?'

'I'll explain,' said David. 'As you're aware, elephants translocate and need lots of space to wander in – but, while Sri Lanka's become very conscious of the importance of conservation, it's a small country, and there's a limited amount of space. Therefore, because of development in the rural areas, some of our farmlands have ended up on the edge of conservations and jungles – like Alighasa. Not all our conservations have good fencing, and for the past three years, the farmers around Alighasa have encountered numerous problems. Unfortunately, some of our barriers, even though we keep strengthening them, cannot restrict the elephants, who break through now and then – resulting in the destruction of the farmers' crops and the loss of money which most of them can ill afford. In retaliation, to protect themselves from the rampaging elephants, they kill them.

'In addition, we face an ongoing tussle with ivory thieves, who kill elephants without compunction, merely to obtain their tusks and sell them; and occasionally, the elephants are dismembered and certain parts sold illicitly for use in traditional medicine. Therefore, one way or another, elephants are being decimated, and while we conservationists are protesting against this, the farmers are petitioning the government to protect their crops.'

Neeka continued the story. 'Five years ago, the Alighasa Board of Directors appointed Lalith to manage the Centre, and he's the best manager we've ever had. He developed the Conservation rapidly and started petitioning the government for more land for the elephants – the land north of the current Conservation is perfect for this purpose. We assured the government that we would fundraise, both locally and abroad, to raise enough money to build strong barriers around the current Conservation and that we would relocate the elephants to the new area so that they couldn't break out and destroy the farmlands.

'Finally, six months ago, the government consented to give us the land. Two months ago, the papers were signed and the property officially handed over to our Conservation. We're now one of the largest conservations in Sri Lanka – here's a rough map of what the NC will be like, and this is the northern boundary of the OC. Sorry – until we find a good name for the new section, OC stands for Old Conservation and NC for New Conservation. The gap between the OC and the NC covers a distance of approximately half a kilometre and we need to move the larger wildlife through that gap into the NC. As you see, there are natural barriers of high, rocky hills on the north, west and east of the NC and a wall is only required in the south, along with a gate.

'We've put up a temporary wooden fence which no other creatures, excepting the elephants, can destroy, and we've moved some of the larger animals into the NC. We're currently working on a cement wall, parallel to the wooden fence. It'll be 3.048 metres deep and 12.192 metres high, and not even elephants can break through; once it's complete, we'll relocate the elephants. The construction site was divided into five sections and two sections in the west are completed; we're now working on the central and eastern segments.'

'But what about the other animals in the OC?' asked Nimal.

'It'll become like the "Harmonious Paradise" at Patiyak,' said Neeka, 'with smaller animals which cannot break out through our fences.

More staff will be hired and the government will get bonus points for creating jobs – a definite selling point for them.'

'That's wonderful,' said Anu. 'So actually, you're expanding, not merely relocating, right?'

'Correct,' said Akki. 'Also, since the half-kilometre gap between the two conservations is part of the Conservation, it'll be developed once we've raised more funds – it's currently barren but we're planning some reforestation later on.'

'What about staff residences, auditoriums and a petting zoo in the NC?' asked Rohan, studying the map.

'The spots marked in red indicate where some buildings will come up, but our first priority is to move the wildlife; we'll deal with the residences later,' said David. 'However, if Mr. Cock-a-doodle-doo continues . . .'

He trailed off as the youngsters exclaimed in one voice, 'Mr. *WHO*?'

'Sorry, that's *our* name for him. His real name is Mr. Kurukulaarachchi and he's a petty government official,' said David, laughing at the looks on their faces.

'Mr. Kuku – kuru – arrarch. Gosh! That's a tongue twister,' said Amy, trying, unsuccessfully, to get her tongue around the name. 'No wonder you've changed it. But why Mr. Cock-a-doodle-doo?'

'Because, in some ways he's just as silly as a rooster, and appears to think he's *the 29th Wonder of the World*,' said Neeka caustically. 'He's the chief troublemaker in *attempting* to turn government officials against us – which is surprising because he supported us when Lalith was appointed manager of the OC.'

'And if not for the firm stand taken by Delo Samaratunge, Jeevana Abeykoon and other wonderful folk, his attempt would have succeeded,' said Akka. 'Delo's a fantastic speaker and from what we heard, she received a thunderous round of applause after she spoke up in favour of giving us the land and, when the voting took place, only Mr. Cock-a-doodle-doo and one other voted against.'

'Yes, Delo's superb,' said Neeka, enthusiastically. 'She invited government officials – all those involved in the decision-making – to visit Alighasa and see for themselves what the OC and NC were all about. We worked hard and organized a detailed educational tour, and the officials had a wonderful time. They learned a great deal, and the papers were full of their glowing reports the next day. You'll meet Delo at the fundraiser since she's one of our chief guests.'

'Did Mr. Cock-a-doodle-doo – or Mr. CADD for short – go as well?' asked Rohan curiously.

'I like your acronym. No, Mr. CADD feigned illness, but he was the *only* person who didn't come,' said David.

'Some of us feel he has an ulterior motive but can't figure out what on earth it could be,' said Akki. 'The land they gave us was lying waste and it's perfect for our needs.'

'How will you move the animals?' asked Gina.

'As Neeka mentioned, some of the animals have already been relocated,' said Akki. 'For the elephants, we're working with a Wildlife Relocation company from Africa who have some new ideas and are working closely with Jack, Jim and Tony Munasinghe, another senior member of our staff.'

'Which animals were relocated?' asked Anu.

'Leopards, wild boar and bears, to name a few,' said David. 'However, reverting to the problems, the day before yesterday, Lalith and Tony were inspecting the building of the wall when they heard an explosion and one of the supervisors from the easternmost section called to say that part of the wall had been blown up and a couple of workers were injured. They rushed across and found a huge hole in the wall. After attending to the injured workers and hiring extra security guards, they set about investigating the explosion.'

'What happened?' said Nimal.

'Somebody had planted a time bomb inside the NC.'

'The labourers refused to work until the entire section had been thoroughly checked for more bombs,' said Akki.

'So Lalith had to hire experts to scour the area and reassure the workers. We spoke to Lalith just before you arrived,' said Kithum, 'and he said the workers would start again tomorrow.'

'Great. But, David, you started to say, "Mr. Cock-a-doodle-doo" and we interrupted you. How's Mr. CADD still involved?' said Anu.

'Well, we seem to keep bumping into him,' said David. 'Sanjay and Tony went into town to meet the bomb experts; after the meeting, they were getting into their Land Rover when a car passed them – a blue BMW with tinted glass. Tony was sure he'd seen the car several times when he was in Colombo, and quickly called Delo to ask if she recognized the number plate. She did; it belonged to Mr. CADD.

'Tony and Sanjay followed the BMW discreetly; it drove towards the poorer part of town, dropped off a man and left. The man disappeared down one of the lanes without seeing Tony and Sanjay, but they recognized him immediately.'

'It was one of the workers,' continued Kithum. 'The day before yesterday that chap told Tony that his wife was very ill; that he had to leave immediately and probably wouldn't return. The man only started work three days ago – they had noticed that he didn't mix with the others and often went off on his own to chat to the security guards along the wall. Perhaps – and this is a *really* long shot – he was the one who planted the bomb. We're checking up on him.'

'We don't want to jump to conclusions, but we can't help feeling that Mr. CADD is trying to delay us,' concluded Neeka.

'Wow, that's some story,' said Rohan.

'It's frustrating. But, it's now your bedtime, folks,' said David. 'We've an early start tomorrow – ready by 5 a.m. – traffic is easier at that time. By the way, I hope you have nerves of steel.'

'Why?' asked Amy anxiously. 'Are the roads dangerous?'

'No,' said Kithum, with a broad grin, 'but Uncle Leo is.'

'Who is he,' asked Nimal, 'and why's he dangerous?'

'He's my mater's youngest brother,' explained David, 'and he's driving us to Alighasa. But why ruin the treat – you'll meet him in the morning.'

They could not get anything more out of the cousins, who just laughed and said, 'Wait and see'.

'Now, here are Gina and Mich, yawning their heads off,' said Akka. 'Goodnight, JEACs.'

'Before you take off, do you want to check your email?' asked Kithum.

'Yes, please,' said Rohan. 'Also, we have a huge favour to ask – if you don't mind.'

'Fire away,' said Akka.

Rohan explained about Umedh, asking if the boy could join them after his course, and Kithum offered to deal with all the arrangements and get Umedh to Alighasa.

'Thanks a ton,' chorused the JEACs.

'He'll be thrilled,' said Rohan, writing down Umedh's email address for Kithum.

They said goodnight and after promising to wake the others at 4:30, Rohan sent a quick email to Umedh and then joined Nimal who was already fast asleep.

CHAPTER 5

Deaf in One Ear and Can't Hear with the Other

'You're punctual,' said Deepthi the next morning, when the children joined the adults in the living room. 'Come and eat something.'

A few minutes later, all of them were tucking hungrily into more delicious Sri Lankan food. As they were finishing off their meal, they heard a vehicle in the driveway and then footsteps in the hall.

'HELLO, THERE!' bellowed someone, making the youngsters jump. 'WHERE ARE ALL OF YOU?'

Hunter started barking.

'WE'RE IN THE DINING ROOM,' yelled back Kithum.

'Sorry,' he said, in a normal tone, 'but Uncle Leo's deaf in one ear and can't hear with the other.'

Gina and Mich took a bit of time to digest this, but the teens caught on immediately and grinned.

As Leo came into the room, Kithum continued, raising his voice again, 'FRIENDS, THIS IS UNCLE LEOPALD – WE CALL HIM UNCLE LEO AND YOU CAN DO THE SAME.'

A grizzled-looking man beamed at the children and shook hands with each of them, talking at the top of his voice all the time. Since he was very deaf, it was no use talking to him unless you also had eye contact. Hunter, who had come out from under the table to see what all the shouting was about, growled and bristled at him, thinking he was about to harm the children. Leo spotted him and bent to pat him.

Hunter barked, and Nimal said quickly, in an exceptionally stern voice, 'Sit, Hunter! This is a friend.'

Hunter looked surprised, but obeyed immediately, holding up a paw to be shaken. Leo fussed over the dog for a while, and Hunter, seeing that his family was not being harmed by this loud being, relaxed and licked Leo's hand.

'SO,' roared Leo, 'ARE WE ALL READY TO GO?'

'WE'RE JUST WAITING FOR AKKA AND AKKI,' shouted David, adding *sotto voce* to the children, 'He's a *really* nice chap but he gives me a pain in my throat.'

'Why doesn't he wear a hearing aid?' asked Amy, trying not to giggle.

'It takes us ages to persuade him to wear it,' muttered Neeka, 'but it's amazing how much quieter he becomes when it's on.'

'We're ready,' said Akka, entering the room with Akki. 'How are you, Uncle Leo?'

Leo, naturally, did not hear her as he was busy drinking a cup of tea, but when he turned around and spotted the sisters, he hollered, 'HELLO, CHANDINI AND RENUKA, HOW ARE YOU? IT'S A GREAT DAY FOR A DRIVE.'

The sisters winced, but Akki said fairly loudly, as the children stifled their laughter, 'We're fine, Uncle, and thanks for driving us to the Conservation.'

'WHAT RESERVATION?' roared Leo. 'DID YOU ASK ME TO MAKE ONE?'

'Watch the fun now,' muttered David to the youngsters. 'This is positively *the only way* to get him to wear his hearing aid quickly.' He faced Leo and pretended to speak.

'WHAT WAS THAT?' yelled Leo, putting a hand to an ear.

Neeka tapped him on the shoulder and he turned to her. She, too, opened and shut her mouth as if she were speaking.

'SPEAK A BIT LOUDER, DEAR,' bellowed Leo, putting both hands behind both ears.

Kithum got his attention next and did the same thing, and then David had another go.

Mich and Gina had to hide under the table – they were hysterical with laughter.

'I MUST BE DEAFER THAN I THOUGHT,' said Leo, in a muted roar. 'Where's that silly hearing aid?'

He fished it out of his pocket, put it in, and said in a normal tone of voice, 'What were you children saying? I could barely hear you – you must learn to speak up.'

The teens had a tough time trying not to laugh, so Anu hurriedly made an excuse about packing and they rushed out of the dining room, followed by Gina and Mich. They collapsed in their room and laughed till they cried.

'This is going to be some trip,' groaned Nimal, wiping his eyes. 'I wonder if that's what they meant when they said he was dangerous.'

'Probably. Can you imagine driving with him if he *isn't* wearing his hearing aid?' gasped Amy. 'We'd be *deaf* by the end of the trip.'

'Yes,' chimed in Gina, 'we'd be deaf in one ear and wouldn't be able to hear with the other.' She had worked that one out and loved it.

'Man, I've got a stitch in my side,' said Rohan. 'Now sober up, folks, and let's take the suitcases out.'

Looking reasonably sober, they trooped outside, gathering around the Land Rover.

'Now,' said Akki, ensuring that Leo was not within earshot, 'who's going to be brave and strong enough to sit in front with Uncle Leo?'

'Nimal and Rohan – you look pretty muscular – well suited for that task,' said Neeka.

'I guess we're fairly strong,' said Rohan, looking suspiciously at the cousins. 'But why do we have to be *strong and brave*? Are you ragging us again?'

'No – more's the pity,' said Akka. 'Uncle Leo doesn't believe in getting his front door on the passenger side fixed. So, whoever sits in front needs to hang on to the door as it might burst open at any time – especially in the city when he takes one of his wild swings around a corner. And there aren't any seat belts.'

'Oh, my hat!' exclaimed Nimal, grimacing comically. 'Surely things like that only happen in movies?'

'They also happen when you're around Uncle Leo,' said David.

'Okay, everybody, in you get,' said Leo.

After thanking Deepthi and Kithum, the conservation-bound group climbed into the vehicle, Rohan and Nimal sitting up front with Leo.

'I'll take a chance with the door first,' muttered Rohan.

'Ready for take-off?' asked Leo, starting the Land Rover.

'Yes!' chorused everyone. They waved to Deepthi and Kithum as the vehicle zoomed out of the compound, Rohan hanging on to the door.

'Now I understand why we need to be brave, David,' muttered Amy. 'What happens if Rohan or Nimal fall out?'

'Oh, we just pick them up and drive on,' said David cheerfully. 'Don't worry. Wait and see what happens when we get out of the city.'

'Jeepers,' whispered Amy to Anu. 'What *more* can happen?'

'Haven't the foggiest,' whispered back Anu, 'but I'm sure getting lots of material for my stories.'

'True!' whispered Amy. '*If you survive to tell the tale!*' Both girls dissolved into giggles.

Leo wove in and out of the traffic. Nimal was tense in his seat, and Rohan hung on to the door for dear life. It was not that the door kept opening; it simply would not close properly and could not be locked. Akka, Akki and Neeka appeared to be quite at ease, as were Gina, Mich and Hunter, seated right at the back with David.

'Aha! The open road at last,' said Leo cheerfully, once they were out of the city. 'Now, in a few minutes, lads, I'll show you just how fast this little Land Rover can go.' He stopped the vehicle and got out.

'We're done for,' muttered Rohan to Nimal. 'Even our so-called "strong muscles" won't be able to hold this door shut if he goes any faster.'

'What on earth is he going to do with that rope?' said Nimal, goggling at Leo who had fished out a strong length of rope from under his seat, and was coming around to the front passenger door.

The JEACs watched, first in horrified astonishment, and then with increasing amusement, as Leo tied the rope securely to the luggage rack. He next wove it through the door handle of the front passenger seat, taking it across to secure it firmly to the front of the vehicle where there was a strong metal cowcatcher.

'Oh, my giddy aunt!' exclaimed Nimal.

'This is hilarious,' giggled Anu, setting off the others. 'What an experience.'

'There we go,' said Leo, climbing back into the vehicle. 'Yell when you want to stop for breakfast, kids. I'll point out places of interest – I act as a tour guide sometimes.'

'That's great, Uncle Leo,' said Rohan, cautiously testing the door – which didn't budge. 'And, do I still need to hang on to the door . . . now that it's . . . er . . . *tied up*?' He kicked Nimal whose shoulders were shaking with silent laughter.

'Oh, no – it's quite secure now,' said Leo, and took off speedily.

Rohan looked over his shoulder at Akka, raising his eyebrows inquiringly.

She nodded reassuringly, leaning over to whisper, 'Yes, it's okay now. Last year, one of his female tourists fell out. She went into strong hysterics, sitting on the road and refusing to get into the vehicle again. He now secures the door on long trips – and *don't* ask me why he doesn't just get it fixed, because I don't have an answer.'

The scenery was breathtaking, and the JEACs loved the rolling hills, green forests and multicoloured flowers. They stopped at 9:30 for a second breakfast of delicious sandwiches, which they ate sitting on large rocks, overlooking a gorgeous valley.

'Here's a map of the OC,' said Akki, handing it to Rohan, and the JEACs pored over the map.

'Why aren't there any bungalows or many trails in the north and central western sections?' asked Rohan.

'It's an extremely dense and unexplored area which nobody's had time to check out yet,' said David.

'Perhaps *we* can explore it,' said Nimal eagerly.

'Good idea,' said Akki, as they climbed into the vehicle and set off once more.

'Now,' said Leo, rounding a curve in the road, 'to your right is the famous *Sigiriya Fortress*. Some historians believe it was built around the year 478 AD, while others say it was constructed prior to 300 BC. It's nearly 183 metres high.

'As you see,' said Leo, taking one hand off the wheel and pointing, while he also looked over at the rock, 'it looks like a crouching lion – so it's also known as *Lion Rock*. We'll take you there after the fundraiser.'

'Uncle Leo,' said Rohan, struggling to keep his voice even, 'you're driving in the lane for oncoming traffic.'

'Ah! I should get back to my lane,' said Leo, quite unconcerned, while Rohan and Nimal breathed again.

'Fortunately there *wasn't any traffic* in the oncoming lane,' said Amy, under her breath. 'Is he always like this, Akka?'

'Most of the time he's worse,' said Akka. 'Akki and I rarely look at what he's pointing to, but concentrate on the road and make sure we grab the wheel if necessary.'

Nimal overheard them and whispered out of the corner of his mouth, while Leo was talking to Rohan, 'I'm not surprised you asked for brave people to sit in front. Frankly, I can't say I feel brave at all; you and Akki must have nerves of steel.'

'You get used to it,' said Akka with a laugh. 'Actually, he's never crashed because the other vehicles on the road recognize him and take extra precautions.'

'I don't blame them,' said Anu. 'But he's a really nice chap and knows a great deal about Sri Lanka.'

'He's okay,' agreed David, 'but you *definitely* need a sense of humour when he's at the wheel.'

They went along merrily, chatting and singing. Now and then Leo would petrify them by wandering into the oncoming traffic lane while pointing out places of interest, but either Nimal or Rohan would grab the wheel and gently draw his attention back to the road. He was a jovial man and did not misunderstand their intentions.

They stopped for lunch at a beautiful picnic spot and Leo had a short nap, after which they continued their journey. The rest of the trip sped past and they soon left the main road and passed the turn-off to a small town.

'That's the road which leads to our schools,' said David.

'Do you both live on the Conservation?' asked Amy.

'No, I have a room on the school premises and come to the Conservation for weekends,' said David, 'and also when I bring my kids on tours.'

'I live on the Conservation,' said Akka, 'but have a little Jeep and drive to school.'

'Wish our schools were close enough for us to live at home,' said Anu.

'Now, sis,' teased Rohan, 'you know you'd miss all those interesting characters, some of whom you can include in your books, if you didn't go to boarding school and have such fun.'

'Yeah, you're right,' said Anu. 'Boarding school *is* great.'

A few minutes later, they pulled up at the south entrance to the OC.

CHAPTER 6

The OC

It was nearly 3 p.m. when the staff at the entrance booths waved in the Land Rover. They drove along a beautiful trail, surrounded by dense jungle and hundreds of flowering shrubs. The canopy of trees was soothing and an occasional glimpse of blue sky, now tinged with orange as the sun went down, was a glorious sight.

'When can we see the new Conservation, and how long will it take to complete the wall?' asked Rohan.

'Perhaps tomorrow – we're hoping the wall will be completed very soon,' said Akki.

'Great,' said Nimal. 'I'm looking forward to seeing how elephants are relocated.'

It took over an hour to reach the large clearing, situated in the central section of the OC, where there were a number of residences. Three people were waiting to meet them. Sanjay untied the rope, which held the front door shut, and the boys leapt out.

'Rohan! Nimal! Welcome to Alighasa!' said Sanjay, greeting the boys affectionately. 'It's great to see you, yaar. You've both shot up and have outstripped me in height.'

He hugged Anu and Gina, and shook hands warmly with the Canadian girls. Hunter licked him joyfully, and then barked happily, as he bounced over to greet the Vijaydasas.

'Welcome to Alighasa, JEACs, which of course includes you, Hunter,' said Lalith. 'We're delighted to have you here and apologize for not being able to meet you in Colombo.'

'Yes, a very warm welcome indeed,' said Priyani. 'I'm sure someone explained why we couldn't be at the airport.'

'No problemo,' said Rohan immediately. 'We're sorry to hear about the situation. Are things okay now?'

'More or less, thanks,' said Lalith, leading the way into the house.

'Thank you so much for having us,' chorused the JEACs.

'Our pleasure,' said Lalith. 'Also, I sent Umedh an email telling him we're looking forward to his visit, and he wrote back immediately to thank me. He sounded very excited.'

'Thanks a ton,' said Rohan gratefully.

'Did you have a good journey from Colombo?' asked Sanjay, winking at them slyly.

'It was an *experience* we won't forget in a hurry,' said Anu as they entered the living room.

'Hello, my dears,' said a bright voice. 'How *nice* to finally meet all of you.' A petite older lady in her late sixties, with snow-white hair, came forward to greet them.

'This is my mother, Matilda D'Silva,' said Priyani.

'How are you, Mrs. D'Silva?' said Anu, greeting her with a handshake and a kiss.

'*Do* call me Aunty Matty,' she said.

'Sure thing, Aunty Matty,' said Anu. 'I'm Anu.'

'I don't need any introductions,' said Aunty Matty. 'I know each of you by name, since Priyani, Lalith and Sanjay couldn't stop talking about you.' She pointed to pictures of the JEACs, their parents and Jack Larkin, which were on the mantelshelf.

Amy greeted her with a kiss, too, saying, 'It's great to meet you, Aunty Matty.'

The others followed suit, and soon they were seated in the comfortable living room, chatting away as if they had known each other for years, which in some cases was quite true.

'Where's Aunty Consy?' asked David. 'She's one of Mum's older sisters,' he explained, 'who also lives here, and she and Mum are good company for each other. Mum actually *behaves* herself when Aunty Consy's around. Priyani and I were very strict in bringing up the mater, but you know what APs are like – she gets out of hand now and then.'

The children glanced at Aunty Matty to see how she had taken this, but she just smiled at David and said, 'Don't get too cheeky, son. I can still give you a good walloping if necessary.'

'I feel as if I'm at home!' exclaimed Gina. 'Our families also tease each other constantly.'

'True, Gina,' said Sanjay. 'When I first came here, I was nervous about being the only "half-breed" in a group of purebred Sri Lankans, especially since most of them are relatives. But once I'd had a good dose of my crazy cousins and their – nearly always and inevitably – crazy mates, I, too, felt as if I was back at Patiyak – quite at home.'

'Are you calling us crazy, Sanjay?' asked David, glowering at him. 'Take five hundred lines and write, "I must NOT call my family crazy". Hopefully that will teach you a lesson.'

Sanjay grimaced at the JEACs and said, 'See what I mean? Aunty Consy's gone to Prithee's home for the next few weeks, David, remember?' He turned back to the JEACs and said, 'She left her apologies that she wouldn't be here to meet you, and a few surprises, which we'll deal with later – she's a sweetheart and great fun. Prithee's another cousin – and they'll all come to the fundraiser.'

'Would you like to see the arrangements we've made for you?' asked Priyani.

'Yes, please,' said the JEACs.

Everyone trailed after her except for Aunty Matty and Leo. Leo had not heard most of the conversation as he had removed his hearing aid once more. He and Aunty Matty had an interesting, confusing conversation until Aunty Matty gave up in despair, turned on the TV, and they settled down to watch a tennis match. Most of the family were sports crazy.

The others went past the main buildings and a short distance along a narrow, well-used trail. Within five minutes they reached a clearing which had a small waterhole; a few birds and rabbits disappeared on their arrival. There, set up a short distance from the waterhole, were four tents.

'What do you think?' asked Lalith. 'Would you prefer to camp out here and come to the house for meals, or would you like to stay in the house – we have lots of room.'

'This is perfect,' said Anu and Amy, and the others agreed enthusiastically.

'We call it *Youngsters' Camping Site*,' said Sanjay.

'YCS! YCS!' yelled Mich and Gina, and the group burst out laughing.

'Exactly! YCS it is. We felt that you'd have a sense of independence, and we want you to thoroughly enjoy your holiday,' said Lalith.

'We're gonna have a blast,' said Nimal.

'And we have another idea for later on this week,' said Akka, twinkling at them. 'Stop right there, you two,' she continued with a laugh, as Gina and Mich immediately clamoured to know what it was. 'No, I'm not going to tell you anything further at the moment.'

'Oooh, Akka,' groaned Mich, 'you're such a tease.'

'Please, pleeease tell us now,' begged Gina.

The others laughed at Akka's prim face as she tried not to give in to the girls.

'Why don't you check out these tents for now?' suggested Priyani.

That distracted the girls, and they ran over to the tents.

'Gee, look, Gina,' squealed Mich, examining the little tent sandwiched between two larger ones, 'this pink tent has only two sleeping bags. Is this for us?' she asked.

'Of course,' said Priyani. 'The blue tent is for the boys and the green for Amy and Anu; they can each hold three sleeping bags so Umedh can share with the boys and, perhaps, Mahesika will join you girls. The brown tent is for storage. You'll be okay since this waterhole is close to the buildings and none of the larger wildlife use it. Hunter can sleep in whichever tent he chooses.'

'Who's Mahesika?' asked Anu.

'Mahesika Jayatilleke, an orphan from a foster home in town, keeps running over here – she's crazy about animals. Her foster parents, who have four other children, know she's safe and don't worry about her. Mahesika's twelve, a little shy, tall for her age, and she'll disappear – sometimes for a few days at a stretch – we haven't a clue where she goes.'

'Does she speak English?' asked Amy.

'Oh, yes,' said David. 'She learned from Mum and Aunty Consy because they told her that if she learned how to read and write, Priyani would lend her books about animals. She's a bright child with a good sense of humour – usually better with older folks than with kids her own age, probably because most of the kids she meets are not as crazy about animals as she is.'

'We're hoping she'll make friends with you, starting with Nimal,' said Sanjay.

'Why me?' asked Nimal, his voice squeaking in surprise.

'Because of your charisma with animals – she's like a little wild animal herself,' said David.

'Oh, man, and here was I convinced it was because of my charm and good looks,' said Nimal immediately. 'Does she know we're coming?'

'Yes, Mum told her. She seemed interested but said she had other things to do tonight,' said Priyani. 'She'll turn up in her own time.'

'Now, are you going to check the other tents?' said Sanjay.

They did. Other than the sleeping bags, each tent contained lanterns, munchies and a water cooler.

'And a walkie-talkie unit, with four handsets and headphones,' said Rohan, coming across it in their tent. 'Why do we need this?'

'Well, we knew you folks like to go exploring and since you don't know this jungle yet, we figured these would be useful in case you get separated and need to contact each other,' said Lalith.

'Also, mobile phone reception isn't very good in some of the denser areas,' said Sanjay, 'and these WTs have a good range – sorry, folks, walkie-talkies.'

'Gee, thanks,' said Amy gratefully. 'You've thought of everything, and we're gonna have a fabulous time.'

'Good,' said Lalith, 'that's exactly what we planned. Now, let's get back to the house and feed you. I'm sure you must be . . .'

'Starving!' yelled Mich and Gina. They ran back to the building ahead of the others.

'What about chores?' asked Anu. 'There are six of us and we don't want to be a burden.'

'Our helpers would be most offended if you tried to do anything,' said Priyani. 'I'll take you to meet the two "chiefs" in a few minutes. They have everything under control – including us. They haven't come out to greet you because they're busy preparing a feast.'

They reached the house and Priyani asked the JEACs to follow her.

'The door's shut,' said Priyani, looking at her watch. She winked at them and whispered, 'Do you mind hanging around quietly for five minutes? It's nearly 8 o'clock and I was told that if we entered the dining room before then, I'd be begging for trouble.'

The youngsters looked intrigued, but agreed willingly.

'Anu, when Lalith and I met you all in Australia, at Jack's new conservation, your mother mentioned that you were going to write a story about your adventure with the dolphins,' said Priyani. 'Have you started writing it yet?'

'Only very rough notes, and an outline,' said Anu shyly. 'I haven't had much time at school.'

'But she's got a title for it: *The Dolphin Heptad*. She's currently editing her first book, *Peacock Feathers*. I've read a few chapters and it's very exciting,' said Amy enthusiastically.

'Well, you know we're all looking forward to reading your books when they're out,' said Priyani kindly.

'Thanks, Priyani. I do have a lot of fun with my writing,' said Anu.

At 8 o'clock sharp, Priyani knocked on the door, which opened promptly.

'*Ayubowan!*' said two women, who were wearing traditional outfits of colourful lungis and white blouses with puffed sleeves. The children greeted them in the traditional manner, too.

'I am Niranjani,' said one of them. '*Aney, okoma lassanai, hamu,*' she continued, gazing at the children admiringly, stroking Gina and Mich's curls and Amy's long hair.

She also said something else, but before Priyani could translate, the other woman spoke up, saying, 'I – Shalini – you like table?'

The children looked at the table; it was loaded with a splendid feast.

'Very nice,' said Anu, smiling at them, and they smiled back.

Nimal sniffed exaggeratedly and looked at the two women with a broad grin. 'Can we eat now?'

'*Mukada qu-ay, hamu?*' asked Shalini, whose knowledge of English was limited.

Priyani translated, and Shalini smiled at Nimal and said, 'Yes – you eat.'

'And Niranjani was admiring all of you and especially liked Amy's long hair, Gina and Mich's curls, Anu's eyes, and the two strong boys,' said Priyani.

'Come, you *babas* sit,' said Niranjani, taking Mich and Gina by the hand and seating them. 'You like I serve you?'

'Yes, please,' said the girls.

Priyani indicated that the others should sit down, too, since the adults were joining them from the living room. They lingered over the delicious meal, and after a wonderful dessert – of not only wattalapan but also chocolate cake – everyone was too full to rise from the table.

'How do you say "thank you" and "great food"?' asked Nimal. Lalith told him, and the boy turned to the women and said, '*Stuthi! Kema hari rassai.*'

The others echoed him, much to the delight of the women, who laughed and cleared the table happily, not allowing the JEACs to assist.

'Now, time for bed, everyone,' said Priyani, noticing that the younger girls were yawning.

'What's the plan for the morning?' asked Rohan. 'Also, what time would you like us to come in for breakfast?'

'You can help yourselves to food any time from 5 a.m. onwards,' said Akki. 'Most of the staff eat here, and grab a bite to eat between five and ten in the morning. Lunch can be sandwiches or rice and curries – either picnic style or at the table – we're very flexible, and you can get it between noon and 3 p.m. Unless otherwise planned, dinner is also whenever you please, between 8 p.m. and 10:30 or 11:30 and, of course, there are always snacks available.'

'Do you want to sleep in tomorrow?' asked Lalith. When a horrified 'No' answered him, he grinned and said, 'Okay, come and grab a bite to eat as soon as you're dressed – you can use the bathrooms and get things from your suitcases whenever you wish. I've got an early meeting in town, but Tony and Sanjay will take you out to the construction site, then bring you back so that you can explore the OC.'

'Would you like a picnic lunch tomorrow?' said Sanjay.

'Lovely, thanks,' said Amy.

'Are we leaving you too much on your own?' asked Priyani anxiously. 'We didn't want to plan a rigid programme for you and, because of the current situation, we're all pretty tied up, but after we've relocated the animals and finished with the fundraiser, we'll take you on some tours.'

'This is all part of the fun,' said Anu reassuringly. 'Please don't worry – we love trekking in jungles and if we've got maps, we'll be fine. But isn't there *anything* you want us to do?'

'Sure is, and I'll call an official meeting about it,' said Neeka. 'Molly and I are in charge of fundraising, while Priyani, Akki and Ken are in charge of the rest, although Ken helps with fundraising, too.'

'Okay,' chorused the JEACs.

Wishing everybody a good night, the youngsters trooped back to the tents, accompanied by Sanjay and Lalith, who ensured they had everything they needed.

Mich and Gina were exhausted and fell asleep almost immediately. Hunter, wondering why they were not in the same 'house' as the older ones, sniffed at the zipped up flap of their tent, pushed against it and whined, looking up at the others anxiously.

'What's up, old chap?' asked Nimal. 'Something bothering you?'

Hunter nosed the tent again, and barked softly.

'I get it,' said Nimal. 'He thinks the kids shouldn't be left alone in the tent and wants to stay with them. Hunter, you're one clever dog.'

He unzipped the flap of the tent, Hunter licked the others and then crept inside quietly, lying down between the two sleeping girls with a deep sigh.

'That's one smart dog,' said Rohan, as Nimal zipped up the tent again. 'Streets ahead of us – imagine realizing that the kids had never been in a tent on their own before?'

'I think it's a great idea,' said Anu. 'They'll be safe as houses with him there. Oooh, I'm getting sleepy, too,' she continued, stifling a yawn.

'Me, too,' yawned Amy.

The girls went to bed while the boys talked for a while, watching some of the smaller animals come to the waterhole for a drink.

'Lots of rabbits and birds,' said Nimal softly. 'And there's a small herd of deer coming down now.'

'Man, that elephant's pretty close,' said Rohan, as they heard a loud trumpeting.

'True – though, you know, it's probably not as close as it sounds.'

'Yeah, of course,' said Rohan. 'I heard you talking to Lalith about the elephants and asking how close they were. What did he say?'

'Nowhere near this spot,' said Nimal. 'He said they have nine herds – fairly spread out at the moment.'

They heard another trumpet.

'Hmmm, that certainly sounds as if there was at least one herd close by,' said Rohan. 'Oh, well, I guess we'd better get to bed.'

The boys turned in and when Sanjay came by half an hour later to check on them, there was no sound from any of the tents.

CHAPTER 7

Exploring

The trumpeting of an elephant woke Nimal, and glancing at the luminous face of his wristwatch, he saw that it was only 4:30 a.m. Without disturbing Rohan, he crept out of the tent, pulled out a mat and lay on it, watching birds and animals flock to the waterhole. It was still dark and, several times, he looked around curiously, sensing that something was watching him, and wondering if there was a cheetah or larger animal close by – but he saw nothing.

A bold rabbit hopped near Nimal, and the boy made a soft sound. The rabbit pricked up its ears, yielded to the fascinating charisma Nimal exuded towards all creatures, and hopped into the boy's arms, nestling there and looking up at him trustingly. Nimal stroked the creature gently and more rabbits loped up, quickly surrounding the boy, as he crooned over them.

Suddenly there was a soft 'plop' to Nimal's left and the rabbits dispersed rapidly into the undergrowth. Nimal looked towards the sound and saw a girl crouched on all fours, as if she had just dropped down from a tree. They stared at one another, neither saying a word. Then, just like the rabbits, the girl moved cautiously towards Nimal, her eyes never leaving his face, her bare feet making no sound. Nimal stayed still and began to talk in a low voice.

'Hello! You must be Mahesika. I'm Nimal. Aren't the rabbits fantastic?'

Mahesika smiled and nodded, keeping her big, brown eyes on Nimal's face as she continued to move towards him. When she reached the mat she sat down in a corner; she appeared to be tongue-tied.

'If we stay quiet for a bit,' said Nimal, still in the same low tone, 'the rabbits may come back.'

Mahesika nodded eagerly and Nimal began to make a soft crooning sound. In a few minutes, the rabbit that had first made friends with the boy came back to him, although it eyed Mahesika warily until it was safe in Nimal's arms. The girl didn't move.

'It's okay now,' said Nimal, cradling the rabbit and caressing it. 'Do you want to pet it? Don't make any sudden movements.'

Mahesika moved closer to Nimal and reached out her hand tentatively. The rabbit lay quiescent in Nimal's arms, and did not flinch or run away when Mahesika stroked it gently. She smiled delightedly at Nimal. After a few moments, Nimal encouraged the creature to rejoin its mates, and it hopped off reluctantly.

'So you like animals, too,' said Nimal conversationally.

'Yes, very much,' said Mahesika shyly. 'But I have never seen animals behave like that with anyone.'

'He has a special gift,' said Anu, joining them on the mat. She had been a silent observer from the time Mahesika joined Nimal. She put out her hand, saying, 'Hi, Mahesika, I'm Anu.'

'I've heard about all of you,' said Mahesika shyly, shaking hands with her. 'Are the others still sleeping?'

'Just waking up,' said Rohan, poking his head out of the tent and grinning at her. 'Big crowd for you to meet. I'm Rohan, *Ayubowan.*'

Mahesika smiled as he joined them, putting her hands together in the traditional greeting, too.

'And here comes Amy,' said Nimal.

'Hi, Mahesika,' said Amy, beaming at her. 'Where did you come from?'

'Hi,' said Mahesika. 'I was in the mango tree and saw Nimal with the rabbits. I wanted to pet them, too.'

'So *you* were the one watching me,' said Nimal. 'I thought I felt eyes on me, but didn't see you till you dropped down. Thank goodness it wasn't a leopard or some other dangerous animal.'

'You'd probably have had the leopard purring all over you and trying to sit in your lap,' said Rohan with a laugh. 'You know, Mahesika, any animal will go to him – big or small. We're waiting to see him with the elephants.'

'Really? Do *all* animals come to you, Nimal?' asked Mahesika, gazing at him in awe. 'You must have some special kind of . . . of . . . scent, which brings them to you. I don't know the right word.' She was fast losing her shyness with the friendly JEACs.

'We call it "charisma",' said Anu. 'It's fascinating to watch.'

There was a bark from the pink tent and when Rohan unzipped it, a black form darted out of the tent and into the shrubbery. Mich and Gina emerged from the tent and came over to greet Mahesika.

'Gee, look at Hunter,' said Mich.

Hunter had come out of the shrubbery, trotted off to a flowering bush, pulled off a flower and was seated in front of Mahesika, holding out a paw. The girl looked at him in astonishment. Then, laughing merrily, she shook hands with him, and he offered her the flower.

'Aney, he is so sweet,' she said, beaming with delight as she took the flower and hugged Hunter. 'Oooh, his tongue is very wet,' she squealed as the dog washed her face with licks.

'Well, Hunter thinks you're special, too,' said Anu with a smile, as Mahesika tucked the flower into her ponytail. 'You must have a way with animals.'

'I like all animals,' said Mahesika, who was now quite relaxed with the JEACs, her arms around Hunter. 'I know you all live on conservations – Aunty Renuka told me.'

Rohan's alarm went off just then and he said, 'It's 5:15, folks. We've got to get ready for the site visit. Hurry!'

They took it for granted that Mahesika would join them, not saying anything specific, but simply including her in their chatter and laughter.

Mahesika was puzzled. She was unused to being included so naturally in a group of children and, intrigued by the rabbits' response to Nimal, was curious to see how other animals reacted to him. Therefore, when they went towards the buildings, she accompanied them.

'Hello, everyone,' said Akki, as they entered the large hall where tables were set out for meals. 'How are you, Mahesika? It's nice to see you. Come along, folks – it's self-service here.'

Soon everyone had a plateful of breakfast and Mahesika enjoyed herself amidst the JEACs as they laughed, joked and teased each other.

'Good morning, JEACs,' said Sanjay, entering the room a few minutes later. 'How were the tents? Hello, Mahesika.'

'The tents were grand, thanks,' said Nimal. 'Mahesika dropped in to visit us early this morning.'

'Would you like to join the JEACs today?' asked Sanjay, turning to the girl who smiled shyly at him.

'Oh, yes, please, please come,' chorused Gina and Mich, before Mahesika could respond.

'You *must* come,' insisted Mich, as Mahesika hesitated.

'Yeah, Hunter and all of us will miss you *desperately* if you don't,' begged Gina.

The older JEACs nodded in agreement and Mahesika agreed shyly, grinning with pleasure as Mich and Gina cheered loudly. None of her peers felt the same way as she did about animals, and she felt comfortable with this group.

'Now, now, what's all this hullabaloo about?' said David, entering the room with a strapping young man.

'Hi, I'm Tony Munasinghe,' said the young man, shaking hands with all of them, including Hunter. 'I've heard lots about you and am here to take you to the construction site – when you've finished breakfast.'

'Thanks very much – we're done,' said Rohan. 'There are three sections of the wall still to be completed, right?'

'That's right,' said Tony, 'and we're working on all of them simultaneously.'

'And when can we bathe the elephants?' asked Mich eagerly.

'Tomorrow morning. Akka will drive you there – she and David have taken half a day off school,' said Sanjay. 'There's a natural bay, outside the OC, in the north-west. Sorry, OC stands for . . .'

'*Old Conservation*, and NC stands for *New Conservation*,' chanted the JEACs.

Sanjay laughed. 'I see you've learned our jargon,' he said. 'Well, tame elephants are taken to the bay, daily, so that tourists can bathe them. Mahesika, would you like to join in?'

'Yes, please,' said Mahesika. 'But we should go early – before all the tourists arrive.'

'Good thinking,' said Sanjay. 'Shall we say 6 a.m. tomorrow?'

'YES,' chorused the children.

'Are there baby elephants, too, Mahesika?' asked Mich.

'Yes, four infants – and they're only a few weeks old.'

'Can't we go *now*?' begged Gina.

'No, dear, we need to arrange things with the mahouts,' said Tony smiling at the eager little girl. 'Will you survive till tomorrow?'

'Guess so,' said Gina and Mich.

'Good. Now, have you decided where you want to go exploring after the site visits?' said Tony.

'The north and central areas in the western section,' said Rohan.

'Okay. We'll drop you off at a waterhole and you can explore to your hearts' content,' said Tony. 'Shall we go?'

The youngsters and Hunter piled into Tony's Land Rover and they set off, Sanjay pointing out various trails leading off the main track they were taking.

'Where does this stream go?' asked Anu, as they crossed it over a small bridge.

'It's a subsidiary of the river where you'll be bathing the elephants,' said Tony. 'It's a long river and its source is beyond the hills which border the north-west side of the NC. Flowing along the outside of the NC, it runs parallel to the rocks bordering the west, broadens into a natural bay between the two sections of jungle – the *Elephants' Bathtub*, as we call it – and then splits in two. One branch meanders into the OC at the north-west corner – it becomes a narrow, shallow stream and breaks out into tributaries, which feed all our waterholes – it's called the *Sustainer*. It finally flows out of our Centre in the south-east.'

'What's the name of the main river,' asked Nimal, 'and where does it end?'

'The Piliangala,' said Sanjay. 'After the bay, it curves away from the OC, running parallel to it but leaving a gap of about three kilometres between the river and the Conservation. The land in that region is extremely fertile and good for farming. The Piliangala makes a wide sweep around the south-west corner of the OC and flows east, meeting the Sustainer approximately fifteen kilometres south of our border. It ends in a lake many kilometres away.'

It took them a while to reach the north end of the OC and exit through the gate. Across bare land they saw the beginnings of another vast expanse of jungle.

'Man,' said Rohan, as they topped a low hill a few minutes later, 'those rocks are humongous.'

'It's a superb, natural area for a conservation,' said Tony, 'and perfect for the elephants.'

'We have to visit all three sites – do you mind?' said Sanjay.

'No problemo, yaar,' said Nimal.

'And here we are,' said Tony, stopping the Land Rover at the first site. 'As you can see, work is progressing nicely, and this section is more than half complete.'

'The wall looks solid,' said Rohan, as everyone climbed out of the vehicle.

The two men went over to talk to the foreman, and the workers stopped to say a*yubowan* to them and to the youngsters. Many of the women looked at Mich's blonde hair and commented on it in Sinhala, pointing at the little girl.

'What are they saying, Mahesika?' asked Anu.

'They say that her hair is like gold and are puzzled as to how it became like that,' said Mahesika.

She said something to the women, who began talking with her.

'I told them that all of you were visitors to Sri Lanka; that four of you were from India and two from Canada. I tried to explain where Canada was, but I don't think they've heard of it,' said Mahesika.

One of the women said something to Tony, and he turned to the children with a smile. 'They want to know if you would pose for a photograph with them, so that they can show their children the little girl with golden hair and all the other "*lassana*" children. Do you mind? They know I have a camera in the car.'

'Not at all,' said Anu and Amy.

'What does "lassana" mean?' asked Nimal.

'Beautiful or nice,' said Sanjay with a grin, and as Nimal grimaced, he continued, 'Hope you feel beautiful, yaar.'

'Haven't had a chance to really do my hair today or to put on my face,' retorted Nimal, patting his hair delicately.

The others chuckled as they posed for the picture. Shortly after that, they piled back into the vehicle and, waving goodbye, set off for the next site.

They did not get out of the Land Rover there but did so at the third site, which was at the south-eastern end of the Conservation.

'The foreman wants a private chat, Sanjay,' said Tony. 'He seems rather perturbed.'

'Excuse me, folks,' said Sanjay.

He and Tony listened to the man, who spoke to them rapidly in Sinhala. After the conversation, Tony and Sanjay shook hands with him, and he went off to continue supervising and instructing his team. Tony said a few words of encouragement to the workers and then shepherded the JEACs into the Land Rover.

'If it's not one thing, it's another, yaar,' said Sanjay, grimacing at Tony.

'Ya, machang,' agreed Tony, turning the vehicle to drive back to the OC.

'Why, what's happened this time?' asked Rohan.

'The foreman says that last night, while the security guards were on duty, one of the men heard a gunshot around midnight,' said Tony.

The children gasped.

'He called a colleague on the mobile, but that chap was quite far away and had not heard anything unusual,' continued Tony. 'So the first chap asked for reinforcements – they're tough characters, these security guards – and two of them went into the NC, along some of the trails, but found nothing. As they returned to the wall, another shot was fired. Sprinting towards the sound, they actually heard footsteps running away, moving eastwards into the forest – but *outside* the NC.'

'They followed quickly and searched the area as thoroughly as they could. However, given that it was pitch dark and they only had torches, they saw nothing,' said Sanjay. 'This morning they told the foreman and asked him to report the matter to us as soon as we arrived.'

'But who do they *think* fired the gunshots?' asked Rohan.

'Poachers, probably,' said Sanjay. 'I'll call up the security company and find out if they can send us more men. We can't have poachers roaming around the NC, trying to get in over our temporary wall.'

'Good idea, machang,' said Tony, waving to the gatekeeper who once again opened the gate for him to enter the OC. 'Now, JEACs, don't worry about all this. I think we'll drop you off near a large waterhole in the north-western area.'

'Do you mind if we explore some of the unknown territory?' asked Nimal.

'Not at all,' said Tony. 'We know you can take care of yourselves and each other. However, would you mind putting that off until we've equipped you with guns and TGs – sorry, *tranquillizer guns* – since there are still a few large animals around, including the elephants?'

'Sure thing, Tony,' said Rohan immediately. 'We'll stay east of the dense area.'

'Here you go,' said Sanjay, giving Amy an extra mobile telephone. 'It's fully charged and though it may not have good reception in a few areas, hang on to it since we didn't bring the WTs. If there are any problems, please call one of us immediately; Lalith's speed dial is one, ours are two or three. Okay?'

'Right,' said Amy. 'We promise to be careful.'

A few minutes later Tony brought the vehicle to a stop and said, 'The waterhole's five minutes away; if we walk, we may see some wildlife at it.'

They jumped out of the vehicle following Tony and soon reached a place from where they could observe the waterhole without disturbing the wildlife. There were plenty of animals around it – spotted deer, sambur, rabbits and lots of monkeys and birds. Hunter stayed absolutely still. Once the creatures had assuaged their thirst, they wandered off into the jungle.

'Oooh, that was super,' breathed Gina and Mich.

'Agreed,' said Tony. He looked at his watch and said, 'It's 9 o'clock now – suppose we meet back here at 5 p.m. – will that give you enough time to explore?'

'Time? Yeah, I guess so,' said Rohan. He laughed at Tony's puzzled expression, and continued, 'Sorry. It's just that we love being in the jungle and there's never *enough* time.'

'Yeah, I know you lot,' said Sanjay. 'Akka said that once we got here I could tell you about the other plans we have for you. Would you like to camp out in the OC in a couple of days?'

'Sanjay – you angel!' said Amy, hugging him impulsively, as the others shouted for joy. 'Tell Akka we LOVE the plan.'

'It'll be superfantabulous,' said Nimal.

'We'll have to find a good spot for you to camp in,' said Tony, leading the way back to the Land Rover.

'And you'll come, too, won't you Mahesika?' said Anu, turning to the girl who had been rather quiet.

'I'd like to,' said Mahesika, a little shyly. 'But I don't have a tent.'

'Don't worry, we'll put up four tents – like at the YCS,' said Sanjay. 'There's never a shortage of tents on our Conservation.'

They reached the Land Rover, and Tony handed out their knapsacks.

'Goody. We can't *possibly* forget our lunch,' said Nimal. 'But what's in that humongous cooler?' he added, eyeing it curiously as Tony and Sanjay lifted it out.

'Priyani and Akki thought you folks wouldn't survive the whole day on just your lunch, so they packed extra supplies,' said Sanjay with a grin. 'The locks are to prevent curious animals – like the monkeys – from opening it and stealing your food. Here are the keys.'

'Mmmch! I kiss my hands to them,' said Nimal.

'We'll stash the cooler in the undergrowth, near this large mango tree. It should be safe there,' said Tony.

'Okay, we're off,' said Sanjay, as they climbed into their vehicle. 'Have fun!'

'We will,' chorused the children. 'Bye, and thanks a ton.'

They waved to the men and then looked at each other in excitement.

'What's the plan, Rohan?' asked Amy, and everyone looked at him expectantly.

'How about this?' suggested Rohan looking at the map. 'We'll follow this stream to some of the waterholes, stop for an early lunch around eleven, take this *other* trail, which leads back here, and have tea around 3:30. What do you think?'

'Whereabouts are we in the Conservation?' asked Anu.

'Somewhere in the north-west of the *centre* of the Conservation,' said Rohan, studying the map. 'Aha – here we are.' He pointed to a spot on the map and the others pored over it.

'We should bring our compasses and WTs when we come camping,' said Nimal, studying the map. 'Let's move, folks – upstream or down?'

'Downstream,' suggested Amy.

It was a beautiful, easy-going trail and they saw plenty of wildlife. They paddled in the shallow stream, until it began to increase in depth, and then walked beside it on the western bank. Hunter got thoroughly soaked, enjoying the cool water. Of course, he shook himself right amongst the children and showered them, too – not that anyone minded.

'Oh, look,' said Anu softly, 'there's a doe and her fawn hiding in the undergrowth.'

As everyone stopped and looked in the direction of her pointing finger, Amy said quietly, 'A newborn – look! It can't stand up and the mother is bleating anxiously because we're too close.'

'Don't move, anyone,' said Rohan. 'Let Nimal reassure the mother first. Hunter, not a sound – good boy.'

Nimal began by bleating like the mother, but in less anxious tones. The doe tilted her head to one side and listened, her body on top of the fawn as she tried to protect it. Nimal continued bleating and then began to talk in what the children called his *special voice*. The doe stopped crying, moved off the fawn and stared at the boy. She did not panic when Nimal moved towards her, but gazed at him out of her huge, gentle eyes, while the fawn turned its head towards Nimal and bleated softly. Nimal reached the doe and let her sniff at his hand before touching her, and the doe, sighing with relief, lay down beside her fawn, looking as if she would be quite happy to spend the rest of the day with Nimal. The fawn licked Nimal's hand and the boy gently stroked its soft fur. He offered both creatures some tender green leaves, which they accepted gratefully, before he moved slowly away from them. The doe lay still, quite at peace, and licked her little one contentedly.

Without a word, Nimal and the others moved away until the doe was out of sight – Hunter was amazingly silent, too.

'Aney, you are a magic boy with animals,' exclaimed Mahesika. 'I wish I had your gift.'

'As do all of us,' said Rohan, smiling at her. 'Later on we'll tell you more stories of the animals he has befriended.'

'It's too bad the fawn was just born,' said Gina, 'otherwise we may have been able to pet it, too. Right, Nimal?'

'I doubt I could have calmed the mother down to that extent,' said Nimal. 'It's not as if they're used to us, you know – unlike animals in a zoo. I wanted to pick it up and cuddle it, but that would have been a mistake for sure.'

'How do you *know* when you can do something like that?' asked Mich.

'Instinct, I guess,' said Nimal. 'Just like I know *instinctively* that it's NOW time to eat,' he added with a chuckle. 'Isn't anyone else hungry?'

'We are,' chorused the others. 'We're *starving*.'

'There's a perfect spot near that tiny waterfall,' said Rohan, indicating a place where a large rock in the stream bed created a miniature waterfall.

They enjoyed a delicious meal, finishing up with a drink of lemonade. Hunter had his own special food and, naturally, everyone shared with him, too.

'Time to move on,' said Rohan a little later, looking at his watch.

They turned north and found the trail which would take them back to the large waterhole they had started out from.

'We're walking north-west now,' said Rohan, looking at the map.

Nimal pointed to his left and said, 'That part of the jungle looks extremely dense – I wonder if there are marked trails in there. Let's have a look at the map again, Rohan.'

The boys pored over the drawing.

'That must be the unexplored section – just waiting for us,' said Nimal.

'No! That's a bad place,' said Mahesika.

'Why, Mahesika?' asked Rohan, looking at her in surprise.

But the girl would not say anything more other than 'there are noises – bad things are in there'.

'Have you been in there?' asked Anu.

'No,' said Mahesika and ran ahead to join Gina, Mich and Hunter in order to avoid more questions.

'Don't push her,' said Nimal, as they gazed after Mahesika. 'She's only just met us and if we push too hard, she may withdraw totally.'

'Good point, yaar,' said Rohan, while Amy and Anu nodded in agreement.

They caught up with the three girls, and Mahesika looked at them apprehensively. However, seeing that they continued to include her and did not ask any more questions, she quickly relaxed again.

The trail was fun; it led them through an area with numerous trees of 'temple' flowers, which filled the air with their sweet fragrance. By

3 o'clock they were back at the large waterhole. Since they had walked many kilometres and were hungry again, they unlocked the cooler and had a grand tea.

'Mmmm, chocolate cake to finish up this feast,' said Nimal. 'Gina and Mich, I'm sure you're *far* too tired to have any.'

'No, we're not,' shrieked the girls, pouncing on him. 'We want our share.'

Mahesika laughed at the way the girls romped with Nimal. 'You're like one big family,' she said to Anu. 'It must be nice.'

'It is, and you can be part of our family, too,' said Anu promptly. 'The only stipulation is that you have to learn our songs and be a little bit crazy.'

'What songs are those?' asked Mahesika. She added with a grin, 'I think the craziness will come naturally if anyone hangs around all of you.' She had completely lost her shyness with them.

'Observant gal,' said Nimal, and then as Amy pretended to glare at him, he added hastily, 'I mean, *womyn*, of course – to be PC about it all.'

'What does it mean, being "PC"?' asked Mahesika.

'It means being politically correct in the way we speak,' said Anu, with a grin. She explained briefly. Mahesika soon caught on and chuckled as Anu concluded, 'As you see, we like to exaggerate being PC since it's carried to a ridiculous extreme at times.'

'So what are the songs?' asked Mahesika again.

'We have a theme song for our group,' said Amy. 'Gina made it up and Mich drew the cartoons to go with the song. Would you like to hear it and may we tell you about our group? You can belong if you like.'

'Yes, please,' said Mahesika eagerly.

She was thrilled to hear about the JEACs and eager to join in. She quickly picked up the theme song, and soon the whole crowd was singing lustily, Hunter joining in with an occasional bark. Then they sang some baila songs, and Mahesika was impressed that they had learned them so soon.

A loud beep made them realize that Tony was back in their midst, and they climbed into the Land Rover, taking turns to tell him about their day.

'I'm glad you had a good time,' said Tony, 'but you must be exhausted after walking so far.'

'Hmmm, I'm a bit tired,' admitted Anu, 'but only because we haven't quite got our jungle legs yet.'

'What are "jungle legs"?' asked Mahesika, looking at Anu's legs in astonishment. These youngsters certainly used some strange expressions.

'Oh, sorry,' laughed Anu. 'I mean that we've been stuck in school for the past few months, and although we play games and exercise a lot there, it's not the same as trekking through jungles.'

'True,' said Amy, 'although karate lessons keep us pretty fit.'

'Here we are,' said Tony, pulling up in the driveway.

'Thanks a ton, Tony!' chorused the JEACs as they jumped out of the vehicle and unloaded the cooler and their knapsacks.

'Aren't you coming in?' asked Amy, when Tony got back into the vehicle.

'No, I've got a number of things to do,' he said. 'But I'll see you tomorrow. Chandini's dropping you at the Elephants' Bathtub, but I'll be picking you up – have fun and enjoy yourselves.'

'We will, Tony, and thanks again,' said the youngsters and waved until he was out of sight.

'It certainly looks like you had a good time,' said Priyani, smiling at them.

'It was amazing,' said Rohan.

The JEACs were soon regaling the adults with what they had done during the day. After dinner and a sing-song, they went back to the YCS. Mahesika said she would see them in the morning, since she could not sleep over; and the JEACs, while assuring her that she would be welcome to share their tents any time, did not question her or try to force her into staying.

CHAPTER 8

Rub-a-Dub Scrub – The Elephants' Tub

'Nimal,' said Rohan, looking across at his cousin who had just woken up, 'do you feel like working out with some karate exercises?'

'Sure,' yawned Nimal. 'What's the time?'

'4:30,' said Rohan, unzipping their tent.

They were soon working out strenuously, finishing off with a mock karate fight. Just as they were about to collect their things for a shower, they heard a loud trumpeting.

'Now, you can't tell me that wasn't near us,' said Rohan, trying to figure out which direction the sound came from.

'Yeah,' said Nimal looking puzzled. 'I wonder if there's a herd nearby. Oh, hi, Mahesika,' he added cheerfully as the girl joined them.

'Hello, there,' said Rohan. 'Did you hear that elephant a moment ago? Do you know if there's a herd near us?'

'Hi, Rohan. There aren't usually herds in this area. What were you doing just now – fighting?' asked Mahesika.

'No – just practising our karate,' explained Rohan. 'It's a form of self-defence and keeps us very fit.'

'Can girls also do it?' asked Mahesika curiously.

'Yeah, sure thing,' said Nimal. 'Amy and Anu are taking classes already, and Gina and Mich start next term.'

The girls and Hunter came out of the tents and greeted Mahesika. 'How nice to see you bright and early,' said Amy. 'Did you hear that elephant trumpeting? It seemed really close.'

'That's what we were discussing, too,' said Nimal. 'But perhaps we'd better get going – it's 5:15.'

After a rapid wash, change and breakfast, they piled into Akka's Jeep, along with David and Akki, and bowled along the trail to the northern gates. Hunter was left behind on this occasion, since dogs were not allowed.

'We're looking forward to seeing Nimal's charisma at work,' said David. 'Also, Akki has a camera and will take pictures.'

'Wish we could have seen the doe and fawn,' sighed Akki.

'Oooh, look!' squealed Mich suddenly. 'Elephants! Lots of them, and teeny, weeny baby ones!'

A herd of sixteen elephants consisting of females, young males and four infants were sauntering majestically along the banks of the river, obviously heading for the bathing spot. Their caregivers – twelve men dressed in sarongs and shirts – waved as the Jeep drove past. They knew that the children were coming to bathe the elephants.

'Are the elephants friendly?' asked Mich.

'I don't know if you'd call them *friendly* as such,' said David. 'They're very obedient and peaceful, and allow humans to throw water on them, feed them, and ride on them, but they won't approach you of their own accord. As for the infants, they're boisterous, but very trusting – as are most infants. And, naturally, they love the bottles of milk everyone gives them.'

'Oooh, are we going to give them milk, too?' asked Gina.

'Of course you are, and bananas as well,' said Akka, pulling up in the car park.

The youngsters ran into the building, changed into swimsuits and rejoined the adults.

'Oooh, they're coming, they're coming,' chanted Mich and Gina, dancing up and down in excitement.

The chief mahout came over to greet the adults, whom he obviously knew, and then greeted the children traditionally. He spoke sufficient English to converse with them.

'Ah, Mahesika,' he said, 'you also with visitors? All elephants like Mahesika because she very good.'

The elephants entered the water and spread out, and the mahout asked the children to observe the animals first. The infants loved the water and frolicked in it gleefully, using their wobbly little trunks to spray each other and their older family members. Some of the bigger elephants lay down in the shallow water.

'Now you come,' said the mahout, and the children followed him eagerly.

With Nimal in the lead, they entered the water a short distance from the largest group of elephants. Each child was given a bucket and a long-handled brush, with instructions to splash the animals with water and then use the brushes to scrub their thick hides. 'Elephants be very happy you do this,' explained the mahout.

However, before they could follow the mahout's instructions, the matriarch of the herd rose to her feet and trundled towards Nimal. The mahout and the other caregivers began to move hastily towards her, assuring the adults that she had never attacked anybody. Rohan signalled to them to stop, asking David to explain that Nimal could handle the situation.

Nimal stood stock-still, completely unafraid, and as the matriarch drew near, he began to speak to her. She reached the boy and put out her trunk to touch him; then she gently patted him on the head, blew down his back, and wrapping her trunk around his waist, lifted him into the air.

The gasp of horror changed rapidly to one of astonishment when she placed the boy gently on her back and flapped her ears with pleasure as Nimal leaned over to stroke her head.

'*Ay yi yo, Hamu.* Mahatya, very clever,' said the mahout, letting out his breath in a sigh of relief. 'No other mahatya can do this. This mahatya – he talk to aliyas.'

He lapsed into his own tongue, chattering away rapidly to the other caregivers who were also looking at Nimal admiringly.

'Aney, that's incredible,' gasped Akka, who along with Akki and David had been petrified. 'Quick! Take pictures!'

'Nimal, can you get her to put you down and see how the infants respond to you?' suggested David.

'I'll try,' said Nimal. He leaned over the elephant's head stroking the beast and talking to it, and when its trunk came up to touch him, he wrapped it around his waist. The elephant promptly brought him down and placed him on his feet in the water, but she wouldn't move away from him. Nimal walked towards the infants, the matriarch following him sedately.

The infants stopped frolicking in the water and looked at the boy approaching them – he did not have a milk bottle in his hand, nor was he one of their human caregivers, but he smelt special. When he spoke to them, they listened to his kind voice and moved towards him.

'Awww, look! They're kissing him,' squealed Mich, as the infants all tried to touch the boy with their little trunks.

'Nimal, can we come and play with them, too?' begged Gina.

'Of course – they're a friendly bunch,' said Nimal.

Soon all the JEACs were cuddling the infants, taking turns to feed them milk, and giving them and the other elephants bananas. After a while, Akka and David waved a reluctant goodbye and went on to their schools.

'Oooh, their trunks are so soft and wriggly. Like . . . like . . . humongous worms,' squealed Gina, as one of the infants tangled his trunk in her curls and got stuck.

A caregiver helped Gina to release the infant. In an excess of exuberance, the baby pushed Gina, who tumbled head first into the water.

They had a fantastic time playing with the infants, going for rides, and bathing the bigger elephants. The huge creatures lay peacefully on their sides in the shallow river, enjoying the feel of the brushes cleansing their hides. The caregivers could not get over the way in which their elephants reacted to Nimal; while the animals obeyed their caregivers, they kept wanting to cluster around the boy.

All too soon it was time to leave, and Tony arrived to pick them up. After a reluctant parting on both sides, the youngsters showered, dried off and dressed. Then they waved goodbye to the caregivers and elephants as Tony drove back to the Conservation.

'I'm not surprised the elephants wanted to adopt Nimal,' laughed Tony. 'Sanjay says he has yet to see a creature that *didn't* want to adopt the chap.'

Back at the house, Hunter greeted them boisterously, and Priyani led them into the dining room where they ate a huge meal and told the adults about their experience with the elephants.

'I *wish* I could have seen you with the elephants, Nimal,' said Aunty Matty.

'I took lots of pictures, Aunty,' said Akki, 'and I'll develop them this afternoon. Now, where's Neeka? She and Molly wanted to talk to the JEACs about fundraising.'

'In the auditorium,' said Priyani.

'Thanks – come on, JEACs, it's about a twenty-minute walk, unless you want someone to give us a ride?' said Akki.

'Oh, no, we'll walk,' said Anu, and the others agreed.

They followed Akki, Amy and Anu picking temple flowers along the way.

'Here's the Cinnamon Centre,' said Akki, as they reached a circular building.

'What's that strong smell?' asked Gina.

'Cinnamon,' said Mahesika. 'It grows wild here.'

'Wow, the smell sure hits you,' said Amy, sniffing delightedly.

'That's only because there's a nice breeze today,' said Akki, ushering them into the building.

'Hi, JEACs. How was the elephant bathing?' called Neeka, as they entered the large conference room where she and another woman were chatting.

'Superfantabulous!' said everyone together.

'This is Molly Liyanage,' said Neeka.

'Delighted to meet you, JEACs,' said Molly, a smart-looking woman, with an abundance of jet-black hair, which reached below her waist.

'Are you *also* one of the cousins?' asked Mich.

'No, dear, thank goodness,' said Molly with a smile. 'I was at school with Neeka. I'm surprised to see you, Nimal – Sanjay said that the elephants would keep you.'

'They nearly did,' said Akki, and she told them about the morning.

'Aney, I'm longing to see you with the animals, Nimal,' said Neeka.

'We're planning to go back some time,' said Rohan. 'Join us!'

'We will,' said Neeka. 'Now, are you sure you want to assist with this fundraising mail-out?'

'Definitely,' said Amy.

Molly laughed as she poured out glasses of juice. 'We obviously don't know these JEACs very well, Neeka. A little bird informed me that they're super efficient.'

'But this is a mailing to 5,000 companies and people, and each package gets four items – here's a sample package,' said Neeka. 'Unfortunately, we're all tied up today and can't help – but we're getting volunteers tomorrow who can complete it.'

'These boxes along the wall have the enclosures,' said Molly.

Anu and Amy had been examining the sample package.

'Is it a general mailing or a personalized one?' asked Anu.

'General,' said Molly. 'Okay, young lady – you have a gleam in your eye. What's up?'

'She's going to make us *slave* – I just know it,' said Nimal. 'Right ho, Aunty. Lead us to it!'

'Mahesika, if I were you, I'd run away quickly,' said Rohan. 'Anu's a terror, to say the least.'

'No, I'd like to help,' said Mahesika.

'Cool it, folks,' said Amy. 'Well, Anu? How soon can we finish it?'

'By this evening. It's 9:30; including Hunter, there are eight of us; if we divvy up into two teams we'll be done around 7 p.m. or so,' said Anu. 'Is that okay, Neeka?'

'Neeka, put your eyes back into their sockets,' laughed Molly.

Neeka stopped gaping at Anu and said, 'That would be wonderful. But we don't want you to spend the whole day indoors. What about relaxing and food and, er . . . just having a good time?'

'We'll have a grand time,' said Gina. 'Anu makes it a lot of fun.'

'Yeah, and we'll have a . . . a . . . sense of a compliment,' added Mich.

'I guess you mean *accomplishment*, honey,' said Molly, giving her a hug.

'Yes, and we've done lots of mailings,' said Mich, not a whit abashed at having used the wrong word. She and Gina loved to learn and use big, new words whenever they could.

'If it's not inconvenient, could we have a few snacks for breaks, sandwiches for lunch, and lots of juice and water in here?' suggested Anu.

'No problem,' said Molly. 'We'll organize the juice and snacks immediately, and lunch will be brought to you around 1 o'clock. Is that okay?' As Anu nodded, she continued, 'What else do you need?'

'Nothing, thanks,' said Anu, accepting the telephone list Molly gave her in case they had questions.

Anu turned to the others and said, 'Okay, folks, you know what to do – let's get ourselves organized – yes, you, too, Hunter.'

Hunter immediately sat up and barked, looking very alert. He had assisted with many fundraising mail-outs.

'Come *on*, Neeka – we're in the way,' said Molly with a laugh, propelling her out of the room.

The youngsters quickly òrganized themselves at two tables, laughing and chatting as they worked. Mahesika had never been involved in anything like this before and had a marvellous time. Hunter wandered from table to table and picked up anything that fell on the ground. He was very clever indeed and never damaged the papers.

By lunchtime, they had completed nearly 2,000 packages. Neeka, who dropped in to have lunch with them, was astounded.

'You folks are amazing!' she gasped, looking at the boxes of completed packages and the way the material was organized. 'I will ask Fareez, one of our staff, to pick these up at 4 o'clock, as well as any others you have ready by then and drop them at the post office this afternoon.'

'Good idea,' said Rohan. 'We'll take a break and help him load them into the Land Rover.'

'Yikes! Was that thunder?' said Gina, as they heard a loud noise.

'Yes – a thunderstorm's been brewing all morning – but it won't hit before nine tonight,' said Neeka.

'Back to work, gang,' said Anu, returning to the tables.

Neeka left them to it and the afternoon sped by. At 4 o'clock they met Fareez, a nice, friendly man, and the boys helped load the boxes into his Land Rover. He had brought them a sumptuous tea, along with instructions to call Lalith once they were ready to return to the residence.

'As you see, the wind's very gusty, and Lalith said he'd pick you up,' said Fareez.

He waved to the JEACs and drove off, and the JEACs settled back to work.

'We're done and it's only 6:30!' said a jubilant Anu. 'Half an hour ahead of schedule, JEACs, and I think it's mainly thanks to Hunter's supervision. Great work, team!'

The JEACs cheered and Amy said, 'Excellent organization as usual, Anu.'

Rohan called Lalith, who picked them up a few minutes later and took them back to the house. Rohan and Nimal had to help Gina and Mich into the building because of the fierce wind.

'Perhaps you should stay in the house tonight,' suggested Lalith, looking out at the stormy clouds and bolts of lightning. 'We'd all be happier to know you're here – okay?'

'No problemo,' said Rohan.

Neeka arrived as they were sitting down to dinner. 'You JEACs are awesome – I can't believe it's finished!' she said. 'We'll take the balance to the post office in the morning.' She turned to the other adults, and described the way in which the JEACs had handled the mailing.

'Here comes the storm,' said Lalith a little later, as a great flash of lightning lit up the room, swiftly followed by a roar of thunder and the heavy patter of raindrops.

'Mahesika, perhaps you should stay here tonight,' suggested Aunty Matty.

'Okay, Aunty,' agreed Mahesika.

The talk turned to what the youngsters would do for the rest of the week. The JEACs offered to assist with more work but Neeka, whilst thanking them profusely, said that there would be lots of help, and that the JEACs should enjoy themselves.

'We'll need your help closer to the fundraiser,' added Priyani.

'Okay,' said Rohan. 'Then could we discuss the possibility of us camping out?'

'Did you have any particular campsite in mind?' asked Nimal.

'Not really,' said Lalith. 'You may find a place south of where the Piliangala River enters the OC. We can drop you near a large trail in that area.'

'Super,' said Anu.'

'You boys had better take some TGs with you,' said Tony.

'Perhaps we should look for a campsite tomorrow, see what you think of it, and then camp there on Wednesday,' suggested Rohan.

'Sure,' said Lalith. 'On Friday morning, we want to send you into town with Akka and David to talk to their schools about the JEACs.'

'Then we'll feed you and drop you off at the museum, while we finish with school,' said Akka, 'after which you can wander in the park until we pick you up. What do you think?'

'Sounds great,' chorused the JEACs.

'Good. That's settled,' said Tony. 'Now, tomorrow, we'll leave around 5 a.m. and I'll drop you at the trail. We'll provide you with lots of food and a phone. Call when you find a suitable place and we'll get there as soon as possible. I have the most flexibility tomorrow, so call me.'

'Good idea, Tony,' said Lalith. 'By the way, the wall's coming up quickly, and we think it should be completed by the end of this week – which means that we can finalize a date for relocating the elephants.'

'So soon?' asked Mahesika in surprise. 'I thought it would take another week.'

'So did we, but a batch of volunteer university students arrive tomorrow,' said Akki. 'That means 200 extra hands.'

Mahesika was very quiet for the rest of the meal, and after a brief sing-song, the JEACs said goodnight and went to bed. They all dreamed of elephants.

CHAPTER 9

JC and TOOJ

The JEACs were in the living room by 4:45 the next morning, and were checking their knapsacks to make sure they had their binoculars and cameras when Priyani looked into the room.

'My goodness, you *are* punctual!'

'Hungry, you mean, Priyani,' laughed Nimal. 'The open air always does this to us.'

'Haven't noticed the *closed* air making you any less hungry, yaar,' teased Rohan, as they followed Priyani into the dining room.

Tony, Sanjay and Lalith were already there, and once the JEACs had finished eating, they piled into the Land Rover – already loaded with everything they needed – and waved goodbye to the adults as they drove off. White, fluffy clouds tinged with orange moved along lazily, and everything looked newly washed as they made their way through the jungle and reached the stream. It was as far as the Land Rover could go into the north-west corner of the Conservation, so Tony stopped the vehicle.

'Where should we put our gear for now?' asked Anu. 'We can't cart things all over the place.'

'How about under this thick bush,' suggested Nimal, pointing to a bush with branches coming right down to the ground. 'It's right beside the stream, and the hamper will stay cool.'

'Good idea, machang,' said Tony, and he and Rohan unloaded things from the Land Rover and handed them to the others to place under the bush.

'Thanks, Tony,' said Rohan.

'Well, I'd better dash,' said Tony. 'Have a great time, keep the TGs with you, and call me when you find a good campsite.'

He drove off, and the JEACs waved goodbye before sorting out the things they would carry with them.

'Which way shall we go to look for a campsite?' said Rohan, looking at the map.

'How about west, to the border, and then south,' suggested Nimal. 'Tony said that they haven't explored around there, and only know that there are some large rocks.'

'We also need to be close to water,' said Rohan. 'All agreed?'

They nodded eagerly, and he led the way with Hunter, Nimal bringing up the rear. The boys and Amy carried the TGs.

Mongoose, monkeys, deer, rabbits, hedgehogs and numerous birds moved out of their way, but didn't appear to be frightened of them, and Hunter, walking quietly with Rohan, did not attempt to chase any of them. Nimal was tempted to make friends with the animals, but since they were eager to find a campsite quickly, he resisted.

There were few trails, and although after reaching the fence, they tried to walk beside it, the heavy underbrush and densely growing trees prevented them from doing so. They ended up walking a fair distance east, before they could go south again, parallel to the fence.

'How on *earth* did they put the fence up?' groaned Amy, disentangling her long braid from yet another bush.

'It was done from the outside,' said Mahesika.

'Makes sense,' said Rohan. 'They didn't have to fight this underbrush.'

They moved on. It was hard work pushing their way through the heavy brush. They were perspiring and bleeding from scratches when Anu stopped.

'Sshh! Listen,' she said. 'I hear water.'

They listened intently and then Mahesika nodded her head and said, 'You're right. It's coming from that direction.' She pointed south of where they were standing.

'Let's go, folks,' said Rohan. 'Anu and Mahesika, *lend us your ears* and lead the way.'

Anu and Mahesika squeezed through some particularly thick shrubbery, and then came to a sudden stop – the others bumped into them.

'Wow! Look at this!' exclaimed Anu as the others crowded around her and Mahesika.

'Yippee!' chorused everyone joyfully, entering the unexpected clearing.

'Who'd have dreamed this was hidden behind that heavy shrubbery,' said Amy.

It was a huge, sandy area, interspersed with occasional shrubbery, and a small stream flowed into the north-west corner of the enclosure, forming a clear, large pool at the foot of some rocks.

'What a fantastic campsite!' said Rohan.

'With those rocks in the west and the dense shrubbery all around, it's completely sheltered, too,' said Nimal.

'Perfect for conservationists to camp in,' said Anu dreamily. 'Just think – running water, a swimming pool, greenery, natural protection . . .'

'And room for staff accommodation,' said Rohan, standing on a rock to get a better view. 'I'm positive it can easily hold 25 large tents for campers, well spaced out; they could also build various facilities.'

'I can't even see where it ends,' said Amy, 'since it curves around the corner in the south.'

'I've never seen *this* place,' said Mahesika. 'And I wander all over the Conservation. I'm sure Lalith and the others don't know about it.'

'No – they've been too busy,' said Rohan. 'These rocks are quite a distance east of the western fence, and the jungle is jolly dense around here, to say the least. Let's see how far it spreads.'

'Wait!' said Anu impulsively. 'Before we start exploring, let's go back and get our gear.'

'Great idea, Anu,' said Rohan.

They made good time back to where they had left their things and, after a quick drink, returned to the clearing – now able to follow the trail created merely by walking along it three times – Hunter leading the way.

Placing everything under an overhanging rock beside the pool, they ran to the southern corner and found another 75 metres of sandy area, interspersed with shrubbery.

'This is amazing – although the bushes around here are pretty dense,' said Anu, looking around happily.

'Let's get back to our things and check the map to see where we are, in relation to the known trails,' said Rohan, leading the way back. 'We have to find a way for the Land Rovers to get here, too.'

'Good idea. Spread the map on this table-like rock and let's have a dekko,' said Amy.

They pored over it and then Nimal, pointing with a twig, said, 'Here's the nearest trail to us – it connects up with the track Tony drove along when he dropped us off on Sunday.'

'You're right, yaar,' said Rohan. 'We need to go due east from here, starting at the south-east corner of this campsite.'

'That means creating *another* trail through this shrubbery,' said Nimal, strapping on his knapsack. 'Let's go.'

'Are you girls coming?' said Rohan, picking up his knapsack.

'No, we'd better stay here,' said Anu. 'Mich and Gina can have a swim; Amy can keep guard; and Mahesika and I will get lunch ready. I know we'll all be hungry by the time you return.'

'Okay, Anu,' said Rohan. 'Keep the TG handy, Amy, just in case. We'll leave Hunter with you.'

'Right,' said Amy, picking up a TG.

The boys set off. Amy sat on a rock, keeping a sharp lookout for any creatures, but other than the monkeys in the shrubbery, there was no sign of other animals; Hunter, knowing he was on guard, prowled around the site.

Moving swiftly, using compass and map, the boys soon met up with the trail they had pinpointed earlier.

'Okay, so if we go east on this track, we'll end up at the waterhole where Tony dropped us off,' said Rohan.

'Correct,' said Nimal, 'and if we go west, we should end up outside the campsite.'

'At least this track, though narrow, is large enough for a Land Rover,' said Rohan. 'C'mon, yaar.'

The track took them through dense jungle and, after about fifteen minutes, it came to a dead end.

'Heavy shrubbery all around – but we should be close to the campsite,' said Rohan, examining the thick bushes.

'Hang on,' said Nimal, listening intently. 'I can hear the girls and Hunter.'

Rohan listened, too, and said, 'You're right, yaar. Let's call them.'

They yelled loudly and the girls, running towards the sound, called back, Hunter barking excitedly as well.

'Only these bushes between us,' said Nimal.

'Perfect,' said Rohan. He called out to the girls, 'Ring Tony and update him. Ask him what time we should meet him at the end of the trail leading south-west of the waterhole where he dropped us off on Sunday – and tell him to bring a couple of saws. We can make a temporary entrance to the campsite without destroying too much greenery.'

'I'll call him immediately,' said Anu. 'Are you going to try and come through now?'

'I've got an idea,' said Nimal. He raised his voice and shouted, 'Hunter, where are you, boy? Come here! Girls, mark the place where Hunter goes into the bushes.'

Hunter, sniffing around on the other side, found the easiest way through the shrubbery and was soon jumping up at Nimal and Rohan.

'Good boy,' they said, hugging the dog.

'Let's try and get through the shrubbery, starting here,' said Nimal, pointing to the place through which Hunter had emerged.

After some hot and sweaty work at both ends, the youngsters managed to make a tunnel through the shrubbery and the boys crawled through.

'Phew! That shrubbery's at least four and a half metres deep,' panted Rohan, wiping his brow.

'Let's have a swim before we eat,' suggested Amy.

Within a few minutes, the JEACs, including Hunter, were in the water. Once they had cooled down, they clambered out of the pool and dried themselves.

'Food as we talk, please,' said Nimal. 'I'm starving.'

'Us, too,' chorused the others.

Sitting on the rocks, they ate heartily, and after their first pangs of hunger had been assuaged, Rohan asked, 'What did Tony say?'

'He'll be here in a couple of hours,' said Anu. 'He was thrilled to hear about our find and said that he would bring a couple of chaps to help make a temporary entrance.'

'Super,' said Nimal. 'Let's explore this place thoroughly and find a suitable spot for our tents.'

'Yeah, and since the boundary meanders haphazardly – there are lots of nooks and crannies – let's divvy up into three groups,' suggested Rohan. 'Gina, Mich and I; Anu, Amy and Hunter; and Mahesika and Nimal.'

After the food was stored away, they split into groups and started exploring, Nimal and Mahesika walking towards the south-west corner, which had some huge rocks in the west and was full of heavy shrubbery.

'This is really thick undergrowth,' said Nimal, holding back the branches of a bush so that Mahesika could get through.

'Ouch!' yelped Mahesika, stubbing her toe. 'And it's full of stones.'

They searched carefully. There were a few small caves – no animals lived in them, but they were too tiny to shelter the JEACs.

'Phew, it's boiling hot,' gasped Nimal, sitting down on a rock after a fruitless fifteen-minute search. He drank some water and said, 'Come and have a rest, Mahesika.'

'Okay, in a minute,' said Mahesika, who was a few metres away.

Nimal stood up on the rock to look for the others and when he turned back, Mahesika had disappeared.

'Hey, where are you, Mahesika?' called Nimal, looking all around.

There was no reply. He jumped off the rock and ran quickly to where he had last seen her – near a thick shrub – but there was no sign of the girl.

'*Mahesika!*' yelled Nimal, cupping his hands around his mouth. '*Where are you?*'

'Right here, Nimal,' said a cheeky voice at ground level. 'You don't have to shout. *I'm* not deaf!'

Nimal looked around wildly and saw her face grinning up at him from under some shrubbery.

He gasped in relief. 'What on earth are you doing down there, young lady? You gave me the fright of my life when you disappeared.'

'Sorry, Nimal. It's just . . . I think I've found the perfect place,' she said, her voice quivering with excitement. 'Come and see!'

She backed into the bushes and Nimal, with some difficulty, followed her through a low, narrow tunnel in the shrubbery. It was tough going, but some small animal had obviously burrowed its way through.

'Oh, man!' he gasped, as he reached the end of the tunnel and was able to stand up and look around. 'This is *absolutely perfect* for us, Mahesika! Pear-shaped area with rocks along one side; heavy shrubbery on the other three sides; and we can make an entrance right where we crept through.'

'Yes, we simply can't keep crawling through that narrow tunnel each time,' said Mahesika, looking ruefully at their badly scratched arms and legs.

'All we'll need to do is to clear away stones and fallen branches – there's no shrubbery in the middle,' said Nimal excitedly. 'What made you crawl through?'

'I saw the narrow tunnel and the shrubbery didn't look too bad around it, so I decided to explore. It was a lucky fluke that I managed to get through, and now we've found this spot.'

'You found it,' said Nimal, giving her a high-five. 'Come on! Let's call the others.'

They scrambled back, and standing on some rocks, yelled for the others to join them.

'What's up?' gasped Rohan as they raced up.

'Boy, you two look as if you've crawled backwards through a hedge,' said Anu.

'We did! Backwards and forwards!' said Nimal with a grin. 'Now, as you know, ladies and germ, we have a beautiful campsite which is suitable for visitors. But, *we* wanted our own cosy, *JEACs'* hideout, sufficient for four tents and about ten of us. So, our local expert, *Ms.*

Mahesika, decided to discover a *beeyouutiful* spot – just for us! Can you guess where it is?'

The others searched eagerly but saw nothing other than dense shrubbery. Rohan climbed on to a large rock and looked around. 'There are more rocks on the other side,' said the boy. 'You can't see them from down there; join me up here.'

The JEACs scrambled up to where Rohan stood, but even Nimal, standing on tiptoes, couldn't see the other rocks.

'Guess we need your inches, Rohan,' said Amy, as they clambered down.

'Where's your discovery, Mahesika?' begged Gina and Mich.

'Where the rocks are,' said Mahesika, with a grin.

'But how on earth do we reach them? More burrowing through shrubbery?' asked Rohan.

'Yes, sir,' said Mahesika. 'That's why we're so scratched up and messy.'

'Feeling strong, Rohan?' asked Nimal.

'I guess so, yaar,' said Rohan.

'Good. We'll have to make the tunnel wider and perhaps break a few branches,' said Nimal. 'Mahesika, since you discovered it, lead the way. I'll come next with Rohan, who'll get stuck if we don't keep an eye on him.'

Everyone crawled in, the boys forcing their way through and making it easier for those behind.

'Oooh! Superb! Amazing! Superfantabulous! Great work, Mahesika!' said everyone, examining the place with pleasure, and Mahesika had to recite her tale of discovery once more. The girl was thrilled at their delight and praise, and happy that she had found a good place for their campsite.

'And lots of company,' said Amy, spotting the monkeys who were peering curiously through the shrubbery.

'Two wonderful discoveries in one morning,' said Rohan gleefully. 'The Conservation folk will be thrilled when they see these campsites.'

'Listen for the mobile,' said Anu. 'In the meantime, let's begin clearing away the stones and branches.'

Soon everyone was busy, including Hunter, who helped by dragging branches over to the pile they were making in a corner. They finished their tasks and looked around with satisfaction. The only thing that remained was to chase the monkeys away, since nothing in the camp would be safe if the monkeys got too friendly.

'Let's see if we can shoo them off,' suggested Amy. 'Nimal, you'd better not join us – they'll come closer rather than going away.'

The others clapped their hands and made loud noises, which sent the monkeys scampering up into the trees beyond the shrubbery.

'Good. Now, hopefully, they won't come into our campsite,' said Rohan.

'Hold on a sec,' said Nimal suddenly, staring into the shrubbery. 'Quiet down, everyone. There's a baby left behind on that branch and it's petrified. I'm going to get it.'

He moved towards the low branch on which a tiny brown monkey was trembling violently, and began to speak softly. The baby stopped trembling to listen, and when Nimal put out his hand, the monkey let him stroke it and then jumped into the boy's arms, nestling against him.

'Gee, wish I could do that with animals,' sighed Amy.

'Will it let us pet it?' asked Mich. 'It's so cute – is it male or female?'

'Female. If you pet her one at a time, she'll be okay,' said Nimal, sitting down on a rock.

They gathered round the boy and took turns stroking the soft fur of the tiny creature who, secure in Nimal's arms, even chattered softly as they touched her.

'I wonder why the others left her behind,' said Mahesika.

'She's probably an orphan,' said Nimal, 'with no one to take responsibility for her.'

'Awww! Poor little thing,' said Mich and Gina in unison, their eyes filling with tears.

'Can we keep her?' asked Amy.

'Looks like she's already adopted Nimal,' said Anu with a grin. 'I doubt she'll leave him in a hurry.'

'What shall we call her?' said Mich, thoroughly excited at the thought of having a baby monkey in their midst.

'Mahesika, think of a nice Sri Lankan name for her,' said Nimal.

Mahesika thought hard and said, 'What about *Chandi*? It means "naughty" in Sinhala.'

'Perfecto!' said Anu with a chuckle. 'I've a feeling she'll more than live up to her name.'

Everyone agreed and Chandi wrapped her little arms around Nimal's neck and hid her face in his shoulder as if she were shy. She was enchanting!

Hunter came up to sniff the tiny creature in Nimal's arms and Chandi, clinging tightly to Nimal, watched the dog intently. But Hunter just licked Nimal and sat down beside him.

'Hunter, this is Chandi,' said Nimal, stroking the monkey and at the same time patting the dog. 'I want you to be friends.'

Hunter gave a small bark and lay down. Chandi, seeing that Nimal was not scared of the big black creature, stopped clinging to him and made a small chittering noise at Hunter, who whined softly back.

'Look, they're talking. They're friends,' squealed Gina.

'Not yet,' said Nimal, 'but they will be, once Chandi gets used to us and sees that Hunter won't harm her.'

'We're going to have a delightful time,' said Anu. 'Chandi's a cutie and Mahesika, you did a great job finding this place. Tony's going to be thrilled.'

'Oh! Oh! How will he get in?' asked Mich. 'He's gigantic!'

'You're right, Mich,' said Rohan. 'We'll have to widen the entrances to both places. We'd better get back to the other side now – they'll call soon.'

'And I need some juice,' said Nimal, as they crawled back into the larger campsite. 'Creating tunnels through shrubbery is thirsty work.'

Everyone had a cupful of thambili. The delicious king coconut juice, with bits of tender coconut in it, was cooling and refreshing – and even Chandi and Hunter enjoyed pieces of coconut.

'That must be Tony,' said Rohan as the telephone rang. 'Hello? Hi, Tony.' He listened intently and then said, 'Okay, we'll meet you at the end of the trail. Bye! He'll be here in 30 minutes, Nimal – let's go.'

Since Chandi had quickly made friends with the others – who spoilt her – she played happily with Gina and Mich.

Two Land Rovers arrived a few minutes after the boys reached their destination and drove along the track to the area just opposite the campsite; Tony, Fareez, Sanjay and Ken climbed out of their vehicles, carrying electronic saws, and quickly made a large entrance. Leaving the vehicles outside, the men entered the main campsite and were delighted at the perfection of the place. They were even more pleased when, after they had sawed their way through to the second section, they were able to examine it as well.

'Hey, a new family member,' said Tony, spotting Chandi on Mich's shoulder.

Chandi allowed the men to pet her and then jumped into Nimal's arms.

'I'm sure you're longing to camp out here as soon as possible,' said Sanjay with a grin. 'Can't blame you – it's a wonderful place.'

'Once we've finished with the wall and the relocation, we'll focus on these two areas. It'll generate more revenue for our projects,' said Ken, who was heavily involved with administration and fundraising.

'It's perfect,' said Fareez.

'How about tea in the main campsite?' suggested Nimal. 'It's nearly 5 o'clock and I'm starving.'

'Sure thing,' said Ken. 'Tea, with the growing numbers of JEACs, would be an honour. Niranjani and Shalini felt sure you must have finished your food, so they sent another hamper for your tea. I'll get it.'

'They packed enough this morning to feed a herd of elephants,' laughed Amy, as she, Anu and Rohan unpacked the additional food.

Everyone, including Chandi and Hunter, sat on the rocks around the pool and enjoyed a sumptuous tea.

'We need names for these two campsites,' said Anu, dreamily.

'True,' said Tony. 'How about naming the smaller one "The JEACs' Camp"?'

'Sounds great – we'll call it JC for short,' said Anu. 'Perhaps, once it's open to the public, groups of *local* JEACs can camp in the JC while their parents are in this section.'

'Excellent,' said Sanjay. 'What shall we call this area?'

'We'll get a good name for it later on,' said Ken, 'but for now, let's call it "Time Out Of Jungle" or TOOJ for short.'

Everyone cheered – and, ultimately, the names were never changed.

'Tony, is there an old tarpaulin somewhere around that we could use?' asked Anu.

'Why would we want that, sis?' asked Rohan.

'The opening into the JC is quite large and, now that there's an entrance to TOOJ, which has a pool, animals might come in,' explained Anu.

'Good thinking, Anu,' said Tony. 'Till there are humans located here permanently, there's a good possibility that animals may use the pool. However, I think temporary gates out of wooden stakes for *both* entrances would be better. We'll take measurements before we leave; call the carpenters so that they can get working on it immediately; and, hopefully, the gates will be ready by morning.'

They got back to work, clearing away the branches they had cut down and making the two entrances easily accessible, and took measurements for the gates.

'Time to head home,' said Tony half an hour later, ushering everyone out to the vehicles. 'We've lots to attend to before tomorrow.'

The adults were thrilled to learn about TOOJ and the JC and happy to meet Chandi who, by then, was so comfortable with humans that she would let anyone hold her. After a huge meal of fruit, she cuddled up to

Hunter and went to sleep. Hunter gave her a gentle lick but Chandi did not move – she was exhausted.

Akki prepared a list of things they would need; the JEACs made their own lists and, within a couple of hours, everything was loaded into vehicles, ready for take-off in the morning. An excited group of youngsters returned to their tents that night.

CHAPTER 10

Mal-li

'Rise and shine, Amy,' sang out Anu. 'I know it's only 4 a.m., but we're leaving in 45 minutes. I'll wake the others.'

The JEACs dressed and packed their knapsacks, which included the WTs and extra batteries – Hunter and Chandi had knapsacks, too. Breakfast over, everyone piled into the three Land Rovers, while Janake and Velu, the carpenters, drove the pickup truck, which held the gates. Neeka, Priyani, Molly and Akki went, too.

On reaching TOOJ, they set to work, and by 9 o'clock everything was in place, including the two gates.

'This is simply super and will attract more people to the Conservation,' said Akki. 'We have lots of ideas as to how we can set it up once the relocation is completed.'

'We'll leave you folks to arrange the rest . . .' began Sanjay, when his mobile rang.

He answered it, listened intently for a few minutes, groaned, and rang off.

'What's up, machang?' said Fareez.

'Bad news! Another tusker's been killed in the south-east – Tony will call back with instructions.'

There was a horrified silence – Mich and Gina burst into tears, while Mahesika gasped and turned pale.

'What happened – can you tell us?' asked Rohan.

'Briefly, Kumar and Sarath, two of our rangers who live in that section, heard a couple of shots and angry trumpeting north of their bungalow – around 4 a.m. – and they hurried to investigate. After searching for an hour or so, Kumar found the body of the tusker with its tusks sawn off. Before he could contact Sarath, or report the incident to

Tony and Lalith, a farmer – whose land is also in the south-east – called to inform him that elephants had broken through the fence and got on to his land around 3:30 this morning. He and his men fired over their heads and scared them back into the jungle. There were tuskers in the herd, but the farmer says they were unharmed.'

'Can he be trusted?' asked Amy.

'Yes, he's one of the good guys,' said Ken. 'What happened next?'

'Kumar contacted the others and – hang on . . .' He answered his phone. After a couple of minutes he hung up and said, 'That was Lalith – we're fixing the fence immediately. Janaka, Velu – you're needed over there; Ken and the ladies are wanted back at the office. Fareez and I will pick up Tony and then meet Kumar and the farmer.'

He turned to the JEACs and added rapidly, 'There are enough cartridges for the guns and darts for the TGs. Given the situation, promise you won't go exploring without the proper equipment and the WTs. Since you'll be here for more than a day, it's no use giving you a mobile phone.'

'We promise,' said Rohan and the others in unison.

'Good luck with finding out who killed the elephant,' said the others.

The adults rushed off and the youngsters discussed the incident; they were upset and frustrated.

'I guess we can't do anything about it for now,' growled Rohan finally.

'Are you okay, Mahesika?' asked Anu. 'You look pale.'

'I'm fine,' said Mahesika abruptly, getting up and moving towards the tents. 'Let's get to work.'

'Good idea,' said Amy, exchanging a puzzled look with Anu as they followed the girl.

'The food and moveable items can go into the largest tent,' said Anu. 'Amy, you and I'll organize that.'

Soon everyone was working hard, Hunter and Chandi helping by picking up various things and offering them to one of the children.

'Chandi, you little wretch! Bring back that hammer,' shouted Nimal suddenly.

The others turned to see Chandi, mimicking Ken who had hammered in tent pegs, trying to hammer a small branch into the ground. The hammer was as big as she was, and heavy, so she could not escape Nimal who rescued it before she injured herself. Knowing her nature, Nimal wisely removed the tiny knapsack from her back, unzipped it, and showed her various small articles which he had placed in it. She was thrilled and spent the next hour in a corner of the campsite, chittering to herself, as she took things out of the knapsack, put them back in and then pulled them out again.

The youngsters felt better as they organized the campsites, laughing at Hunter and Chandi's antics. Heavy items that could not be carried off by monkeys were left outside, but everything else was put away in the tents.

'Time for grub – it's 12:30,' said Nimal, looking at his watch.

'We're hungry, too,' chorused the younger girls.

They were enjoying their meal when an elephant trumpeted.

Nimal glanced at Mahesika and said, 'That sounded pretty close.'

The girl shrugged, and Nimal did not push her. The group moved into TOOJ and sat on the rocks, dangling their feet in the water.

'Once they organize this, it'll make a superfab resort,' said Anu. 'And if they have a petting zoo in one corner, it'll be perfect for children to play with baby animals and learn about them.'

'Yeah, and Mahesika, you'll have to write and tell us about it, and send us pictures,' said Amy.

'Sure,' said Mahesika who had been very quiet.

'Okay, folks. What shall we do next?' asked Rohan. 'I'm in the mood to go exploring but am open to other suggestions.'

'Exploring for me, too,' said Amy and Nimal simultaneously, and the others nodded.

'Where shall we go?' said Rohan, pulling out his map.

After poring over it for a few minutes, Anu said, 'How about south-east? It looks very dense and there aren't any marked trails, but we may find some to add to the map.'

'Good idea, Anu,' said Rohan. 'Shall we see how far we get in a couple of hours?'

'Sounds fine, yaar,' said Nimal. 'Do we take tea with us?'

'You've just finished a huge lunch,' teased Amy. 'Do you mean to say you'll be hungry again in two hours?'

'I'm always hungry, Amy,' began Nimal mournfully. 'It's one of the saddest stories of my life! I . . .' He trailed off as the others threatened him with extermination. 'Well, I figured that by the time we walk two hours south, in dense jungle, and then return, it'll be way past our tea time. What do you say, Mich and Gina?'

'For once, you're right, Nimal,' said Mich cheekily.

'All right! With you hungry lot, we'll have no peace unless we take food,' said Anu. 'Bring over your knapsacks and load up.'

With the gates shut firmly behind them, they headed south, Rohan and Nimal each carrying a gun, while Amy had the TG strapped across her shoulders. They took their WTs.

The jungle was dense and they followed a narrow trail until they came, unexpectedly, across a shallow stream. They walked in it for a fair distance and saw several species of wildlife, including a leopard, who moved away quickly. A little later, they heard the steady tramp of heavy bodies.

'Elephants!' breathed Nimal. 'Ahead of us – c'mon – we've *got* to see them. Be as quiet as you can – Hunter, stay with me.'

He led the way out of the stream and they crouched in thick underbrush, grateful that the breeze was wafting their scent away from the elephants. Soon, moving majestically through the jungle, appeared a herd of eight elephants – two of which were tuskers. Once the herd had passed, the youngsters breathed a collective sigh of bliss.

'Gee, that was some sight,' said Amy, who had never seen elephants in the wild before.

'Awesome,' said Mich.

'I guess *you're* quite used to seeing them in the jungle, Mahesika,' said Amy.

There was no reply and they looked around – Mahesika had disappeared.

'Blow! She's gone again,' said Rohan. 'Does anyone remember when she was last with us?'

'When we saw the leopard – hope she's okay,' said Anu. 'She's been extremely quiet ever since we heard about the tusker.'

'Yeah, I can understand how she feels about the animals in *her* jungle,' said Nimal.

'Should we try and find her?' asked Gina.

'No point – she's fast and is probably far away by now – she knows her way around better than anyone else,' said Rohan. 'She'll join us when she wants to. Come on, let's carry on.'

A little later Anu came to a halt, saying, 'Time for a break – we've walked for two hours.'

They sat beside the stream, munching chocolate and talking about the elephants and the other animals they had seen. Then Nimal, looking at his watch, said, 'Shall we do another hour's trek or are you all tired?'

'I'm fine – what about you lot?' said Rohan.

'Let's go,' chorused the others.

'Man, this jungle's getting denser than ever,' said Rohan sometime later, as they reached some shrubbery that was impassable. 'We'll have to go a bit further east and then south again.'

They tramped on for about ten minutes and then Nimal said, 'We're in that *bad place*, according to Mahesika, close to the trail we took the first day.'

'You're right,' said Rohan. 'Let's be extra careful. Should we go further?'

'Better get back to TOOJ, I think,' said Amy. 'It'll be dark soon.'

So they turned back, pleased that they had added some new trails to the map and happy to have seen so much wildlife. They were nearly at TOOJ when they heard a loud trumpeting.

'Gee, that sounds *really* close,' said Amy. 'Do you think the elephants are coming our way?'

'I doubt it,' said Nimal, who was listening intently. 'I don't hear the thud of their feet.'

Back in the JC, as they bustled about preparing a hot meal, Anu said, 'Let's not pester Mahesika with questions when she returns – okay?'

'Agreed, Anu,' said Nimal.

'Do we wait for her before we eat?' asked Gina hungrily.

'We'll wait a bit,' said Amy. 'But you and Mich can each have a hot dog – they're ready.'

'Yes, please,' said the girls.

Half an hour later Mahesika turned up, looking quite cheerful. She did not say a word as to where she had been and the others refrained from questioning her.

'Do you want me to get the plates, Amy?' asked Mahesika.

'Yes, please,' said Amy, smiling at her.

After a hearty meal, they sat around a campfire and made further plans.

'I'd like to check out that dense area – perhaps at midnight, after we've had a rest,' said Rohan.

'Which one?' asked Mahesika.

'The one we passed the first day we went exploring,' explained Nimal. 'You said it was a bad place – we saw it again this afternoon.'

'Oh, that one,' said Mahesika, looking nervous. 'I usually try and avoid it because I've heard guns and lots of angry voices.'

'Really? Are you sure it wasn't some of the staff?' asked Rohan eagerly.

'No, I'd recognize their voices. Also, none of the staff were out that night – I checked.'

'Didn't you tell Tony or someone else about it?' asked Amy.

'No. Anyway, it was more than a year ago – perhaps it's safe now.'

'OK – so, what do you say, JEACs – shall we go exploring tonight?' said Rohan.

'We're game,' chorused everyone.

'Can we take a midnight picnic?' asked Gina.

'Naturally, chicken,' said Amy. 'Are you *sure* your real name isn't Nimal?'

The discussion ended in laughter, and since it was nearly 8 p.m., they went to sleep immediately, Rohan promising to wake them at midnight.

At 11:30 Nimal woke with a start. 'Wake up, yaar!' he said urgently, shaking Rohan. 'Listen!'

'What . . .' mumbled Rohan, but was up in a jiffy when he heard the loud noises. He scrambled out of his sleeping bag and grabbed the nearest TG, already loaded with a dart.

As they crept out of their tent, the three older girls and a growling Hunter, held back by Anu, joined them. Amy had the TG, which she handed to Nimal. Moonlight filled the campsite.

'Something's trying to get in – and it sounds pretty big,' muttered Amy nervously.

'It's at the entrance to TOOJ,' said Nimal, unlocking the gate to the JC and stepping into TOOJ.

'Let's . . .' began Rohan and then stopped as a loud trumpeting filled the air, and the gate shook violently.

'Elephants!' breathed Nimal.

Everyone stood stock-still for a split second and then Mahesika sped towards the gate.

'Come back, Mahesika!' yelled Rohan. 'STOP – it's dangerous!'

But she took no notice, and the others, with one accord, ran after her. However, she had a head start and, upon reaching the gate, opened it quickly. A huge bull elephant stood there, stamping his feet, his trunk raised above his head – he had a magnificent pair of tusks!

Rohan trained his TG on the animal. 'Blow,' thought the boy, realizing that he had grabbed the smaller TG. 'This dosage will be useless if he charges.'

'Oh, my hat!' breathed Anu.

Nimal, thrusting the TG back at Amy, moved swiftly towards Mahesika and the elephant, Hunter at his heels.

The others, knowing that any sound might anger the creature further, froze.

Mahesika reached the elephant first. He trumpeted again, then wrapped his trunk around the girl, and lifted her on to his head. While the others gaped silently, Mahesika bent over the elephant's head, whispering in his ear, and stroking him. Then she said something to him in Sinhala and he put her back on the ground and stood there quietly. Nimal stopped in his tracks, and commanded Hunter to sit.

'I'm really sorry,' said Mahesika, smiling apologetically at the others. 'I didn't mean to frighten you. He's perfectly tame and very gentle – he just came looking for me – please, may he come in? His name's "Mal-li".'

'O-of c-c-course. Y-you mean h-he b-belongs to you?' stuttered Anu dazedly.

'Not really – he's with one of the herds,' said Mahesika, leading Mal-li into the campsite. Nimal closed the gate behind them. 'Over a year and a half ago, when I was wandering in the jungle, near that section which you folks want to explore tonight, I heard a gunshot and, as I mentioned earlier, loud voices. I climbed a tree quickly and a little later Mal-li staggered underneath and fell down. He'd been beaten and poked with sharp objects, and shot in his left hind leg – look, you can still see the scar. He was scared and distrustful, but in so much pain that he let me help him. I left him there, ran back to one of the staff bungalows, stole some bandages and medicine, and returned to him. I looked after him for two weeks. After that, we adopted each other. Although he's so big, he's as gentle as a lamb. I *know* he'll make friends with all of you, especially Nimal.'

'Phew,' said Rohan, wiping his forehead. 'You're a most extraordinary girl, Mahesika. Lots of things are beginning to make sense: like why we often heard an elephant trumpet when you were around.'

'What's happening?' asked two sleepy voices.

Gina and Mich emerged from the JC and stared at the group, Chandi on Mich's shoulder. The girls woke up completely when they saw the elephant standing next to Mahesika, his trunk wrapped lovingly around her waist.

'Is that *your* elephant, Mahesika?' they said in unison.

'That's right, kiddies,' said Amy with a grin. 'What did you call him, Mahesika?'

'*Mal-li*,' said the girl. 'It means younger brother. He's my family. I'm really sorry I couldn't tell you the story earlier.'

'No worries – we understand, Mahesika,' said Anu.

The others nodded, and Mahesika smiled gratefully at them. 'Thanks,' she said.

'Does he often wander away from his herd?' asked Nimal.

'Only if he knows I'm in the jungle, then he'll stay with me for a few days. I call him, and he comes as soon as he can.'

'Gee, you're so lucky to have an elephant brother,' said Mich.

'Can we make friends with him, too?' asked Gina eagerly.

'Of course,' said Mahesika.

Naturally, Mal-li took to Nimal instantly, and even lifted the boy on to his back without being told. He made friends with the others, too, blowing gently down his trunk at Hunter before they solemnly touched paw and trunk. When Chandi boldly scampered on to his head, holding up his ear and chattering into it, Mal-li remained calm – he was used to monkeys. He was quite unlike a wild elephant, and Mahesika, who had spent lots of time at the *Elephants' Tub* before she met Mal-li, had taught him a number of things that the domestic elephants did.

The youngsters were ecstatic. They led Mal-li to the entrance of the JC, and since he was too big to enter the campsite, they sat beside him, just outside the gate. Gina and Mich insisted on Mahesika repeating the story of how she had become friends with Mal-li.

'How did he follow you here, Mahesika?' asked Anu, patting the elephant.

'When we heard about the dead tusker, I was terrified that it was Mal-li – there are a few tuskers in his herd. Then an elephant trumpeted while we were eating. I knew it was Mal-li and went to find him – he was near the source of the Piliyangala. He wasn't too happy when I left him again, and I guess he came looking for me.'

'So now we know why you kept disappearing,' said Nimal with a grin.

'Yes, sorry,' said Mahesika again. 'I *was* going to tell you some time and I'm grateful that you didn't question me. I'm used to being on my own and not sharing my secrets, and even though I liked all of you a lot, I wasn't sure how you'd react.'

'We're thrilled,' chorused the JEACs.

'Also,' continued Mahesika, now eager to explain everything to her friends, 'I wasn't sure how I'd be able to visit Mal-li whenever I wanted to once he was in the NC and the gates were in place. I thought I had more time, but then Lalith said it would be completed this week.'

'But can't he stay here – in the OC?' asked Gina.

'He likes to spend time with his herd, too – and it would be safer for him,' said Mahesika.

'Yeah – especially since elephants are being targeted for their tusks, and he has a super pair,' said Nimal. 'Well, now that your secret's out, you can easily visit him when the herds are moved to the NC.'

'Yes, that's a big relief,' smiled Mahesika.

'Perhaps he can come with us tonight,' said Rohan, thoughtfully. 'If there are crooks in the OC, they won't try anything funny with Mal-li around. He's just too humongous for words.'

'Good idea,' said Anu. 'Do you think he'll come, Mahesika?'

'Of course, even though he doesn't like that particular part of the jungle,' said Mahesika.

'Do you *really* think there are crooks in that section, Rohan?' asked Amy

'Not sure – but we *do* know there are nasty folks around – causing lots of trouble. They appear to work mainly at night and, as we know, nobody has had time to check out that area.'

'You think they're *in* the Conservation?' asked Mahesika.

'Possibly,' said Rohan. 'It's easier for them to stay here rather than creep in and out, taking the risk of somebody seeing them and questioning them.'

'Makes sense – like the crooks we caught in Patiyak,' said Anu. 'It makes me mad!'

'I could be wrong,' said Rohan. 'But, let's move – Mahesika, will Mal-li stay put while we collect our equipment and other items? We could leave the gate to the JC open.'

'Yes. Now he knows I'm close by, he'll obey me,' said Mahesika. She spoke to Mal-li in Sinhala and he blew down his trunk at her, his little eyes gleaming intelligently.

When the JEACs went back into the JC to collect their things, Mal-li stayed where he was, Hunter lying down beside him while Chandi curled up on Mal-li's head and went to sleep.

CHAPTER 11

What's Going On?

The JEACs set out shortly after midnight – Mahesika, Anu, Nimal and Rohan carried WTs, and everyone had a torch. Mich, Gina and Chandi rode on Mal-li's back, Mal-li tramping along happily as they made their way to the dense area.

'We're nearly there,' said Rohan, sometime later. 'Let's take extra precautions.'

'I'd rather not take Mal-li too close,' said Mahesika nervously.

'Why don't we find a nice, safe . . .' began Anu, and then stopped. 'Gosh . . . is that thunder?'

'Sure is,' said Amy. 'Let's find shelter and then decide what to do.'

'Here's a good spot,' said Mahesika, quickly leading them off the trail into heavy jungle.

They sat under a thick canopy of trees, Mal-li lying down beside them.

'Phew, what a storm,' said Anu, gazing up through the treetops, where faint flashes of lightning could be seen now and then. 'Good thing the trees are so thick here – there's hardly any rain coming in.'

Suddenly Hunter growled, and Nimal put his hand on the dog's head. 'Sshh, I hear voices,' whispered the boy.

They froze as they heard male voices, talking in Sinhala. There was a brief silence and then the voices spoke again. There seemed to be two men, but it was apparent that they were moving away from the group of youngsters. Hunter stopped growling, and the group relaxed.

Rohan whispered to Mahesika, 'Did you recognize the voices? What did they say?'

'They're not Conservation folk – they saw our torchlight and wondered who was around. One of the men said, "Who's there?" and the other chap gave his name – "Pala". They assumed that they had seen each other's torches and decided to go back to their camp to dry off. Also, though it makes no sense, the man called Pala said he was tired of being a monkey and would be glad when this was over. The second chap said that the others were nearly finished for the night and would return to camp in an hour and that they would not leave until tomorrow night.'

'Now what?' said Amy. 'Rohan, do we still try to explore the DA – sorry, folks – *Dense Area*?'

'I'd love to – but we'd better wait till daylight,' said Rohan. 'Also, the men will probably be in hiding at that time, so we're less likely to bump into them. How tired are you two?' he added, turning to Gina and Mich.

'We're okay,' said the girls, though they were both stifling yawns.

'Here's an idea,' said Nimal. 'Since the storm's over, it's not a bad night for sleeping in the open; we've got Hunter and Mal-li to warn us of danger and protect us. Let's move deeper into the jungle, further away from this area, find a snug place and get a few hours' sleep. Then we're right on the spot to start our search in the morning.'

'Brainwave!' said Anu. 'I vote for that.'

'I second it. We've got to solve this mystery,' said Rohan.

'Yes,' chorused everyone excitedly.

'Once we find a place, I'll run back to camp with Hunter, leave a note for whoever brings food, to say we've gone exploring, and bring back more food,' said Rohan.

Within fifteen minutes, they had found a nice, dry spot, and Mich and Gina dropped off to sleep quickly.

Amy and Anu opted to go with Rohan and help bring back food. They returned soon and everyone slept soundly until Rohan's watch alarm went off at 8 a.m. and he woke them. After a quick meal, they set off, skirting the DA as they attempted to find a way into it.

'This is useless,' said Anu, at last. 'Let's split up – form two groups – Rohan, Nimal, Amy and Gina, you go south-west with Hunter; Mich, Mahesika, Mal-li and I will go east. We'll communicate via WTs.'

'Okay, sis,' said Rohan. 'But stick together in your groups.'

They split up and started searching for an entry. Anu's WT beeped twenty minutes later, and she answered it promptly. 'What's up? Over.'

'We think we've found the entrance,' said Rohan. 'We're ten minutes south-west of where we parted from you – we'll wait for you under a large cinnamon tree. Hurry, and beep if you need more directions. Mahesika, try to leave Mal-li behind. Over.'

'Will do,' said Anu. 'Over and out.'

Mahesika whispered to Mal-li; it was incredible how the creature understood her, because he stayed put. The groups met and followed Rohan, who stopped in front of a thick section of shrubbery, pointing silently to where a fragment of clothing clung to one of the bushes.

'People have gone through here,' whispered Rohan. 'But since Hunter hasn't made a sound, I'm sure it's safe to explore.'

'Let's try,' said Anu, 'but I can't see how on earth anyone can squeeze through.' As she spoke, the girl pulled at the bush and jumped in surprise as the thick shrub came away easily.

'Golly, it's only stuck in the ground,' said Nimal, helping Anu.

The others joined in and quickly uncovered a gap in the bushes. Filing through cautiously, Rohan and Hunter in the lead, they found themselves standing in a grove of mango trees, which grew so closely together that their abundant foliage prevented even a patch of light from penetrating through.

'Let's cover the entrance,' said Nimal.

They replaced the shrubs and branches as they had found them, and looked around. There was heavy undergrowth but, as they moved further into the grove, they discovered some narrow trails.

'Look, footprints,' said Nimal. 'The ground's damp and these were made recently.' He made some quick sketches of the prints.

'Keep an eye open for signs of people camping here,' whispered Rohan. 'But stay in groups of twos or threes – if you find anything, beep over the WT and we'll go outside the mango grove to discuss it.'

'And don't walk *on* the trails – but beside them. We don't want to leave *our* footprints for others to discover,' said Anu.

They split up: Rohan, Gina and Mich formed one group; Amy and Mahesika another; and Anu, Nimal and Hunter the third. Chandi leapt off Nimal's shoulder and vanished into the treetops, looking for fruit.

Anu and Nimal, checking out the south-west corner of the grove, moved silently as they searched for footprints or clothing – but they found nothing.

After twenty minutes, Hunter suddenly stopped and growled softly.

'Quiet, boy,' whispered Nimal, placing his hand on the dog's head.

Hunter subsided immediately, and the teens listened intently. They had arrived in a section of the grove where the trees grew even closer together. After five minutes Nimal said to the intelligent dog, 'Hunter, go and see if there's anyone around.'

The dog immediately went forward, the teens close behind him, but he did not growl again, and they continued to move south until they saw a clearing ahead of them where four trees had been felled, leaving behind just the stumps. In the middle of this clearing was a firepit.

They sent Hunter into the clearing, and when the dog sniffed around but did not bark or growl, Anu and Nimal cautiously checked the area, discovering several empty cans and a large sack of tinned food, cunningly hidden under a thick bush. Around the firepit they found numerous footprints.

'Two of them are identical to the earlier ones,' muttered Nimal, checking them against his drawings.

'No sign of tents or the usual camping equipment,' muttered Anu after they had searched for a further fifteen minutes.

'Maybe there were people here earlier, and Hunter heard them,' said Nimal. 'But they obviously left soon and seem to have disappeared.'

Puzzled, they finally beeped the others, asking them to regroup at the entrance to the grove. Once outside, the entrance carefully hidden once more, Nimal led them into some thick bushes and gave them an update.

'I'm positive they've *got* to be hidden in that GOMT,' said Nimal.

'What?' said Mahesika.

'Sorry, it's too long to say *Grove of Mango Trees* all the time, so I shortened it.'

The others chuckled, and Amy said, 'But you didn't see tents or camping gear – perhaps they use that area just to cook meals, but camp elsewhere.'

'Well, it's a large GOMT and we haven't searched all over yet,' said Anu.

'Yes – I'm positive they're camping *in* the GOMT and, most likely, somewhere in the south-west section,' said Rohan. 'They wouldn't go to all the trouble of camouflaging an entrance, cutting down trees to make a firepit and hiding cans under a bush, if they were camping far away. The GOMT is humongous – we could all, including the crooks, hide there and if everybody's very careful, we'd never see each other.'

'Now what?' asked Mich. 'Nimal, where's Chandi? I haven't seen her for a while.'

'She's probably stuffing her face with fruit,' said Nimal with a chuckle. 'She'll return when she's had her fill.'

'Unfortunately, we can't search any more today,' said Rohan, looking at his watch. 'Tony's coming to pick us up at 6 p.m. I think we'd better return to TOOJ – it's nearly 2 o'clock and I'm sure everyone's hungry.'

'Gosh, I'd forgotten that we're going to the schools tomorrow,' said Anu. 'Are we going to keep this to ourselves?'

'Oh, yes. It's *our* mystery!' chorused Mich and Gina, and the others agreed.

They made good time back to TOOJ, picking up Mal-li on the way. He stayed inside TOOJ and was spoilt by the JEACs.

Sanjay had left them a note informing them that Tony would be half an hour later than agreed and that there were fresh samosas and a large cake in the green cooler he had left for them. As they sat down to a hot meal in TOOJ, Hunter, who was sniffing around the shrubbery, suddenly barked welcomingly. An excited chittering announced the arrival of Chandi, who leapt on to Nimal's shoulder.

'Golly! Where did she get *those* things?' exclaimed Gina.

They stared at Chandi who was wearing a strange assortment of garments – a white vest, draped artistically over her arms and trailing behind her and a hunting cap grasped in one paw, since it was too big for her head. The vest had several rents in it.

'Where on earth . . .' began Rohan, as he and the others burst out laughing at the comical sight.

'Hey, look at this,' said Anu, unpinning a clothes peg from the vest. 'She must have got it off a washing line.'

'But who'd do laundry in the jungle, and where on earth would she find a washing line?' asked Amy.

'Let's try a process of elimination,' said Rohan thoughtfully. 'Conservation staff don't do laundry in the jungle and they wear dark green, peaked caps with their uniforms; the security guards wear brown caps – this cap is *black*. So, considering that we're looking for thugs, and Chandi disappeared shortly after we entered the GOMT, these could belong to the crooks – which, again, brings me to the conclusion that they're somewhere in that area.'

'Jolly good reasoning, Rohan,' said Anu. 'But where? We didn't see laundry lines.'

'We must go back and investigate more thoroughly,' said Nimal. 'When do we return here?'

'It's easy to lose track of days when you're in the jungle,' said Amy, pulling out a little calendar from her pocket, 'so I've been crossing them off. Today's Thursday, tomorrow we go to the schools, and we return here on Saturday morning.'

'OK, so we'll have to wait till then. Let's get ready for Tony; he'll be here soon,' said Rohan.

'Chandi, come here,' said Gina. 'You can't wander around wearing that vest.'

'That's right, Gina,' said Nimal. 'Tony will ask where she got it.'

Gina tried to remove the vest and cap, but Chandi shrieked loudly, attempting to escape. However, Nimal grabbed her, and cleverly distracting her with his cap, quickly removed the garments.

Tony arrived shortly afterwards, was introduced to Mal-li and chortled over Mahesika's humongous secret. After a fond farewell to Mal-li, whom they left outside TOOJ, they drove back to the residences.

Back at the bungalow, everyone was amused at Mahesika's secret, and eager to meet Mal-li; and Mahesika, relieved that no one was upset with her, became unusually sociable. After a relaxing evening and a lively sing-song, the JEACs organized their clothes and badges for the next day and had an early night for a change.

The next morning they set out with Akka, leaving Hunter and Chandi behind. There were huge turnouts at both schools and Mahesika was very proud to be with the JEACs, taking delight in translating for her peers when they wished to speak to her friends. Not all the children were equally comfortable speaking English, although they understood it well enough.

The JEACs' theme song was received with cheers, and many badges were handed out that day, with children signing up and wanting to start participating immediately. Akka and David had already done some preliminary organization and gave their students dates of upcoming meetings.

At noon, the JEACs were treated to a sumptuous lunch in town.

'Now, folks,' said David, as they ate dessert, 'Akka and I have to finish off at school, but we should be back around 4 p.m. There's a superb museum nearby and then, perhaps, you'd like to wander around the park – we'll meet you beside the water fountain.'

'Sure, David, sounds like fun,' said Amy.

Waving goodbye to Akka and David, the children visited the museum, which was excellent.

'It's only 2:45,' said Rohan, looking at his watch when they came out of the museum. 'Let's check out the park.'

There was a lot going on; acrobats performed stunts on stilts and ropes, jugglers and clowns were up to all kinds of tricks, and the dancers were superb. The children watched them for a while before moving towards the water fountain, which was at the other end of the park. They reached a section which had three soapbox speakers – each speaker raised above the crowd on impromptu platforms – and paused to listen to each of them, but since the men were speaking in Sinhala or Tamil, only Mahesika understood what they were saying.

As they strolled within hearing range of the third group, Mahesika gasped in shock and tried to get the others to move away. However, before she could explain, the speaker pointed at them and yelled something in Sinhala, before changing to English. Everyone turned to look at the JEACs, who stared back in astonishment.

'And those people, my friends,' yelled the speaker, 'are the ones who waste money and land to protect animals – and so we poor farmers suffer because our crops are destroyed by elephants and we're not allowed to shoot them.'

Some of the crowd began moving towards the children. The JEACs backed away, but had to stop because more people had gathered behind them.

'Who's that man, Mahesika?' asked Rohan urgently.

'I don't know. He was saying nasty things about the Conservation and animals before he saw us, and he mentioned Lalith and Priyani, as well,' said Mahesika uneasily.

The crowd, with a typical herd mentality, glared angrily at the children, booing and hissing at them, although most of them had no idea what was going on.

The speaker continued in English, interspersing his remarks with expletives in Sinhala, 'Do you see those children – they are part of the group who want to steal our lands – let's teach them a lesson.'

A few of the more boisterous youths advanced towards the JEACs threateningly.

Mahesika yelled out in Sinhala to the people behind them, 'Call a policeman, quickly, please.'

A man standing nearby had already pulled out his cellular telephone. He called the police and then went to stand with the JEACs.

Sensing trouble, some of the women and children dispersed quickly, but the speaker egged on the boisterous youths to *teach those thieves* a lesson. A group of seven males moved towards the JEACs, leering at the girls and challenging the boys. Rohan and Nimal placed themselves in front of the girls and stepped forward to meet the gang who advanced, grinning at the prospect of thrashing the boys. Although Amy and Anu were good at karate, too, there would be no one to protect Mich, Gina and Mahesika, if they joined the boys.

The man who had called the police stood beside the boys and muttered, 'Cops on their way – hope they get here soon. Know any of the martial arts?'

'Karate,' said Rohan abruptly, his eyes on the gang.

'Good! Same here,' said the stranger.

'Come on,' screamed the speaker, 'let's see some action. They're stealing food from the mouths of our children and destroying our farmlands.'

Seconds later a vicious fight ensued. Most of the crowd stood by and watched while the gang of seven attacked Rohan, Nimal and the stranger. However, it soon became apparent that the three karate experts were gaining the upper hand. The local youths, who had no martial arts skills whatsoever, did not stand a chance.

The crowd screamed encouragement to both sides, and by the time the police arrived, only two of the gang members were still on their feet, unable to run away since the crowd hemmed them in. Right behind the police were Akka and David.

The police put an end to the fight in short order, dispersed the crowd and asked for an explanation.

'My name's Jagith Weerakody,' said the man who had helped the JEACs. 'I witnessed the whole thing – these youngsters are innocent.'

The troublemakers had nothing to say, and were taken off in a van, while an Inspector of Police stayed to get the complete story from Jagith and the JEACs.

'What happened?' asked David.

'That speaker seemed to know who we were,' said Amy shakily, giving Rohan her handkerchief to staunch his bleeding lip.

'Which one is he?' asked the Inspector.

'He disappeared down one of the streets,' said Rohan, who was able to look over most of the heads around him.

Sure enough, the speaker, along with his colleague, had vanished.

'I don't know the speaker's name, but his companion is a Mr. Kurukulaarachchi,' said Jagith. 'He's been in the park before, with his speaker buddy, and they *always* criticize the conservationists. But I didn't worry about it since they haven't mentioned names before. Everyone's entitled to freedom of speech, and I figured they couldn't do much harm by shouting about the farmers' rights.'

'Mr. CADD! We should have known,' growled David under his breath.

'You're bruised,' said Akka, looking at the boys anxiously.

Rohan's lip was still bleeding, Nimal had a cut on his forehead and their helper had a black eye.

'We'll be okay, Akka,' said Rohan.

'Let's go over to my place – I live close by – you'd better come too, Inspector,' said Jagith. 'I'm a keen conservationist and visit Alighasa frequently. I've met Lalith a couple of times.'

'Thanks very much,' said Akka, gratefully accepting his offer.

They trooped along to Jagith's house, which was opposite the park, and Akka attended to Rohan and Nimal's bruises. Jagith's mother produced tea and cakes for his guests while Jagith quickly bathed his eye before joining them in the drawing room.

Mr. and Mrs. Weerakody, Akka, David and the Inspector listened to their story in silence. The Inspector took detailed notes and then left, promising to report it to his superior.

'So Mr. CADD is causing more trouble,' said David.

'I've seen him frequently over the past three years – his blue BMW is unmistakable,' said Jagith. 'Some of my friends and I are convinced he's up to no good.'

'Like what? Drugs? Gun running?' asked Rohan.

'Not sure, but there's an increasing problem with drugs and illegal exports in this part of the country, and your Mr. CADD is pretty friendly with some of the people suspected by the police. Oh, I nearly forgot – Mr. CADD's very pally with one of the farmers, whose land lies just outside the Conservation – my father and I have seen them together.'

'Would it be possible for you to find out a bit more?' asked Anu. 'For instance, where exactly his farmer buddy's land is located?'

'Sure thing,' said Jagith who was in his early twenties and of an adventurous nature. 'One of my buddies works at the hotel where Mr. CADD stays when he comes here – I'll ask him for some leads and go from there.'

'Please do,' said David, 'and get back to Lalith or Tony as soon as possible.'

'Of course,' said Jagith. He grinned and added, 'My middle name's *Sherlock* and I'll fish out my magnifying glass, violin and trench coat!' Everyone laughed as he pretended to play a violin.

Jagith said he would be at the fundraiser, but hoped to see them again before that. They thanked him for his assistance, said goodbye, and piling into Akka's car, set off for home.

'How did they know we belonged to Alighasa?' asked Amy.

'Word gets around,' said David. 'I'd like to know what Mr. CADD's up to and hope Jagith will have information for us soon. Thank goodness he was there to call the police and help you out.'

'Yeah, we'd have been rather stuck otherwise,' said Rohan. 'We were quite outnumbered.'

'I'm glad you didn't join the fight, girls, even though you're good at karate,' said Akka.

'We knew it would be rough on the boys,' said Anu, 'but if they'd both gone down, we'd have rushed in – I was so glad Jagith joined them.'

'That crowd was scary,' said Amy. 'But you guys were really cool.'

'I was trembling inside,' confessed Nimal.

'I guess our biggest advantage was our karate skills,' said Rohan. 'In our previous adventures we've had a bit of experience in karate fighting.'

'Thanks for protecting us,' said Amy gratefully, and the girls echoed her.

'We were just lucky – not really plucky,' said Rohan modestly.

'And now you're a poet, too,' said Anu.

The group dissolved into laughter and the tense atmosphere relaxed.

'Don't mention the fight in front of my mater,' requested David. 'She'll just worry and get into a flap.'

'No problemo,' said the youngsters.

'We'll update the others after Aunty Matty goes to bed,' said Akka.

They reached the Centre around 7:30 and Hunter and Chandi welcomed them enthusiastically. After dinner, they adjourned to the living room and told the adults about the schools and the museum, managing to evade Aunty Matty's questions about the boys' bruises.

Lalith's mobile rang and he left the room to take the call, returning a few minutes later to signal Sanjay and Tony to join him outside the room.

'What's up, machang?' asked David, following them.

'Sabotage at the NC, again,' said Lalith angrily, updating them quickly. 'Tony, call the security company and tell them we want an extra ten guards immediately. David, tell the others, and make it light so Mum doesn't get upset. Let's go.'

Rohan, who was returning from the bathroom, saw the men run outside, and asked David what had happened.

'A bomb blast in the south-west corner of the Conservation – part of the wall's been blown away,' said David.

'Good grief! Weren't any of the guards in that area?' asked Rohan.

'No. Although it's patrolled regularly, the guards don't stay in one place,' said David.

'And that section was completed, right?' said Rohan.

'Yes. Some of the guards jumped into their Jeep and drove towards it, but when they reached the south-west corner, there was nothing to be seen. Let's go and tell the others. It's nearly Mum's bedtime so I'll just say that Lalith and the others had to deal with an emergency at the NC and leave it at that – we'll update the others once she's gone to bed.'

So David, in the understatement of the century, said, 'The boys went to deal with a minor emergency at the NC, Mum. You know how excitable those guards are.' And Aunty Matty went to her room shortly afterwards, convinced that the *boys* would be back soon.

After she left, David told the others what had happened – they were shocked and upset.

'Do you think it's that awful Mr. CADD again?' asked Neeka angrily.

'I wouldn't be surprised,' said Akki.

'And we have further evidence of his animosity towards our Conservation,' said David. 'Tell them what happened this evening, JEACs.'

'Anu, you tell it,' suggested Rohan.

Anu told their story, and as she finished, the main line rang. Priyani answered it and returned to the group, saying, 'That was Sanjay. The bomb created a huge gap and it'll have to be rebuilt – it can't simply be patched up. That's going to take time.'

'Don't worry,' said Neeka. 'We'll contact our volunteers and get help. Come on, Akki – we'll talk to the others.'

'Can we help?' asked Rohan.

'That's kind, dear,' said Priyani, 'but we'll be okay since our volunteers have the required experience. You youngsters should return to TOOJ tomorrow morning – try not to worry about this – it's just another attempt to delay the relocation of the elephants.'

'Okay,' said Nimal, 'if you're sure you don't need us.'

'Positive, thanks,' said Priyani. 'Akka, could you and David drop the JEACs off tomorrow? Niranjani and Shalini have already prepared the hampers.'

'Sure,' said Akka. 'Ready by five, JEACs?'

'No problemo,' chorused the group. They said goodnight and hurried off.

'Talk in your tents,' said Rohan. 'We'll have a general confab at our campsite tomorrow.'

'Right,' agreed the others.

Although no one felt they would be able to sleep, it was not long before all discussions stopped and the JEACs dozed off – Hunter sleeping with one ear open.

CHAPTER 12

In the 'GOMT'

'I'm looking forward to seeing TOOJ,' said David, as they headed off in Akka's Jeep, after an early breakfast.

'It's superfantabulous,' said Gina.

'Will we have the honour of meeting Mal-li?' asked Akka.

'Definitely,' said Mahesika. 'If he's not there, I'll call him.'

'How do you call him, Mahesika?' asked Mich, envisioning Mahesika whistling for Mal-li as she would for a dog.

'I have a special call,' said Mahesika.

They reached the campsite, and since Mal-li was nowhere to be seen, Mahesika went to the gate, cupped her hands over her mouth and sent out a call that sounded like *Tarantara-ooo-iii*! It was loud, high-pitched and clear and sounded a little bit like an elephant trumpeting. After a few minutes, they heard an answering trumpet call and an elephant pounding through the jungle. Finally Mal-li arrived on the scene.

'What a handsome creature,' said David admiringly.

'He's simply enormous!' exclaimed Akka. 'Are you sure he's safe?'

'Watch,' said Anu.

The elephant came to a halt in front of Mahesika, blew gently at her hair and then, winding his trunk around her waist, lifted her on to his head. She whispered in his ear, and he immediately walked to the entrance of the JC, patting Nimal on the head in passing, and lay down contentedly.

They surrounded Mal-li, petting and stroking the creature, and Hunter and Chandi greeted their new friend happily.

Akka and David gave Mal-li some of his favourite fruit, while the JEACs bustled about and brought out snacks and hot drinks.

'This is a beautiful spot,' said Akka, looking around her with pleasure.

Soon after the meal Akka and David said they had to leave, and the youngsters thanked them for the ride. The large coolers were unloaded, and Akka and David gave Mal-li a final pat before they climbed into the Jeep.

'Stay safe, please,' said Akka. 'Everyone's tied up for the next couple of days, and we won't be in touch until Monday morning, when somebody comes to pick you up. Too bad we couldn't leave you a mobile, but you wouldn't be able to charge it.'

'So, stick together and if there's any problem at all, go to Romesh's bungalow – it's closest to you,' added David.

'Don't worry, Akka,' said Rohan. 'We've got Mal-li and Hunter to protect us, and we're pretty good at looking after ourselves and each other.'

'Okay, I don't mean to fuss,' said Akka, smiling at the youngsters.

'We'll be very careful,' promised Nimal.

The others added their assurances, and Akka and David drove off.

'Now, who'd like a cup of hot chocolate with marshmallows?' asked Anu.

'Me! Me! Me!' yelled everyone.

Settled comfortably on the ground beside Mal-li, Rohan called the meeting to order. 'Right, JEACs – let's confab!' He looked around expectantly.

'I was thinking about Chandi's findings and wondered if we should return to the GOMT and search for a hideout – it must be somewhere around there.'

'You're absolutely right, Nimal,' said Anu. 'I've been thinking along the same lines.'

'I'm wondering *why* this situation exists and what it's about,' said Amy. 'A crooked official connected with crooked farmers?'

An animated discussion ensued, Rohan making notes as they spoke.

'You haven't said anything, Rohan,' said Amy.

'I'm listening to all of you and trying to piece it together,' said Rohan.

'Tell us, yaar,' said Nimal.

'Okay, but remember, these are merely possibilities,' said Rohan, glancing at his notes. 'We know that Mr. CADD doesn't want the NC to be functional – he's tried to set the government and the public against it. On the other hand, he supported Lalith's appointment as manager of the OC. Then there's yesterday's incident and Jagith's information about the people Mr. CADD associates with. The rocks in the NC are impassable and once the wall's up, people can't enter the Conservation except through the gates.'

Rohan paused and looked around the group.

'Go on, Rohan – I'm with you,' said Anu encouragingly.

'Right. When I look at the facts so far, I conclude that Mr. CADD, perhaps a corrupt farmer (or two), and some others, are up to no good. They don't care whom they hurt as long as they can carry on their business. One possibility is that they're ivory traders and, when the relocation's completed, they won't have access to the elephants.'

'That's it!' exclaimed Anu. 'But, it's all speculation. We have absolutely no proof.'

'How do we get proof?' asked Mahesika, who was unused to thinking in this way. 'Do we call the police?'

'Not yet,' said Nimal. 'Let's go exploring in the GOMT and see what we discover.'

'Let's spend tonight there,' said Amy. 'It'll be more convenient than going back and forth between here and there.'

'Brilliant!' said Gina.

'Also, since they don't appear to wander around the GOMT during the day, except to get food, if we get to the firepit this afternoon and hide, we may be able to follow them to their hiding place after they've had a meal,' said Rohan. 'Let's organize what we need and get going – it's already 11 a.m. and we should get there ASAP.'

'What's *ASAP*?' asked Mahesika.

'Sorry. It stands for *as soon as possible*,' said Rohan.

Mahesika laughed and said, 'I can't help noticing that you folks *love* your short forms.'

'True, we love acronyms,' said Anu. Then, seeing the puzzled look on Mahesika's face, she explained, 'An *acronym* is a word made up from the initial letters of other words.'

'Hmmm,' said Mahesika, thoughtfully. She grinned cheekily and said, 'Okay, JEACs, let's pack up in the JC, not forgetting our WTs, lock the gate to TOOJ and set off ASAP, going past the DA to the GOMT!'

'You bet, *machang*!' said Amy, as everyone burst out laughing.

'What about Mal-li?' asked Gina. 'Is he coming?'

Everyone looked at Mahesika.

'Well, perhaps it would be better to send him off now – we couldn't get him through the entrance to the GOMT anyway.'

'True,' said Rohan, 'but we have lots of things we need to take, and if we strapped them on to him we could move much faster.'

'Good idea, Rohan,' said Mahesika. 'We'll do that, and I'll send him off from there.'

They bustled about and soon Mal-li was loaded with sleeping bags, minimal camping gear and, of course, lots of food. They took their WTs, extra batteries, rope and all other necessary equipment and then, locking both gates, set off for the GOMT, moving swiftly but quietly. They knew the trail pretty well by now, and made excellent time.

'We're just ten minutes away – quick confab, JEACs,' said Rohan, stopping and moving off the trail into the dense jungle.

'Someone should go ahead and be a lookout,' suggested Amy. 'We have to be sure the men aren't around.'

'I'll take Hunter and go ahead,' offered Nimal. 'Once inside, I'll page you: one beep if it's okay, and two if there's a problem and you need to stay hidden.'

'Go for it,' said Rohan.

Nimal handed Chandi over to Gina, called Hunter, and went off. Upon reaching the entrance to the grove, he let Hunter sniff around, but the dog did not growl. Nimal removed just enough of the barricade for the others to get through in single file, and entered the GOMT before he beeped the others, who arrived quickly.

Hunter stood on guard while Mal-li's load was distributed among the JEACs. Then the patient creature was sent off and the entrance blocked once more.

'We should first find ourselves a good hideout,' whispered Anu.

'Agreed,' said Rohan. 'Let's find a spot in the north-east corner of the GOMT – the crooks must be somewhere in the south-west, near the firepit.'

'Good idea, yaar,' said Nimal.

'What kind of a campsite should we look for?' whispered Mahesika nervously, as they set off. 'And what if the crooks creep up on us?'

'Don't worry,' said Anu softly. 'Hunter will warn us if there are any strangers around, and it's so dark in this grove that we won't be easily seen.'

Mahesika nodded. She was very brave where animals in the jungle were concerned, but men with guns were a different matter. She admired the others for being so cool about everything and tried to follow their example. 'I guess it's because they've had adventures of this kind before,' said Mahesika to herself.

After trekking through the grove for about twenty minutes, Rohan, who was in the lead, whispered, 'We're coming to the end of the GOMT in this direction – the trees are thinning out. I'm turning further east.'

He took a slight detour off the trail, struggled through some heavy shrubbery and came to a halt in a small clearing, which surrounded a particularly lush mango tree whose branches reached the ground. There were no mangoes on the tree.

'This looks perfect,' said Nimal.

'The shrubbery around us is so thick that you'd never guess there was a clearing,' said Amy softly.

'I'm going to climb the tree,' said Nimal, and disappeared, Chandi on his shoulder.

Rohan called Hunter, pushed his way out of the clearing and checked a wide circle around it. The dog did not growl at all, and Rohan returned to the group.

'This'll work,' he said. 'I had a tough time pushing through the shrubs surrounding this spot.'

'We heard you,' said Anu.

'We could easily camp here and no one would know,' said Amy. 'What's it like being Tarzan, Nimal?' she called softly.

Seconds later, Nimal joined them, grinning broadly. Chandi sat on his shoulder and chattered excitedly. 'Wonderful,' he said. 'Hunter! On guard! Good boy. The rest of you, come on up – it's easy.'

'It's like our tree house at home,' said Gina, thrilled with her perch.

'I wish I could have an arboreal existence for a while,' said Anu dreamily, lying comfortably on one of the branches and peering out through the thick foliage. 'We could keep a lookout from here to see if anyone approaches our hideout.'

'It's super,' said Rohan. 'We can post lookouts with WTs, sleep and cook under the tree, hide all our things in the thick shrubbery – and, if necessary, all escape into the tree.'

'But what about Hunter?' asked Mich. 'He can't climb a tree.'

'No problemo, Mich,' said Nimal. 'If necessary, we'll haul him up by rope. Now, all of you stay here and keep absolutely still. I'm going to climb down and see if I can spot any of you. Hang on to Chandi, someone.'

He reached the ground, moved away from the tree and on to the trail. Looking hard at the tree and the surrounding shrubbery, both with and without his binoculars, he tried to spot the others. He even stood right under the tree, peering up into its foliage.

'It's *perfectly* safe,' he said, shinnying up once more. 'Unless you climb up, you can't see a thing. Could you see me?'

'Easily, yaar,' said Rohan. 'Okay, let's confab, but remember, we need to be extremely cautious.'

'Could we do this over a meal?' asked Nimal pathetically. 'I'm simply starving.'

Everyone chuckled.

'Sure we can,' said Amy.

The JEACs prepared to climb down, but Rohan said, 'Let's post a lookout immediately – we don't want to be taken unawares. Who'll do the first shift?'

'We will,' said Mich and Gina together.

'We'll face different directions and cover a wide area,' said Gina.

'Great! Thanks, you two,' said Rohan. 'Use your binocs and croak like frogs if you spot anything.'

Chandi stayed with the girls while the older JEACs descended. They prepared a meal while making plans as to how to get Hunter up the tree if necessary and what their next course of action should be.

'Once we've eaten we should scout around the south-west section where the firepit is,' said Anu. 'This time at least we know we must be extra quiet, and perhaps we should split up into groups of twos or threes.'

'I think someone should also stay *here*,' said Nimal, 'just in case our presumptions are incorrect.'

'Yes, I agree,' said Mahesika. She hesitated, but when the others looked at her encouragingly, she continued. 'Compared to me, you four are much better at this sort of thing and know what to look for. Suppose I stay here with Gina and Mich – we can keep watch from the tree, while you others go off with Hunter. We could hide everything before you leave.'

'Super idea, Mahesika,' said Anu. 'Rohan, do you think the WTs are powerful enough for us to contact each other over the distance?'

'Should be okay,' said Rohan. 'They have an excellent range. Do you have extra batteries, Mahesika?'

'Yes,' said the girl, checking her knapsack.

'Let's do it,' said Nimal. 'How shall we divvy up?'

'I'll go with Rohan,' said Amy promptly.

'Okey-dokey, Amy,' said Nimal, 'and if you, Rohan and I each carry a WT and Mahesika has one here, we can communicate easily. Do we go with one beep if things are okay and two if there's a problem?'

'Sure, yaar,' said Rohan, 'and make sure everyone wears the earpieces.'

'Food's up,' said Anu, handing out hot dogs, samosas and carrots. 'Who's going to take some up to the girls?'

'I'll do it,' said Nimal.

He gave Mich and Gina their meal, updated them about the plans and then came down, Chandi on his shoulder. After the meal, they carefully hid away all their equipment, keeping out only the TGs, WTs and binoculars.

'All set?' asked Rohan, settling the larger TG in its shoulder strap.

'Aye, aye, mate,' said Amy.

'Mahesika, call immediately if there's a problem,' said Anu. 'And, naturally, you'll hear everything over the WT.'

'And don't forget, JEACs,' said Rohan. 'All the WTs are currently on the same frequency so, if you are caught – though I sure hope not – and don't want to let on that there are others around, try and give the double beep for danger, and then nobody say a word – just listen for an *all clear*. We can only hear each other on band 3.65. Also, you can always pretend that the WT is a transistor radio since it has music channels.'

Mahesika nodded – she had never used a WT before. The others set off with Hunter and Chandi, while Mahesika joined the girls in the tree. It was just after 4 p.m.

CHAPTER 13

Moosik

The teens followed the trail, moving swiftly and silently, Hunter up ahead with whoever was leading. Upon reaching the south-west corner, Nimal and Anu took the lead, searching for familiar landmarks.

'Mahesika, we're approaching the firepit, over,' Nimal whispered into the mouthpiece of his WT.

'We're sticking to the shrubbery, but will take a dekko. Over and out,' muttered Rohan.

They stopped under a heavy bush, west of the firepit, and Rohan said softly, 'Hunter, go see if there's anyone around.'

Understanding immediately, Hunter crept out and sniffed around the area before approaching the firepit. He returned to the children, wagging his tail.

'All clear! Let's see if the sack of food's still there,' whispered Nimal, leading the way to the firepit. 'Hunter, on guard!'

While Hunter kept a sharp watch, the JEACs searched for and found the food in the same spot where Anu and Nimal had discovered it previously.

'Is it possible they've moved on and not taken the food with them?' said Amy.

'Unlikely, but you can also tell that they've cooked a meal here very recently,' said Rohan, who was examining the firepit.

'How do you know, Rohan?' asked Amy.

'Because these are freshly opened cans of fish and there are grains of cooked rice on the ground,' said Rohan, pointing with a stick. 'See, the fish around the edge of the can is still fresh and soft. Also, the ashes are slightly warm.'

'Could they be watching us?' said Anu.

'Back into the shrubbery,' said Rohan abruptly. Once they were out of sight of anyone who might have been watching the firepit, he continued, 'Good point, sis. Warm ashes means the crooks are close by – let's be extra cautious as we search for their hideout.'

The youngsters informed Mahesika of their intention, split into pairs and agreed to keep in touch every half hour. Rohan and Amy skirted the firepit, going north, taking Hunter with them; Nimal and Anu went south-east, Chandi riding on Anu's shoulder.

'Gee whizz, Rohan,' said Amy, a while later, sitting down on a tree stump, 'we've been searching for ages. I can't imagine where these crooks are hiding. Should we return to camp and come out at night to see who uses the firepit and catch them red-handed?'

'It's an idea,' said Rohan, offering her a drink of water, 'but if you're not too tired, let's look around a bit more.' He gave Hunter some water, too.

'Of course,' said Amy, rising immediately. 'I'm not tired – just frustrated that they're so elusive.' She smiled and added, 'I don't mean to complain, you know . . .'

'Sure do,' said Rohan understandingly. 'Let's check-in with the others before we move on.'

'Good,' said Amy, hearing the *all okay* from Nimal and Mahesika. 'Let's go, *yaar.*'

Rohan laughed and followed Amy, who led the way into another section of the GOMT, Hunter sniffing ahead of them. Half an hour later they had still not discovered anything new.

'Perhaps we should go back to the firepit,' said Rohan, mopping his brow. 'Phew! It sure is hot!'

'Yeah,' said Amy. 'Shall I beep the others?'

'Go ahead,' said Rohan.

Amy beeped once and Mahesika's voice came over the air immediately. 'All okay out there, Amy? Over.'

'Sure is,' said Amy softly. 'Rohan and I are returning to the firepit – haven't found any trace of a campsite. Anything new at your end?'

'Nope – the girls are making sandwiches. Over,' said Mahesika.

'Good thinking,' said Rohan. 'Hello, Nimal. Anything cooking? Over.'

There was no response. Rohan tried again, and then four more times, but there was no answer.

'Where are they?' said Amy anxiously.

'Don't know,' said Rohan. 'Mahesika, we're going off the air – hopefully Nimal's WT connection is just loose or something. Over and out.'

Rohan and Amy looked at each other. What could have happened? Calling softly to Hunter, Rohan silently led the way back to the firepit.

They were nearly there when their WTs beeped twice and a male voice spoke angrily. 'You tell me that transistor? I not believe you. Where moosik?'

Rohan and Amy froze. Anu's voice came over the air cheerfully, 'Now, Nimal, I told you the transistor had good music on channel 5.5. Sorry, chaps, I'll show you how it works.'

'Yes, you show us soon, or you be very sorry,' said another male voice. 'Give girl radio.'

'Nimal, hand it over,' said Anu. 'Why did I ever wish I could be an arboreal being? And even if I did, why do my wishes have to come true?'

Her voice went off the air, and Rohan and Amy stared at each other.

'Oh, no,' groaned Rohan. 'Nimal obviously turned the WT on speaker. Did you hear that, Mahesika? Over.'

'Yes,' whispered Mahesika. 'What's happened to them? Whose was that other voice? Over.'

'They've been caught,' said Rohan grimly. 'I think the voice speaking in broken English was the same one we heard the other night. What do you think, Amy?'

'Absolutely,' said Amy. 'What next?'

'We'll try and discover where they are, and then update you, Mahesika,' said Rohan, thinking quickly. 'Also, if the WT beeps twice don't make a sound – just listen hard. Over and out. Let's go, Amy,' he continued, running in the direction of the firepit, Hunter and Amy at his heels. It was 6:15 p.m.

Upon reaching the firepit, they hid in the shrubbery and, using their binoculars, searched for signs of a struggle.

'Nothing to be seen, and Hunter's not making a sound,' whispered Rohan finally. 'Hunter, find them, boy. Sniff 'em out!' He said to Amy, 'Even if he doesn't find Nimal or Anu, he'll follow the scent of the crooks.'

The dog crawled out of the shrubbery, sniffed around and went south-east from the firepit, Amy and Rohan on his heels. They had not gone far when their WTs beeped twice, and they stopped immediately, listening hard. Rohan grabbed Hunter's collar to prevent him from going on.

Anu's voice said impatiently, 'Really, Nimal, if it isn't *just* like a boy! You had to go channel surfing! Why couldn't you be satisfied with the channel I found?'

'Sorry, sis. Can you fix it, please? Oh, excuse me, but will we be getting some food soon? I'm hungry,' said Nimal.

'You shut up, boy,' said a harsh voice. 'We go to firepit at ten. If you good – you get food.'

'But it's only a ten-minute walk from here,' groaned Nimal.

'You put moosik on and shut up,' growled another voice. 'If you no shut up, I take your radio.'

'Moosik it is,' said Anu quickly, and the WT went off the air.

'Smart kids to let us know they're close to the pit,' muttered Rohan, as he and Amy waited, hopefully, to hear Anu or Nimal again.

But the WT was silent. Rohan spoke briefly to Mahesika, who had also heard the conversation.

'Let's go back to our campsite and make some plans,' said Amy, who was very upset.

'Okay, come on, Hunter. It's now 6:45, Amy, and we should try and get back to this area before ten tonight,' agreed Rohan.

They hurried back to the mango tree, and the others descended quickly – all of them anxious about Anu and Nimal. Hunter, once fed, was put on guard while the others prepared a meal and made valiant attempts to eat it.

'How are we going to rescue them?' asked Mich, who was toying with her food.

'Eat up, chicken,' said Amy, trying not to sound worried, 'and you, too, Gina. We must keep up our strength if we're to rescue them. I'm sure Rohan already has some ideas – right, Rohan?'

'Er . . . yes,' said Rohan. 'Let's confab.' He continued around a mouthful of food, 'Facts: we know there are at least two men; their hideout is ten minutes away from the firepit; they'll be going there around ten this evening.' He looked at his watch, 'It's eight now – let's leave around nine, make our way to the firepit and watch to see if they bring Nimal and Anu along.'

'But what can we *do*, Rohan?' asked Gina.

'If they bring Anu and Nimal to the firepit, they'll have to untie their hands so they can eat. I doubt they'll think two kids are much of a problem, and knowing those two and their powers of invention, they would have come up with a great story as to why they had a TG and why they were in the jungle in the first place. Don't forget, we're fully equipped and we have Hunter. We'll play it by ear and see if we can rescue them.'

'I have another suggestion, Rohan,' said Amy.

'Go ahead.'

'Let's attempt to locate the crooks' hideout first, in case they *don't* bring Anu and Nimal to the firepit. Once we find the CH, we can watch to see when the men take off, and then try for a rescue.'

'Hmmm . . . yeah . . . you're right, Amy,' said Rohan. 'Let's go with your plan – we'll head for the firepit, get our bearings and then start looking for the CH.'

'CH – Crooks' Hideout?' queried Mahesika, who was catching on fast.

Rohan nodded. They finished their meal, cleared everything away, and set out once more. No moonlight pierced the dense grove as Rohan led the way with Hunter, flashing his torch on and off occasionally to make sure they were still on the trail. Mich and Gina went next with Mahesika and Amy brought up the rear. They took both TGs with them, and walked extra cautiously, knowing that the men might be close by.

'Sshh – no noise now,' said Rohan a while later. 'We're close to the firepit.'

They moved on silently, and then Hunter growled softly. Everyone froze in their tracks. Three male voices, speaking in Sinhala, were heard, and Mahesika translated softly.

'A man who sounds like one of those who shouted at Nimal earlier, asked if "the children had more friends in the jungle". The chap named Pala said he thinks they're from the Conservation and that they are very frightened. Then Ranjan told both men to stop talking so loudly and get cooking so that they could eat and then take a meal for the others. He also warned them not to make a sound on the way back to, or in, their campsite – just in case staff members were roaming the jungle, looking for the children.'

'Blow! It's only 9:45 – they're here earlier than planned and haven't brought Nimal and Anu,' whispered Rohan. 'I can see a faint glow through these bushes – guess it's from the firepit. Let's make a wide circle around it and see if we can find the CH.'

They wound their way through another trail, moving south of the firepit, and the voices faded.

'Good thing they were talking so loudly,' muttered Amy. 'At least we know where they are.'

'Gee, I wish we could call out for Anu and Nimal,' said Mich. 'They may be close by and could answer.'

'I would think they're tied up and gagged,' muttered Rohan under his breath to Amy. He then continued softly to Mich, 'That won't help at the moment, kiddo, and we might only put them in more danger.'

They searched, unsuccessfully, for twenty minutes before Hunter growled again.

'Quick, into the shrubbery,' said Rohan, grabbing Hunter by his collar and telling him to be quiet. 'Amy, I think they're coming this way and I'm going to tail them – we've *got* to see where they go. Stay put, everyone, and hang on to Hunter.'

They had barely hidden in the shrubbery when they saw torchlight on the trail. Hunter, Amy's hand on his head, did not make a sound, but Amy felt him bristle.

As the men passed the JEACs, it was obvious that they wore dark clothing, but there was not enough light to see their faces since the torches were focused on the path.

Rohan followed them silently, returning fifteen minutes later.

'What happened?' whispered Amy.

'Lost them,' said Rohan frustratedly. 'I followed their torchlight into an area where there were some massive trees, growing very close together – five minutes away from here. Then they turned off their torches, and appeared to stop moving, too. I listened hard but heard nothing but a swishing sound. After a few minutes, I crept out very quietly and went over to the trees wondering if they had climbed them, but since the branches only start about four and a half or five metres off the ground, the men couldn't have climbed up without a ladder – and I didn't see one anywhere around.' He paused.

'And then?' asked Mich eagerly.

'And then – nothing,' muttered Rohan. 'I searched for five more minutes, looking for possible entrances which could lead to a CH – like a hollow in the trunk of a tree or an underground cave, but didn't find a thing. Not one clue as to their whereabouts – they seem to have vanished into thin air.'

'Let's return to our hideout,' suggested Amy. 'We can talk more freely there.'

'Okay,' said Rohan, leading the way back.

It was a dispirited group of JEACs, who reached the campsite around 11:30 that night. Hunter sniffed around, looking for Nimal and Anu; he finally sat down, between Gina and Mich, and they put their arms around him. Amy made a hot drink – nobody felt like eating anything.

Rohan insisted that they roll out their sleeping bags and get into them before any discussion. He knew Gina and Mich were exhausted. Sure enough, although they tried hard to stay alert, they nodded off as soon as they lay down.

'What now?' asked Amy.

'Let's put on our thinking caps,' said Rohan. 'We've looked all around the firepit; we've followed the men, who obviously have a campsite close to where I last saw them; but there's absolutely *no* trace of them. How did they disappear just like that?'

They thought hard and then Mahesika said hesitatingly, 'Sorry, I know this may be a strange question to ask just now, but what does "arboreal" mean?'

'It means "living in trees",' explained Amy. 'Why did you suddenly think of it?'

'Because Anu used it twice today,' said Mahesika. 'First, when we were all here, up in this tree, she said she wished she could be an arboreal being for a while. The second time she used the word was after they were caught, when she and Nimal were talking over the WT, and she said, "Why do my wishes have to come true?" I just wondered . . .'

Rohan stared at her intently. 'Hold it! I think you're on to something there, Mahesika. Let's retract a bit. What *exactly* did she say over the WT – I need to write it down. Amy, shine your torch over here so I can see what I'm doing.'

She did so; he pulled out his notebook and looked at the girls expectantly.

Amy said slowly, 'I think she said something like, "Why did I wish I could be an arboreal being? And even if I did wish it, why did my wish have to come true?" Does that sound right?'

'Absolutely,' said Mahesika.

'More or less,' said Rohan jubilantly. He had been writing busily as the girls spoke. '*Now* we know where they're being held and where the CH is!'

'Where?' asked Mahesika and Amy, staring at the grinning boy.

'Sometimes Anu uses words very deliberately,' said Rohan, 'and I think she was trying to give us a message without the crooks catching on. So she used *arboreal*, which is not a word many people know, especially if English isn't their first language. "Arboreal" – "living in trees" – get it?'

'You mean . . .' gasped Amy and Mahesika together, 'they're up in a tree?'

'Of course! Makes sense, right?' said Rohan. 'She said it was too bad that her wish to be an arboreal being came true – the men I followed disappeared suddenly and we were unable to find their hideout. What if they're living in a tree? They'd be safe and sound – a couple of planks across some branches would make a great platform – and *nobody* would find them.'

'Oooh!' gasped Amy. 'Mahesika, didn't you say that one of the chaps was grumbling about being tired of living like a monkey?'

'He did,' said Mahesika excitedly. 'If we go back to where you lost track of them, Rohan, and start checking out the trees, we'll find them. Shall we go now?'

Hunter, sensing their excitement, whined softly and put his paw on Rohan's knee.

'I know all of you want to set off immediately,' said Rohan, patting the dog, 'but I think we'd better leave it for tonight.' He nodded at the two sleeping girls. 'I'd rather we all stick together. Also, the men are probably up and about and we don't know how many of them there are. So let's leave it till morning. We know they'll probably sleep during the day.'

'Okay,' yawned Amy, snuggling into her sleeping bag. 'But I hate to think of Nimal and Anu in their clutches.'

'Me, too,' said Mahesika.

'Don't you worry about them, ladies,' said Rohan, more chirpily than he felt. 'You know what those two are like. They're probably cooking up schemes for escaping and giving those chaps a hard time.'

'Do you really think they're in a tree, Rohan?' asked Amy, once Mahesika had fallen asleep.

'Yeah, I'm positive our guess is correct.'

'What time should we set out tomorrow? Will you wake us?'

'Sure thing,' said Rohan. 'I'll wake you up around 5 a.m. G'night, Amy.'

'G'night, Rohan.'

Hunter, puzzled as to why Nimal and Anu were missing, stayed on guard and dozed lightly.

CHAPTER 14

An Arboreal Existence

Anu and Nimal, when they parted from the other two, decided to re-explore the section they had checked previously. Chandi had disappeared once more, but they knew she would return sooner or later.

They crept south-east, keeping a sharp lookout for anything that might look like a campsite, but nothing caught their eye.

All at once Anu, who was just behind Nimal, put out her hand and touched him on the arm. 'Look over there, Nimal – to our right – in that large mango tree with tons of mangoes. Isn't that Chandi?'

Nimal looked in the direction she was pointing and chuckled softly. 'Sure is,' he muttered. 'And she's still wearing her knapsack, little wretch that she is!'

'She's also wearing another strange garment,' whispered Anu. 'Should we try and get her or let her be?'

'Better leave her alone – she'll come when she's ready,' said Nimal, watching the little monkey as she ate part of another mango and threw it away. 'Let's check out the trees in that clump over there – they're quite close together and would make a good hiding place for a campsite.'

It was 5:50 p.m., and as they moved into the area, treading softly, two men suddenly swung down from a tree and knocked Nimal over before he could do a thing to defend himself or protect Anu. Kicking the gun out of his reach, the men grabbed him, twisting his arms painfully behind his back. A third man, appearing from behind a tree, made a grab for Anu, but she immediately took up a karate stance.

'Back off!' said Anu fiercely.

'You lookit here, missie,' said one of the men holding Nimal, 'if you no be good, we break you frien' arm and leg. You be good?'

Anu relaxed her stance, glared at the man, and replied, 'I'll be good. Don't hurt my brother.'

'Okay, now you climb tree,' he replied, pointing to the rope ladder that was hanging down from one of the trees, and indicating that both youngsters should climb up. 'Pala,' he said to the other man who had helped capture Nimal, 'you go first, then this missie and her brother. We come last.'

Nimal and Anu obeyed. The branches of the tree began way up above the ground, and it would have been impossible to climb it without the ladder.

At the top of the ladder, they stepped on to a large platform. Sturdy planks of wood were nailed across the branches and it was, all in all, a snug retreat. The heavy foliage gave them perfect cover from prying eyes and protected them from the elements, although they had tied some plastic sheets above the planks so that not a drop of rain could reach the platform. A clothes line was strung across one section of the tree house, and a few articles of clothing were hung out to dry.

Two more men were in the CH – they spoke no English at all. The youngsters were pushed into a corner of the CH, and their feet were tied, while Nimal's gun was placed beyond his reach.

'My name, Ranjan,' said the man who had captured Nimal. 'You not Sri Lankan. What you do here?'

They played innocent. 'I'm Nimal, and this is my sister, Anu. We're on holiday from India, visiting friends at the Conservation.'

'How you find way here?' asked Pala.

'We got lost,' said Anu briefly.

'Why you carry gun?' asked Ranjan, who was obviously the leader.

'In case any of the animals attacked us,' explained Nimal.

'What that?' asked Ranjan, pointing at the WT.

'Transistor radio,' said Nimal.

It was then that Nimal and Anu first attempted to send a coded message to the others to let them know that they had been captured and were up in a tree house. How they hoped the others would catch on. After this little episode, Ranjan was satisfied that they only had a radio.

The youngsters were not badly treated, and only their feet were tied, but they were informed, sternly, that if they tried to yell or escape, their hands would be tied, too, and they would be gagged. They were given a drink of thambili, and were told that they could listen to their transistor radio, but that the volume should be low; this was the second time the teens tried to send a message to the others.

The men conversed in low tones, in Sinhala, so Anu and Nimal were unable to understand anything; however, the word *aliya* occurred frequently.

At 9:40, Pala, Ranjan and Karan, the third man who had assisted in capturing the teens, went off to cook a hot meal for everyone, including the children. Ranjan decided that it was too risky to take Nimal and Anu along in case people were out looking for them. He also gave the men strict instructions not to speak loudly, and that the kids should not turn on their radio since sound travelled clearly in the still night.

It was on their return to the CH, around 10:25 p.m., when Rohan had tried, unsuccessfully, to follow the three men. After a silent meal, the youngsters were given a couple of mattresses to lie down on, but their feet were kept tied. Then the men played a game of cards, while Anu and Nimal fell asleep.

At midnight, Karan lit an oil lamp and the men had cups of tea from a large flask. The youngsters, who had slept very lightly, woke up at the sound of movement in the tree house, and watched as four of the five men climbed down the rope ladder, Ranjan warning Karan, who was left behind to guard the teens, that there should be no noise from the tree house.

Nimal and Anu looked at each other. Since Karan could not speak much English but *understood* a fair amount, Anu and Nimal spoke in Hindi. Karan could not understand them, but seeing that they were speaking softly and not attempting to escape, he left them alone and lay down on his mattress to read a newspaper.

'Do you think they're smuggling something or other?' asked Anu in Hindi.

'Absolutely,' replied Nimal. 'There's a pile of stuff in that corner, covered with the plastic. I wouldn't be surprised if they were ivory traders – remember their conversation? They used the word for elephants, in their language, quite often. And, when one of the men lifted the sheet slightly to slide my gun under it, I glimpsed what looked like a tusk.'

'That makes sense,' said Anu, in a low voice. 'These crooks kill the poor ephalunts, saw off their tusks, and sell them to the ivory traders for humongous amounts of money. The same guys are probably sabotaging the NC wall because once that goes up and the ephalunts are relocated, they won't have access to them.'

'Yeah,' groaned Nimal. 'We've simply got to escape and do something about it.'

'I hope they don't kill any more ephalunts tonight,' said Anu angrily.

'Let's be practical and think up an escape plan,' said Nimal. 'Also, we should get some sleep now so that we're alert when the men return.

'Okay,' said Anu. 'Try and get as comfortable as pos. We'll catch these crooks, one way or another.'

'Definitely. G'night, Anu,' said Nimal.

Despite the uncomfortable positions they had to lie in because of their bonds, they soon fell asleep.

Around 6 a.m., Anu and Nimal, who were awake but lying down and pretending to be asleep so that Karan – who was pottering around – would not notice, heard the sound of leaves rustling. The men had returned, tired and dirty, carrying nothing but their guns with them. Karan poured out cups of tea. The crooks, taking no notice of the teens, sat in a circle, carrying on a low-voiced, heated argument. Nimal stealthily moved his hand towards the WT which was near him, turned it to channel 3.65 and beeped twice. Anu raised her eyebrows. *How* they hoped Mahesika would hear the argument – she was the only JEAC who could understand Sinhala.

Ranjan, in a filthy mood, was obviously ticking the men off. He spoke angrily until Pala finally yelled at him. Ranjan hastily told him to speak quietly, and calmed down himself. A general discussion ensued for another 45 minutes, and after it was over, the men lay down on their mattresses and went to sleep. Not one of them was concerned that the youngsters might escape. Such a possibility would be inconceivable – these were just kids.

Nimal quietly turned off the WT and winked at Anu.

Anu nodded over to where Pala was stretched out, his mattress lying on top of the rope ladder – no chance of escape yet.

'Oh, well, might as well get a few more hours of shut-eye,' whispered Anu, in Hindi.

Nimal nodded. By 7:15 a.m. there was no sound in the hideout except for heavy breathing and loud snores from some of the men.

CHAPTER 15

Chandi Wears Socks

Earlier that morning, at 5 a.m., Rohan woke the younger girls. 'Rise and shine, kiddos,' he said, shaking them gently.

'Are we going to rescue Anu and Nimal now?' asked Gina sleepily, rubbing her eyes.

'We're definitely going to try,' said Amy, who was preparing breakfast, while the others bustled about, hiding everything in the bushes.

Over a cup of hot chocolate and sandwiches, they discussed their plans and outlined their ideas to Gina and Mich.

'We need to be extra quiet as we make our way to the firepit,' said Rohan, as they prepared to set out just after 6 o'clock. 'For all we know, they could be wandering about the GOMT since . . .'

He trailed off as the WTs beeped twice, and raised his hand in a signal for the others to stop.

Rohan, Amy and Mahesika listened hard through the earpieces. They heard men's voices raised in argument, speaking in Sinhala. Rohan and Amy gazed at Mahesika whose eyes had widened in shock as she absorbed what the men were saying. The JEACs sat down quietly, Mich and Gina hanging on to Hunter, and nobody made a sound.

Once the voices had died down, and it was clear that Nimal and Anu had tuned out, the youngsters looked expectantly at Mahesika. But before she could say a word, Hunter growled softly and the youngsters froze.

'What is it, boy?' said Rohan in a low voice, kneeling beside the dog.

Hunter sniffed the air and then whined.

'It's like he's scented a friend,' said Gina. 'He always makes that funny little sound.'

Everyone peered out of the shelter in an attempt to see if anyone was close by.

'Oooh!' gasped Amy.

The others turned to her and gaped at the tiny monkey seated on her shoulder.

'Chandi, you little wretch,' said Rohan, gently stroking the creature, who leapt on to his shoulder and tugged his hair affectionately. 'Where on earth did *you* drop from?'

Chandi chattered into his ear.

'She's wearing another strange garment,' said Mich, pulling at the shreds of a T-shirt. 'I wonder where she keeps finding these things.'

'Probably belongs to the crooks,' said Rohan, taking the garment off the monkey and examining it. 'Perhaps she goes to their hideout and steals their clothes when they're not around.'

Chandi leapt from shoulder to shoulder, making little chattering noises. Finally she leapt on to Hunter's back and whispered in his ear. He shook his head and she scampered up into Gina's arms, hiding her face in the girl's shoulder and making a small whimpering noise.

'Oh, don't cry, Chandi,' said Gina softly as she stroked the little creature. 'I'm sure we'll find Nimal soon.'

Rohan stared at Gina. 'Why did you say that, kiddo?' he asked.

'I don't know,' said Gina, looking at her brother. 'But she's so crazy over Nimal and when she seemed to be looking for him and began to cry, I thought perhaps she was sad that he wasn't with us.'

'You're probably right, pet,' said Amy, giving her a hug.

'Why can't we get Chandi to lead us to Nimal and Anu?' said Mahesika suddenly.

'Brilliant, Mahesika!' said Rohan. 'Gina, hang on to Chandi – she's good at disappearing suddenly, and we need her – let's confab.'

Gina wrapped her arms around the little monkey, who snuggled against her and went to sleep.

'Fire away, Mahesika,' said Rohan, as they seated themselves underneath the mango tree once more. 'What *were* those guys saying?'

'Here's the gist of their conversation,' said Mahesika. 'Basically, the man who spoke first – his name is Ranjan – was mad at the others. He said that because they had to leave Karan on guard with Anu and Nimal, they were short-handed for their job that night. And guess what they're doing? *They're the ones killing elephants for their tusks!*'

The others gasped in horror, but Rohan said, 'Questions later, folks, if you don't mind. Tell us the rest, Mahesika.'

'They're going out tonight in one last attempt to get more tusks. Karan will stay behind because of Nimal and Anu, but apparently someone called Mr. K. will send extra men to help them, and they'll meet at the mid-west section of the fence, which is weak and unguarded. Then a herd, with tuskers, will be driven towards that spot. As soon as the elephants reach the fence – around 1:30 or so – Mr. K. and others will be there to shoot them and take their tusks. Someone asked about the farmer the land belongs to, and Pala said that the farmer was in on the deal and would say he *had* to kill the elephants because they were dangerous.'

'Wicked, wicked men,' sobbed Gina, and Mich put her arm around her consolingly, although she was crying, too.

'We have to stop them,' said Amy angrily. Also, didn't Mr. CADD's name begin with a K – something like Kurukul?'

'You're right, Amy, it did,' said Rohan. 'But we can't jump to conclusions about him. Let's focus on protecting the elephants first. Here's a map, Mahesika – did they say exactly *where* mid-west of the Conservation is?'

'Yes, it's the section directly west of this GOMT. Fortunately, one of the other guys didn't know the area and was given detailed directions.'

'No other names, by any chance?' asked Rohan.

'Sorry, no.'

'No problemo,' said Rohan. 'Let's think this through. We simply have to protect the ephalunts. Most of the men will be leaving the CH tonight – we can easily deal with one chap. We need to get a message to Anu and Nimal; tell them what the men are planning; say we're going to try and rescue them and then we'll all rush off to the fence with Mal-li to save the ephalunts. Anu and Nimal will be alert and on their toes, too. What do you think?'

'Hmmm, let's get a message to Nimal and Anu first,' said Amy. 'Do you think Chandi would be like Hunter that way and "scent" Nimal out?'

'It's a good idea, Amy, and worth a shot,' said Rohan. 'She'd be better than us or Hunter, because she can swing through the trees, and I'm sure she'll find him. I guess we'll have to return to TOOJ, find something of Nimal's – like a sock – and give it to Chandi.'

'Chandi's clever enough to find Nimal,' said Gina, and Mich nodded in agreement.

'Should we tell Lalith and the rest?' Mahesika asked.

'Not yet,' said Rohan. 'They're weighed down with other problems. Let's do this on our own and only resort to involving them if we can't rescue Nimal and Anu this evening.'

Mahesika looked nervous but said, 'We can get Mal-li to help us.'

'Super, Mahesika,' said Rohan. 'With Mal-li around, nobody would dream of messing with us. Let's go, folks.'

Back at TOOJ, Rohan rummaged through Nimal's bag and found an extra pair of socks. He knotted them together, and tied them around Chandi's waist. The little creature was thrilled with her new clothes. She knew they belonged to Nimal and wandered all around the campsite searching for him unsuccessfully. Then she returned and leapt on to Rohan's shoulder, whimpering in his ear. He tried to soothe her.

'How are we going to tie the message to her?' asked Mahesika.

'Let's put the message into one of the socks – written in Hindi,' said Mich.

'Brilliant!' said everyone. Rohan quickly wrote a message in Hindi, and tucked it into one of the socks.

'Now let's go for a walk and see what she'll do,' said Amy.

They set out from TOOJ, Chandi riding on Mahesika's shoulder.

Mahesika kept stroking the tiny creature, and saying in a low voice, 'I wonder where *Nimal* is, Chandi? Can you find *Nimal*? Take our message to him . . . I know he's missing you . . . *where is Nimal?*'

Chandi listened to the girl and looked around for Nimal. When he did not appear, she suddenly leapt off Mahesika's shoulders and scampered off into the trees. The children followed her easily for a little while because they could see the white socks. However, she soon outstripped them and was lost to sight.

'Well, she's gone now and I hope she finds them soon,' said Rohan.

'We'd better go back to TOOJ and finalize our plans for this evening,' said Amy, turning back.

'Yes, and we should try to get some sleep,' said Rohan, practically. 'We need to be alert and fighting fit tonight.'

'But it's only noon,' said Gina, looking at her watch. 'Are we going to sleep the whole afternoon and evening?'

'No, of course not,' said Rohan with a laugh. 'Here's what we'll do – and tell me what you think, folks. The first part of our plan is to have a big, hot meal, make some sandwiches for later on, and get a few hours' sleep. The second part is to rescue Nimal and Anu, go to the mid-west fence – which isn't too far from us – and save the elephants. What do you think?'

After firming up the plan with a few more suggestions, by which time they reached TOOJ once more, the JEACs carried out the first part of their plan, and went to sleep by 3 p.m. Rohan set his alarm for nine that night.

CHAPTER 16

Back to Earth

The day crawled by for Anu and Nimal. How they hoped that Mahesika had heard what the men were saying.

The men woke up at noon, untied Nimal and Anu and allowed them to wander around in the tree house for a short time. But space was limited and, when all the men were up and about, Nimal asked if they could climb down for a little while. The men consulted together and agreed to take them to the firepit for a hot meal.

'But you be good. If you no behave, I break your sister's arm,' said Pala nastily.

They agreed to behave.

The rope ladder went down with a swishing sound, and everyone descended quickly. Then, as Anu and Nimal watched in amazement, Karan hid the rope ladder out of sight. Concealed in the shrubbery was a long pole with a hook attached to one end of it. Using this pole, Karan draped the rope ladder on a high branch of the tree, where the leaves hid it completely.

'Come,' said Pala, once he was satisfied that the ladder was out of sight.

As the party walked towards the firepit, Nimal said to Anu in Hindi, 'So *that's* why we couldn't find a trace of where these guys were hiding. Even the ladder was concealed.'

'True,' said Anu. 'Let's be extra careful. They're not as dumb as we may think.'

The youngsters were glad to stretch their legs and kept a sharp but discreet eye open for the others – but, unfortunately, saw no signs of them. After a quick meal, they were taken back to the tree house and their feet were tied up. It was a boring time for Anu and Nimal since the men merely played cards for a little while before lying down again for a nap. Pala, confident that the teens could not climb down without waking up the men, did not bother to tie their hands. He simply placed his mattress on top of the rope ladder and dozed off.

Nimal and Anu spoke softly in Hindi.

'I wonder what the others are up to and if they heard the men earlier,' said Anu with a sigh. 'This sure is tedious, just sitting around.'

'We could free our legs,' said Nimal.

'What's the use?' said Anu. 'We can't escape at the moment without waking Pala, and there are too many chaps for us to take on.'

'True,' agreed Nimal. 'It was just a thought. I wish Chandi would appear,' he continued.

'Why don't you try signalling her?' suggested Anu. 'If the men wake up they'll just think it's the monkeys chattering in the trees.'

'Good idea,' said Nimal, lying down with his back towards the men.

He pursed up his lips and made a low, chattering sound. Anu listened in awe. Nobody would *dream* that a human being was making those noises. The men were fast asleep, and Nimal kept calling for about five minutes.

All of a sudden there was a rustling in the leaves above them – and down dropped Chandi.

She scampered on to Nimal's shoulder, crooning with delight and making her funny little chittering noises, nibbling at his ear and tugging his hair affectionately. Nimal and Anu were thrilled, and spoke to the little monkey very softly in Hindi. The men slept on.

'Look at her funny garments – two socks tied together. I wonder where she got those from?' said Anu with a chuckle.

Chandi jumped into Anu's arms, and the girl stroked her gently.

'Hey! They're *my* socks,' said Nimal.

'Are they? Gosh, I can feel something in one of them,' said Anu excitedly.

Making sure the men were still asleep, Anu pulled out the note written by Rohan. She and Nimal read it quickly.

'Good old Mahesika. But this means we've simply got to get away from here this evening,' said Anu. 'How are we going to escape?'

'When they go off tonight, we'll see if we can tackle the guard,' said Nimal. 'I have a penknife in my knapsack and can cut the ropes around our feet.'

'But they're sure to tie our hands, as well, especially if they're all going off,' breathed Anu.

'No problemo,' said Nimal, as he stuffed his socks under the mattress. 'Let's lie down and pretend to be asleep and we'll find a way to rescue ourselves. Look – Chandi's fallen asleep, cuddled up under my sheet.'

The men awoke at 6 p.m. and after a brief discussion in Sinhala, tied the youngsters' hands behind their backs, collected guns and prepared to descend. They did not notice Chandi who was still hiding under Nimal's sheet.

'Now you be good. We going for food, and Karan bring some for you,' said Ranjan.

A few minutes later, all the men were gone.

'A chance in a lifetime,' said Anu.

Nimal grinned as he struggled over to his knapsack. 'They're really dumb to leave us alone like this,' he said. He reached his knapsack and, looking over his shoulder, found the zip and managed to open it. 'Hah! Got my penknife.' He inched his way back to Anu and said, 'Turn around, old thing, and hold still while I set you free.'

In a few minutes, Nimal's Swiss army knife had sliced through the ropes tying Anu's wrists together. She then took over the knife, freed her feet and cut the ropes binding Nimal.

'Now for the rope ladder,' said Nimal, going to where it was attached to the tree. 'Blow!' he muttered a minute later. 'We can't get it off the branch they anchor it to without the hooked pole. We'll have to think of an alternate plan.'

'Let's assume only Karan comes back,' said Anu. 'The others had their guns with them so they'll probably set off for the rendezvous after their meal. If they all return, we'll have to rethink our plan.'

They finalized their ideas and then gathered what they needed.

'Grab that rope from the corner, Anu,' said Nimal, picking up his gun and hiding it within easy reach of Anu. 'Cut a couple of lengths and knot them so that we can slip them over our hands when Karan returns.'

Anu got the rope ready, and they waited anxiously, wondering if their plan would work. Chandi was busy inspecting the tree house.

A little later they heard the sound of someone climbing up the rope ladder, but no voices.

'Good! He's alone,' muttered Nimal, in Hindi. 'Are you going to be okay with the gun? The safety trigger's on and you can just pretend you're going to shoot.'

'I guess so,' murmured Anu.

They were tense with anticipation. They had tucked their legs under the sheets and wrapped the rope around their wrists.

Karan came up the ladder, a container of food hanging from a rope around his neck. He placed it on the platform, pulled up the rope ladder, and said to the youngsters in his broken English, 'Others gone, but I bring you food.'

He turned to fetch some plates and saw Chandi who was playing with a cup, trying to put it on her head.

He shouted at her, and Chandi, frightened at the angry sound, scampered behind Nimal for safety. Karan followed in an attempt to catch her.

As he knelt down on Nimal's mattress, the boy kicked out and caught Karan a nasty crack on the jaw. The man fell backwards with a thud that knocked all the breath out of him. Nimal was on him in an instant, and Anu, thankful that she did not have to use the gun, helped to tie him up quickly.

To make sure he could not set himself free as they had, he was secured in one corner of the platform, and they ran the rope around a thick branch so that he could not move more than half a metre.

They stood up, and Nimal said, 'I won't gag you since you'll have to remain like that for a long time. We're leaving now, but if we hear you shouting, we'll come back and gag you. You understand me?'

Karan spat out a "yes". He knew they had the upper hand for the time being.

Nimal and Anu grabbed their knapsacks and the WT, and then checked out the tree house quickly. Under the tarp they discovered a crate filled with tusks. Nimal also found a notebook with names and telephone numbers and slipped it into his pocket. They loosed the rope ladder and climbed down quickly, leaving it hanging down – in full sight of anyone who may pass by.

'Straight back to TOOJ?' questioned Anu.

'Yep, let's move,' said Nimal.

They were very pleased with themselves.

'I was wondering if we should call the others on the WT,' said Anu, 'but we don't know exactly where they are, so perhaps we'd better just go and see. What do you think, amigo mio?'

'Agreed,' said Nimal.

They ran through the jungle and were soon at TOOJ where they opened the gate quietly, crept towards the JC, and peeped through the open gateway. The others were fast asleep outside their tents, stretched out on top of their sleeping bags.

As Nimal stepped forward, mischievously wanting to give them a fright, Hunter, who was lying beside Rohan, leapt to his feet and, barking joyfully, raced over to greet them.

CHAPTER 17

Caught in the Act

The others woke in a fright and Rohan reached for the gun, but when they saw Nimal and Anu, they rushed over to join Hunter.

What a reunion! Hunter, shushed several times by Nimal, finally lay down, stretching out over Nimal and Anu's legs, and the JEACs were able to discuss their adventures.

'So we *were* right – they're ivory traders,' said Rohan, once everyone had told their stories. 'I'd love to catch them red-handed and hand them over to the police. Including that chap you left at the CH.'

'What do you suggest we should do?' asked Anu eagerly. 'Those guys must be herding the elephants towards the fence as we speak. We've got to stop them and it's already 8:30.'

'Put on your thinking caps, JEACs,' said Rohan.

They thought hard, discussing possibilities and options.

'I guess it's time to call in the cops,' said Rohan finally, albeit a little reluctantly.

'But it'll take the police at least three to three and a half hours to reach the mid-west fence,' protested Nimal.

'Yeah, but there are, as far as we know, more than five dangerous men trying to kill the elephants,' said Rohan, thoughtfully. 'Right – I have an idea.'

Half an hour later, plans finalized, Rohan, Nimal and Amy were fully equipped. Anu put her camera, which was loaded with high-speed film, into her knapsack. Outside TOOJ, they waited while Mahesika sent out her weird call to Mal-li.

A little later, the huge beast trundled up to the JEACs, greeting them affectionately, and in no time at all, Mahesika, Gina and Mich were seated on Mal-li's broad back. At Mahesika's command, he took them rapidly towards Romesh's bungalow in the south-west corner of the Centre. Mahesika and Mich had WTs.

'Let's hope they get there fast,' said Nimal, looking at his watch. 'It's 9:30, and by the time they get to Romesh's, contact the police and Lalith, and reinforcements arrive at the mid-west fence, I should think it'll be around one in the morning.'

'True,' said Rohan briskly. 'Hopefully, the elephants won't get to the fence before that. Let's get to the rendezvous ASAP.'

They set off – Rohan and Nimal leading the way with Hunter, Anu and Amy close behind. Chandi rode on Amy's shoulder.

They reached the western fence and struggled through the shrubbery, making their way south. It was slow work since there were few trails and they had to force a way through.

'Gosh!' said Nimal, as they heard trumpeting in the distance. 'Those elephants sound pretty angry.'

'Hurry,' said Rohan abruptly.

The fence curved further west, and twenty minutes later, the group came to an abrupt halt. It was 11:35.

'What's that buzzing sound?' whispered Amy.

'Sounds like a saw – softly now,' muttered Rohan, creeping forward with Hunter.

Within minutes, Rohan stopped and pointed. A faint light glowed ahead, the buzzing noise was louder and they heard male voices. Moving cautiously, grateful for the strong wind that shook the bushes and masked their progress, they came to a halt at the edge of the shrubbery – which had thinned out considerably – and peered at the scene before them.

'The thugs,' whispered Amy angrily. 'They've made a humongous hole in the fence.'

'And look! The bottom half of the fence is jagged and will injure the elephants as they go through – making them even more vulnerable,' said Anu. 'We have to do something to stop them.'

'Four guys altogether, and the chap in the Jeep giving the orders must be Mr. CADD,' muttered Rohan. 'I wish we could grab them all.'

'He's obviously a coward,' said Nimal. 'Ready for a quick getaway if the elephants can't be controlled by the others. And that chap in the blue shirt is Ranjan – the chief guy from the hideout.'

'Too bad we can't understand what they're saying,' said Amy. 'They're not bothering to keep their voices down or anything.'

'Well, they've no reason to suspect that there'll be trouble,' said Rohan. 'Ranjan has probably told them that Anu and Nimal are tied up in the CH with no chance of warning the Conservation staff. There's no staff bungalow close by and, to add to everything, the farmer whose land is beyond the fence is in cahoots with them. All in all, I'd say they feel pretty secure.'

'I'm glad they're noisy,' said Anu. 'Keeps them from hearing my camera click.' She had been taking several pictures of the men, including Mr. CADD.

'Okay, I've got enough proof to assist a police case. Obviously, I can't use a flash, but with the high-speed film and the light from their lanterns, the pictures should be fine,' she added. 'But we've simply *got* to do something. Think hard, folks.'

'It's 12:30 now,' said Rohan, 'and no news from Mahesika. Hopefully, this means that they've made contact with the adults. I hope they're okay.'

'Are you sure she's out of range for the WT?' said Amy.

'Yeah – Romesh's bungalow is too far away,' said Nimal.

Five minutes later the men finished their task and sat around chatting and smoking while they had a drink. Mr. CADD did not join them but lay back in the seat of his vehicle.

'Follow me – I have a plan,' said Rohan, moving back into the shrubbery. The others crowded around him, and he continued, 'I don't hear anything to tell us that a herd's in the vicinity – how about making the crooks a little nervous?'

'Good idea, yaar,' said Nimal immediately. 'If we can capture the men – their guns weren't beside them – we may be able to prevent the elephants from breaking out and getting injured.'

They made their plans and then Amy and Nimal took a WT and crept away through the shrubbery. Hunter and Chandi went with them.

Rohan's WT beeped in his ear fifteen minutes later.

'We're right opposite you,' whispered Amy. 'Nimal's just unloading the gun. Over.'

A minute later, a shot rang out, and then another one. Both boys had fired blanks.

The men stopped talking immediately and stood up, looking into the jungle expectantly. But there was no sound of stampeding elephants or shouts from the men herding them in the direction of the fence. After a few minutes, Mr. CADD called out something to Ranjan, who looked at his watch and shook his head. Ranjan spoke to the men who relaxed once more with their drinks and cigarettes.

The moment they were comfortable, Rohan and Nimal ran out of the shrubbery, shouting loudly and pointing their TGs at the men, Anu and Amy at their heels. The men gaped at them but, before they could do more than stand up, the boys had thrown away the guns and tackled the two bigger men, bringing them to the ground. Anu and Amy went after Ranjan but, as they neared him, Anu tripped over a root and fell flat on her face. Amy was distracted for an instant, and Ranjan managed to get to his gun, which was three and a half metres away from him.

Amy, knowing she could not take Ranjan on her own, tried to access the TG strapped to her back, but Ranjan pointed his gun at Anu, who was on her knees, and yelled at the boys saying, 'You no let go my men, I shoot your sister.'

The boys, unwilling to take the risk, released the men who quickly grabbed them in turn, twisting their arms behind their backs. Amy helped Anu to her feet. Mr. CADD did not approach the scene of action, but stood up in the Jeep bellowing instructions – to which nobody paid any attention.

'How you two get loose? Where Karan?' yelled an infuriated Ranjan.

'Tied up in your hideout – he's nice and safe,' said Nimal cheekily. It earned him a cuff on the ear from his captor, but he was past caring.

'Where's Hunter?' asked Anu in Hindi, as she and Amy were herded across to join the boys.

'I told him to stay put,' replied Nimal, also in Hindi. 'Didn't know if Mr. CADD had a gun.'

'What you saying? You talk English only,' shouted Ranjan. 'How many more you are?'

'The Conservation staff and the police will arrive soon,' said Rohan angrily, glaring at Mr. CADD.

'Police?' yelled Mr. CADD. 'You are lying, boy. Nobody will come at this time of the night. You're just trying to frighten us and it won't work.'

'Have it your way,' growled Nimal.

'*Ranjan, mehe ende*,' said Mr. CADD.

Ranjan was just about to hand over his gun to one of the others and go over to Mr. CADD when a loud trumpeting was heard close by.

Everyone froze, the men as well as the youngsters.

CHAPTER 18

An Elephant Never Forgets

Another trumpet sounded and then they heard the heavy thud of an elephant crashing through the jungle.

'Mal-li! STOP! Mal-li, come back! Oh, please, please stop!'

The teens looked at each other in horror. Mahesika, Gina and Mich – what on earth was happening?

Ranjan trained his double-barrelled gun on the boys, ordered his men to let them go, and told them to collect their guns, which they hastened to do.

'I think more children and other elephants, with our men chasing them,' said Ranjan. 'Not Conservation staff or police,' he added nastily to the JEACs.

'It's Mal-li,' muttered Nimal softly, and the others nodded in agreement.

There was a tense moment and then . . . Mal-li crashed into the clearing. He charged towards Ranjan – trumpeting deafeningly. It was a spine-chilling sight!

'Rogue! Rogue!' yelled the other men, throwing down their guns and scrambling to get out of Mal-li's way.

Ranjan stood his ground for a moment and emptied both cartridges at the elephant. But, since his hands were shaking badly, the bullets went astray. Before he could reload or run away, Mal-li reached him, picked him up in his trunk and flung the man nearly five metres away. A nasty crack was heard and Ranjan screamed as his right leg broke at the knee. He yelled for assistance, but the men, attempting to run away, tripped each other up, and the boys promptly took karate stances over them.

'Hunter! Here, boy, quick!' yelled Nimal.

The dog bounded from the shrubbery and stood guard over Nimal's man, growling ominously.

Seconds later, Mahesika, Gina and Mich rushed into the clearing, Mahesika yelling for Mal-li to stop, but for once, the elephant was disobedient. Gina and Mich clung to Mahesika in a desperate attempt to prevent her from reaching the angry animal. Anu and Amy ran to help restrain the anxious girl.

Mal-li stomped over towards where Ranjan was lying, stopping one and a half metres away from the man. He trumpeted angrily once more – immobilizing the entire group, except for Nimal, who approached Mal-li, moving fast but smoothly. When he was three metres away from the elephant, he began to speak in the special voice he used for animals.

To add to the tension, Conservation staff, with the Chief Inspector of Police and his men right behind them, were now entering the clearing. Lalith, in the forefront, took in the situation at a glance and ordered the group to stop immediately, and everyone watched the extraordinary drama unfolding before their eyes. Four Conservation staff trained their TGs on Mal-li.

'Please, *please* help me,' begged Ranjan, trembling with fear. 'He will kill me!'

'*Shut up!*' growled Rohan fiercely. 'Don't move.'

'Mal-li,' said Nimal calmly. 'You know me . . . I won't let anyone harm you. You're a wonderful creature. *You* don't need to debase yourself by killing that horrible man. Come now. Let's move away and calm down.'

Mal-li heard the magical voice and flapped his large ears in acknowledgement of his friend. But he still, desperately, wanted to get at Ranjan. This man had a nasty smell and voice – and Mal-li recognized him as the man who had beaten him with a stick, poked at him, and then shot him when he tried to escape. Mal-li had done him no harm – he had just been with his herd when this man had attacked them.

He trumpeted again, stamping a huge foot, but it was obvious that he was listening to Nimal. Ranjan cringed, expecting the worst to happen any second.

Nimal stepped between Ranjan and Mal-li, still murmuring in a low voice. 'Now, you just come with me, Mal-li. He's a bad man, and we'll let the police take care of him. He can't run away because his leg's broken – you've done your part. Is he the one who tried to kill you and your herd? Is that why you hate him?'

As Nimal reached the huge animal, everyone tensed – would Mal-li listen to the boy and save Ranjan from a certain death or was his desire for revenge too strong?

Confidently, still talking soothingly, Nimal put out his hand and touched Mal-li's trunk. The elephant stood still – Nimal stroked him gently and then, as Mal-li finally turned his head to look at him, the boy grasped the rope tied around the elephant and led him away from Ranjan. Mal-li went without protest, caressing the boy's head with his trunk and blowing gently down his neck. Six or seven metres away from Ranjan, at Nimal's command, the elephant stopped.

'Mahesika,' called Nimal, 'if you, Mich and Gina come over and stay with him, I think he'll be okay.'

The girls ran over and Mal-li greeted them lovingly, wrapping his trunk around Mahesika, as if to apologize for disobeying her earlier. She told him to lie down and he obeyed immediately. Chandi, who had been hiding in the trees, came down to sit on his head.

A loud cheer went up from the staff and police, who were relieved beyond words – they had been terrified that Nimal would be killed.

'How on earth did that elephant find this crook?' asked one of the police officers.

'Ranjan was shouting loudly, and the breeze was blowing his scent towards Mal-li,' said Nimal. 'Mal-li recognized him immediately; remember the saying, *An Elephant Never Forgets.*'

The police rounded up the three crooks, and Hunter was released from guard duty. He joined Mal-li and licked him affectionately.

One of the staff, along with a police officer, got directions from Nimal and Anu as to where, exactly, the CH was located, and went off to get Karan.

Rohan suddenly turned around, looking beyond the fence for Mr. CADD. 'Blow! He's escaped!' he exclaimed.

'Who has?' asked Tony.

'We think it must have been Mr. CADD,' said Rohan gloomily. 'I guess he drove off during all the commotion.'

'Mr. Who?' asked the Chief Inspector of Police.

'One of the leaders,' said Nimal.

The Chief Inspector questioned the crooks in Sinhala, then turned to Rohan and said, 'It was a Mr. Kurukulaarachchi.'

'That's him all right,' said Rohan.

'Don't worry, young man,' said the Chief Inspector, 'there's only one road he could have taken, and some of our chaps were using that route to get here. They had instructions to take anyone on the road at this time of the night to the police station for questioning.'

'Great!' said Anu. 'I do have pictures in my camera, but it would be more satisfactory if you were able to catch him tonight. What about the farmer? Is there proof that he's involved?'

'We're checking on that, miss,' said the Chief Inspector, 'and we'll let you know what happens. We should have information soon.'

'Jagith called us today – or rather, as it's now close to 2 a.m., yesterday – to tell us about his discoveries,' said Lalith. 'But, for now . . .'

He trailed off as angry trumpeting, and the unmistakable sound of a herd of elephants crashing through the jungle, was heard – Mal-li lumbered to his feet and trumpeted back.

'The other crooks and the herd,' yelled Nimal, over the trumpeting. 'We've got to head them away from here! C'mon! There's no time to lose. Mahesika, I've got to take Mal-li! Maybe he can stop them. I'll ride him.'

'Along with two of us,' said Lalith, immediately signalling Tony to join him.

Mahesika stepped back at once, and Nimal wrapped Mal-li's trunk around his waist and was lifted on to the broad back. Lalith and Tony were lifted up next, along with their TGs.

'Mal-li, let's go meet the herd,' said Nimal, patting the elephant's huge head. With the JEACs and everyone else following closely, Mal-li headed into the jungle, going towards the sound of the stampeding elephants; he seemed to understand exactly what Nimal wanted him to do.

Recognizing his herd, Mal-li trumpeted loudly once more and the herd trumpeted back; they appeared to be very close. Nimal brought Mal-li to a halt and all three descended from Mal-li's back. Both men had their TGs ready.

'Let Mal-li meet them on his own,' said Nimal. 'I'm sure he's communicating with them. Go on, Mal-li!'

Mal-li went forward, trumpeting loudly. There was a single, answering trumpet and then the leader – a huge male tusker – came into view. Seconds later he was joined by three other tuskers and four younger males.

They had to stop since Mal-li was blocking their path and, after all, he was part of their herd. They appeared to communicate silently for a few seconds. Then the leader, with a final, angry trumpet, turned south and led the herd away. Mal-li did not go with them.

A few minutes later, five panting men arrived on the scene. They were quite unprepared for their reception committee and, as they were too exhausted to run, the police rounded them up at gunpoint and led them away.

Everyone returned to the clearing near the fence. Mal-li was praised and petted, and he loved the attention.

'Here's the rest of our team,' said the Chief Inspector, as they reached the fence and saw three police Jeeps on the other side. 'I believe they've got your Mr. CADD.'

'Yes,' said Lalith, recognizing the cowering crook.

'Yippee!' yelled the JEACs, and the staff joined in the cheer.

'You JEACs are something else!' said Lalith. 'Thanks to you, and the information Jagith gave us, I think we have finally rid the Conservation of all the bad guys – at least, for the next few years.'

'I would like to hear the full story, sir,' said the Chief Inspector. 'I need it for my report and the case hearing.'

'Does it have to be tonight, Chief Inspector?' asked Sanjay, glancing at the girls who all looked pale and exhausted.

'No, of course not. We'll come over tomorrow, after these youngsters have had a rest. We'll have our hands full for now, getting statements from the thugs.'

'Then I think it's time we returned to the house,' said Lalith. 'Let's all have something hot to drink and . . .' He broke off with a laugh as the JEACs yelled . . .

'Tons and tons to eat! We're simply STARVING!'

'Okay! I was going to say *sleep*, but you can sleep *after* you've been fed,' laughed Lalith. 'Right – jump into the Land Rovers, JEACs – and let's get back.'

'I'll see you in the morning, folks,' said Tony, who had been busy on the mobile. 'Romesh and I are going to stay here until the fence is repaired. I've called the carpenters, and they're on their way. It shouldn't take too long. Excellent work, JEACs – see you later.'

More staff arrived and stayed on to help mend the fence.

'What about Mal-li?' said Sanjay, stroking the huge beast affectionately.

'Why don't you and I take him to the house?' said Kumar.

'Right, yaar,' said Sanjay.

They mounted Mal-li, and set off, while the Land Rovers took the JEACs back to the main bungalow, which was ablaze with lights.

'Thank goodness you're all safe,' said Priyani, hugging them. 'What would we have said to your parents if you'd been injured?'

Everyone wanted to know what had happened, but seeing how exhausted the JEACs were, they fed them and bundled them off to their tents. Gina and Mich had fallen asleep at the table and were carried to their tent by Lalith and Sanjay.

'Don't set any alarms,' were the last words Rohan heard as he changed and tumbled into his sleeping bag.

CHAPTER 19

Reunions, Recountings and Relocations

It was almost 11 a.m. when Rohan awoke, feeling completely rested and ready for more action. He unzipped the flap of the tent and peered out to see if the girls were stirring, and saw Anu, seated on a log near the waterhole, chatting with Umedh as they watched the rabbits playing around in the grass.

'Hey, yaar, great to see you,' said Rohan joining them and greeting his mate with a friendly punch. 'I thought you weren't due till 3 p.m.'

'Well, firstly, I couldn't get a seat on the same flight as your pater; and secondly, I was dying to see all of you as soon as possible. So, since my flight arrived last evening and Kithum was scheduled to attend a 10:30 meeting here this morning, he offered to bring me if I didn't mind leaving in the early hours of the morning. We got here around ten, since there was hardly any traffic.'

'And, you know what's weird, Rohan?' said Anu.

'You?' teased Rohan.

'Pest! I dreamed that Umedh was here earlier than expected; that he had turned into an elephant and was trumpeting outside our tent. I woke up with a start and couldn't help giggling, which, of course, woke Amy. I told her about the dream and then, since we were both up, I got dressed first. It was about 10:15 when I came out and sat here, and a few minutes later – guess who turns up!'

'Spooky, to say the least,' said Umedh with a wide grin.

'Get used to it, yaar,' laughed Rohan, winking slyly at him. 'She has some bizarre dreams.'

'I wonder what's taking Amy so long?' said Anu, looking around. 'I thought she'd be dressed and out here ages ago.'

'Here she comes,' said Rohan, hiding a smile.

Amy greeted Umedh with a hug and a kiss and, after hearing his explanation as to his early arrival, said teasingly, 'I'm glad you came early, *yaar*. Found us far too enticing to wait and come up with Uncle Jack and Uncle Jim, eh? Did you dream about our adventures?'

'Definitely, *yaar*. Anu's been telling me the story. Next time, though, don't you dare leave me out, or I'll turn very grouchy,' said Umedh, pretending to frown.

'Peace, buddy! Yes, I think you'll have to be part and parcel of our adventures from now on,' said Amy. 'What do you say, Anu?'

'That depends. Can you *sing*, sir?' said Anu, glaring at Umedh mockingly.

'I can but try, ma'am,' said Umedh meekly. 'But surely you don't expect me to sing right now?'

'No way! If you do, it'll scare the rabbits away from the waterhole, and all the other creatures for miles around,' mocked Rohan.

'Yeah, poor things,' said Amy.

'He may not be a Pavarotti, Anu, but he's definitely a "Q" – invents the most amazing gadgets,' said Nimal, joining them and shaking hands with Umedh. 'We call him "U" at school!'

The girls chuckled heartily, while Chandi, seated on Nimal's shoulder, shook hands with Umedh in a very prim and proper manner, much to everyone's amusement.

'I guess we can *consider* him since Chandi seems to like him,' said Anu. 'But the final say should be Gina and Mich's, if they ever wake up.'

'Here they come,' said Nimal.

Gina and Mich shrieked with joy when they saw Umedh, running up to hug the boy boisterously, while Hunter licked him lavishly.

'That's it, then, yaar,' said Rohan, slapping Umedh on the back. 'You're stuck with us for good.'

Umedh wiped his face, once Hunter had finished greeting him, and turned to speak to Mahesika, who had come up behind Mich and Gina. 'I'm *so* happy to meet you, Mahesika – I've already met Mal-li – man, what an amazing creature he is. Such a friendly soul! You have to tell me the story of how you found him.'

'Sure,' said Mahesika, warming to him immediately. 'But we should go to the bungalow now because the girls told me they were . . .'

'ABSOLUTELY STARVING!' yelled Mich and Gina, who had far too much energy to keep still and were dancing around the others.

'Me, too!' said Nimal. 'Let's go. All stories must wait – stomachs first.'

'Good afternoon, JEACs! Come on in. We have no laurel wreaths to crown you with, but we *can* offer you food,' said David, who was the first to spot them as they arrived at the door of the living room.

They laughed at his teasing and walked into the room, which was crowded with adults.

'Are you *sure* you're awake?' teased Neeka.

'Very much so,' said Nimal, 'and, though I don't want to inconvenience anyone, the kiddies are – shall we say – fairly ready for – er – ummm ...'

He trailed off with a grin and joined in the yell of 'WE'RE STARVING!'

'I'm sure *even Uncle Leo* heard that!' grinned Lalith. 'And he's about an hour's drive away at the moment, bringing Jack and Jim to join us.'

'Let's feed them first,' said Priyani, ushering the merry group into the dining room, where the table had been expanded to accommodate everyone.

'Stories when everyone's here,' said Lalith firmly.

Niranjani and Shalini had obviously gone to town where the meal was concerned, and it was a satiated group of JEACs who finally rose from the table. They thanked the two women for the wonderful food and then went into the back garden to greet Mal-li. He was perfectly content since the kitchen staff were spoiling him with lots of fruit, and, after spending a little time with him, the JEACs followed the adults to the Cinnamon Centre and joined Tony, who was standing outside.

'It's easier for large groups to meet here,' explained Tony, when Amy asked him whether Aunty Matty would not be joining them. She had been very keen on hearing the story, too. 'Aunty Matty and Priyani will come along with Uncle Leo, Jim and Jack. Plus, there are going to be at least 50 to 60 members of the relocation team joining us soon. They arrived last night and are camping around some of the other staff bungalows.'

'Did they all come from Africa?' asked Gina.

'No, Gina,' said Tony. 'There are fifteen Africans and the rest are Sri Lankans, experienced in relocating animals and eager to assist us.'

'Everybody wants to hear your story – from start to finish,' said Lalith. 'Jagith will also be here shortly, to report on his findings.'

'Good,' said the Chief Inspector who, along with some of his colleagues, had just joined the group. He was delighted to meet the JEACs again. 'It will help us to put the case together once we have all the facts.'

His officers joined the stream of people filing into the auditorium; Ken, Kithum, Molly, Akka and Akki were directing people to seats.

The JEACs saw the group of Africans go into the auditorium; then, a little later, they met up with Jagith, who had heard about the capture of the crooks and was eager to hear the story. The JEACs, in turn, wanted to know what he had discovered. However, Jagith was shepherded into the auditorium with Fareez and Sanjay, while the others waited for Leo's Land Rover, which was just driving up.

'Dad! Uncle Jack! Uncle Jim! Uncle Leo!' yelled the JEACs. Hunter's joyful barks and wet tongue added to the exuberant reunion, while Chandi chattered excitedly and leapt from shoulder to shoulder.

'Whoa! You folks haven't changed a bit,' said Jack Larkin, beaming at everyone and trying to stop Hunter from knocking him over. 'We hear you've been causing more trouble, as is inevitable when you're together. You *do* realize that you're getting a bad name among crooks the world over, don't you? In fact, you're overworking the poor police force.'

'You also appear to be considerably more energetic than usual and have been adding to your menagerie,' said Jim Patel, cuddling Chandi who, taking a sudden liking to him, had leapt straight into his arms. 'I assume you are Mahesika,' he continued, as he and Jack shook hands with the girl. 'Where's this famous Mal-li?'

'He's over at the bungalow,' said Mahesika shyly. 'You'll meet him later.'

'Okay, folks, now that everyone's here, it's time to start the meeting,' said Kithum, coming out to greet the newcomers and usher everyone into the auditorium.

The JEACs and Jagith, along with Chandi and Hunter, were seated in the front rows since they would have to go on stage to speak into the microphones. Chandi was in Umedh's arms while Hunter sat beside him.

When requested to do so, the JEACs narrated their story, and everyone listened in absolute silence, enthralled by their tale of adventure. They were astounded at how the youngsters had dealt with the many challenges facing them. Anu, as usual, was elected as the chief narrator, and she made sure that all the JEACs, including Mahesika, participated in recounting the tale.

The diary, which Nimal had found in the CH, was a wealth of information and the police had already made some arrests based on its contents.

Jagith's information was new to the JEACs and filled in important details. He and his friends had made inquiries about Mr. CADD and the farmers who owned the land just west of the Conservation. Fortunately, there was only the one corrupt farmer – and the police had already received incriminating evidence against him.

'We managed to find witnesses who knew when and where Mr. CADD and the crooked farmer met,' said Jagith. 'Also, one of the waiters at the hotel where Mr. CADD stayed whenever he came here had been bribed to keep his mouth shut. However, when questioned, the waiter was eager to confess that he'd felt really bad about the whole situation. He handed over all the money Mr. CADD had given him and asked that it be donated to the Conservation, since he'd never felt comfortable enough to use it. He's also willing to appear as a witness for the case and gave us names and descriptions of everyone who met up with Mr. CADD. Man! It sure is a mixed group. Apparently the waiter's daughter, who's crazy about animals, had been crying because so many elephants were being killed and had begged her father to help the police to catch the crooks.'

'And remember the worker who left in a hurry after the bomb explosion?' said Tony. 'We wondered if he had any connection with Mr. CADD – and he did! He confessed everything when the police questioned him this morning. He, too, had been heavily bribed by Mr. CADD, and since his wife is extremely ill, he was tempted by the money which would pay the medical bills. His wife will be given good, free medical attention, and the man is willing to testify at the hearing, too.'

'Were they only after ivory, or were there any other criminal activities?' asked Umedh.

'It's a massive racket,' replied the Chief Inspector. 'We don't have the complete picture yet, but ivory trading was only a part of their scam. We believe they're involved with drugs and other illicit trading, including gun running.'

'Whew! That's some adventure,' said Lalith, when all the many questions had been answered. 'I think the JEACs, Jagith, Hunter, Mal-li and Chandi, in particular, and all the others who helped in one way or the other, deserve a hearty cheer.'

He led the packed auditorium in three rousing cheers, which nearly raised the roof.

'Something we have realized, very clearly, is that we need to take more stringent security measures in ensuring that people who enter the Conservation, to visit or work, have actually left at the end of the day; or we should have a record of why they're still here, and where they are,' continued Lalith. 'To this end, we've already spoken to Greg Patel, who's agreed to write a computer program – as a donation to us – to enable us to keep better records. We'll also have a rubber stamp, probably of an elephant, which will be placed on the back of everyone's hand, and we'll use a different coloured stamp for each day of the week.'

'That's a great idea,' said the Chief Inspector. 'I have a brother who makes rubber stamps, and he's crazy about animals, too. I'm sure he would be willing to donate the stamps to the Conservation.'

'Thank you,' said Lalith. 'We'd be most grateful.'

After a few more announcements, one of which was that the wall was completed – in record time, thanks to the volunteers – Tony took over from Lalith.

'We're going to break for lunch, and then please return here so that we can discuss the relocation process. I know a number of you are involved in this, but even if you aren't, feel free to stay on if you're interested in hearing the plans. It's now 1:30 and we'll reconvene in an hour.'

The meeting dispersed. Aunty Matty, David and Leo came up to speak to the JEACs and Jagith, prior to returning to the bungalow.

'The things you children get involved in,' said Aunty Matty, sounding quite shocked. 'Someone should write a book about all your adventures.'

'We're hoping Anu will do that, Aunty Matty,' said Amy. 'She's writing about the other two adventures as well.'

'Who's not well?' asked Leo, hearing the tail end of Amy's comment. He had turned off his hearing aid after the meeting.

'We're all as fit as fiddles, thanks, Uncle Leo,' said Rohan.

'Riddles? Who's going to ask them?' said Leo.

'TURN ON YOUR HEARING AID, UNCLE LEO,' roared David, making everyone within five metres of him jump in fright. 'Otherwise,' he continued *sotto voce*, winking at the JEACs who were struggling to hold back their laughter, 'the conversation will be more confusing than a riddle!'

Leo heard him, turned on his hearing aid, and said mildly, 'No need to shout, my boy. I'm not *quite* deaf yet. Now, what was it you were saying, Matty?'

'Never you mind,' said Aunty Matty. 'Let's go and get some tea. Goodbye, children – we'll see you later.'

The JEACs waved to her and Leo and then burst into laughter.

'What's the joke, kids?' said Jack, coming up just then.

'Just Uncle Leo,' chuckled Anu.

'Hmmm, great chap; awfully confusing to talk to at times,' said Jack with a grin. 'JEACs, I'd like you to meet the leaders of our relocation team. This is Tswalu, the manager.'

'I am very pleased to meet all of you,' said Tswalu, bowing from the waist as he shook hands with each of them. He was a giant of a man, at least six foot five inches tall. 'Allow me to introduce my colleagues –

Lana, Mulalo, Kwazulu and Modupe. We were very interested in your story and think that you can assist us with relocating the elephants. Would you be willing to brainstorm with us?'

'Of course,' said Nimal, immediately. 'What do you want us to do?'

'Once the main meeting is over, our team, along with Jack, Jim, Lalith, Tony and others, will be gathering to discuss a new and innovative idea. Would you join us after that so that we can share our ideas with you and get your input?'

'Sure thing. We'll do whatever you wish,' said Rohan, and the others nodded eagerly.

'What time do you want us and where?' asked Nimal.

'I believe this is the best place to meet,' said Jack, 'and it'll be a couple of hours before we're ready for you.'

'Righto!' chorused the JEACs.

'During that time we'll go back to the bungalow and return with Mal-li, so everyone can meet him,' said Anu. 'Is that okay?'

'Excellent idea, Anu,' said Jack.

After a quick lunch, the meeting reconvened, the leaders of the African Relocation Team taking the stage, along with Lalith, Jack and Jim.

It was interesting to hear about the way in which elephants were relocated.

'There are, as most of you know, various methods used to relocate elephants. Briefly, they can be darted with anesthetic, moved into crates, revived with the reversal agent and then loaded on to trucks; or they are tranquillized and a crane lifts them, by their feet, and loads them into the trucks and, I'm sure, depending on the country and expertise of the teams, there are many other ways of relocating them. We're a little unconventional and use a combination of these methods along with some of our own ideas,' said Tswalu.

'We herd the elephants into a clearing and hem them in by surrounding the area with working elephants. We have found that the working animals calm down the wild ones.

'Then we dart the adults and teenage males with a dose of anesthetic; when they fall asleep, with the assistance of the working elephants, and sometimes a crane – if we can get one – we put them on to conveyor belts which carry them into large trucks. The infants just follow their parents.

'Once inside the trucks, the elephants are given a reversal agent and, when they revive, we tranquillize them to keep them calm, and we also provide them with lots of food. The loaded trucks are driven to the new location and the elephants are encouraged to move out of the truck –

which they are only too glad to do – and then they wander off into their new home.'

'Man – that must be a sight to behold! But how will you know that all the elephants have been moved?' asked Jagith, who was fascinated by the whole idea of relocating elephants.

'We have tagged all the elephants in the herds and know exactly how many there are,' replied Lalith. 'There are nine herds in this jungle – a total of 127 elephants, including Mal-li and the infants.'

'That'll be quite a task, won't it?' said the Chief Inspector, who had stayed on.

'We have a team of 60 experienced people,' said Lana. 'We split into smaller groups, and each group is responsible for a single herd. It is our responsibility to move that herd to the designated clearing at the scheduled time. All things being equal, we should be able to move the elephants, over a period of eight or nine days, to the new location.'

'I know it's a great deal of hard work, folks,' said Jack, 'but we have experienced workers and some new ideas which may make the relocation even easier.'

'May I come and watch some of it?' asked the Chief Inspector eagerly.

'You would be most welcome, and also any others here,' said Tswalu, politely, smiling at the group. 'I am sure you won't put yourselves or anyone else in danger by not following instructions.'

'Will you be relocating any other animals?' asked Amy.

'The Sri Lankan team have their own experts in that area,' said Mulalo. 'However, depending on how smoothly the relocation of the elephants goes, we may stay to assist with the other animals, too.'

'Which other animals will be relocated?' asked Umedh.

'Limited numbers of sloth bears, leopards and wild boar,' said Lana. 'Since there are plenty of birds, monkeys, deer and other small wildlife in the NC, none of them will be relocated.'

The team leaders waited for more questions, but none were forthcoming. Most of those present were eager to watch the actual relocation of the elephants.

'And, Tswalu, once your work is completed, you must stay on for our fundraising event,' said Neeka. 'It's on a Saturday – about eleven days away.'

'We would like that very much indeed,' said Tswalu with a bow. 'Thank you.'

The meeting dispersed and the JEACs went back to the bungalow, Jagith and the Chief Inspector joining them for a late tea.

It was 5:30 p.m. when they returned to the auditorium with Mal-li. The leaders of the Relocation Team were outside, waiting to meet them.

Mal-li enjoyed all the attention and his little eyes twinkled as he allowed everyone to fuss over him. He lay down and waved his trunk at them, trumpeting in delight.

After a little while, leaving Hunter and Chandi to keep Mal-li company, everybody went inside and Lalith asked Jack to take the lead.

'We have a very simple plan which, we believe, could be highly effective,' said Jack. 'The elephants have been traumatized a great deal over the past few months, and we'd like to avoid causing them more grief. Based on Nimal's ability to deal with animals, Mal-li's friendship with Mahesika and the way he listens to both her and Nimal, and the fact that we have a great team who are open to new and innovative ideas, we have come up with an unusual plan of action.'

'It's actually a bit of an experiment,' said Tswalu. 'Jack and Jim suggested it this evening, after we had heard about Mal-li.'

'You mean you're not going to move them as you normally do, Tswalu?' asked Neeka.

'That's right, ma'am. We're convinced that the new plan is more humane, and if it works – great! If not, we'll revert to our usual routine.'

'Tell us, please,' said Nimal eagerly.

'As you all know,' said Jack, 'a section of the jungle has been cleared around the fence in the north of the OC, and tonight, a gap will be made in the fence. This gap is close to the road, which leads to the entrance of the NC, and trucks will be in place, not only blocking the gap, but ready to transport the elephants. Our teams, riding on working elephants, will drive one herd at a time into this clearing. Once the elephants are in the clearing, we'll have tranquillizer shots ready – if required – to keep them calm. But first, we'd like to see if Nimal can "charm" the leader of each herd and make friends with him or her, keeping Mal-li beside him as a token of good faith towards the elephants.'

'Oh, Nimal can do it – easily,' said the other JEACs immediately.

'Also, we thought Mahesika could ride on Mal-li and give him his commands, one being that if Tswalu sees the slightest sign of any danger to Nimal or Mahesika, he will tell Mahesika, and she will immediately instruct Mal-li to grab Nimal and move out of the way while we use the working elephants and tranquillizers,' continued Jack.

'B-b-ut,' stammered Mahesika, 'I don't know if I can control Mal-li like that. Nimal would be better.'

'You can do it, Mahesika,' said Nimal encouragingly.

The rest of the JEACs also assured the girl that they had the utmost confidence in her ability to work with Mal-li.

Mahesika looked around shyly. She simply could not let them down. 'Okay – I'll do my best.'

'We know you're both up to the challenge,' said Jim. 'If this works, then the next stage will be for Nimal to guide the leader into the truck. Once the rest of the herd see their leader befriend Nimal, they will, we're almost positive, follow their instincts and trust him, too, allowing him to lead them into the other trucks. We will have lots of fruit, injected with mild sedatives, to tempt the animals and calm them down without knocking them unconscious.'

'There will also be a space between the driver's cabin and the main body of each truck, for some of us with tranquillizers – just in case we need them,' continued Tswalu. 'Nimal will be in the truck which has the leader of the herd, who will be able to see, smell and hear him.'

'Awesome,' breathed Anu. 'It will certainly be less traumatic for the elephants, but won't it take longer?'

'Actually, no,' said Tswalu. 'It's much more time consuming to follow our normal procedure and move unconscious elephants. We think that, if this experiment works, we can move all the herds within six days – or even less.'

'Man! That'll be some sight,' said Umedh, and the others agreed.

'So, Nimal, what do *you* think?' asked Tswalu.

The boy had been very thoughtful for the past few minutes.

'I like the idea. It's a snapper!' said Nimal with a grin. 'I guess I only have one question at this point. If the elephants are going to eat all those goodies, where do I come in? I need food to keep me calm, too.'

The meeting broke up in a shout of laughter. Nimal was assured that they would have tons of snacks for him, too – *without* hidden sedatives – and that he would be well fed.

'May I take pictures?' asked Anu.

'Of course you may,' said Tswalu. 'It's always great to have extra pictures. Our camera crew and the Sri Lankan crew will be here soon. We always keep records of our relocations, especially new ideas – it assists us when we review them, and we constantly search for ways in which to improve our methods.'

'Glad I brought my camera, too,' said Jagith and Umedh together.

'When's kick-off?' asked Rohan.

'As we speak, the working elephants are being taken to the various locations. After an early dinner, the teams will move out to join them,' said Lana.

'By tomorrow morning around 5:30, the first herd should be ready for relocation,' said Kwazulu. He smiled at the astonished exclamations and explained. 'Lalith's staff have a good idea of the current location of each herd, and we'll start with those closest to the northern border of the Conservation.'

'The Land Rovers will leave around 3:30 a.m. from our bungalow, so as to reach the site in good time. Sanjay, who has bonded very well with Mal-li, will take him over this evening to the residence near the northern gates. The clearing's only half an hour's walk from there,' said Lalith. 'You JEACs and Jagith can come with us. Chief Inspector, you can stay at the northern bungalow and come with Sanjay.'

'Now, we've got lots to do, so let's move,' said Tony.

'Man! I'm *so* glad I'm here,' said Umedh, as the JEACs walked to the bungalow with Jagith and Jack. 'I wouldn't have missed this for the world.'

'We're glad you could come, too, yaar,' said Rohan. 'Plus, you haven't seen Nimal with the larger animals.'

'Early night for all of us,' said Amy. 'I don't want to be late tomorrow.'

'Definitely,' said Jack, looking at his watch. 'It's nearly seven and I'm POSITIVE you won't want to miss dinner.'

'Of course not,' shouted Gina and Mich, excitedly. 'Nimal's simply *starving!*'

Nimal chased them into the bungalow and after a quick meal, the JEACs ran off to their tents. Umedh would share the tent with the boys, while Jagith had a room in the house.

****

They were up at 2:30 a.m. and after a mug of hot chocolate and some sandwiches, everyone piled into the Land Rovers, wide awake and raring to go.

They reached the site and found three humongous trucks parked in the gap, their ramps easily accessible to the elephants. Each truck could hold four fully grown elephants and, fortunately, none of the herds had more than ten adults. Mal-li was already there with Sanjay and the Chief Inspector, and there were also twelve working elephants, along with their mahouts. After the JEACs went over to pet Mal-li, Nimal quickly made friends with the other elephants – who, naturally, wanted to follow him – but since they were very well trained and obeyed their mahouts implicitly, they merely blew affectionately at Nimal, and stayed in their allotted places. Members of the relocation team stood around patiently, drinking hot tea and munching on snacks. The camera crews had already set up their equipment, and some of them were perched in the surrounding trees.

Everything was in place and Nimal waited for instructions from Tswalu, while Mahesika and Mal-li stood beside Lana.

Around 5:10, Tswalu's mobile rang. After listening intently, he rang off and said, 'Absolute silence now, please, and everyone take your positions. They're fifteen minutes away.'

Soon the sound of elephants moving through the jungle reached their ears. Nimal entered the centre of the clearing, Mahesika astride Mal-li, a few metres behind him. Four of the working elephants moved to either side of Mal-li – everyone else, other than the eight remaining working elephants and their mahouts, moved out of sight, and the team members were alert, TGs at the ready.

Nimal was quite calm. As soon as the leader of the herd, a humongous matriarch, reached the entrance to the clearing, Nimal began to speak as he moved forwards, making sure his scent was wafted to her. Everybody watched in awe, wondering at the boy's fearlessness and his wonderful gift of being able to communicate with any animal – tame or wild – and make them trust him. He made no hurried movements and just spoke in the low special voice he used with animals. The matriarch stopped and listened intently. She liked the scent of this boy and knew instinctively that he meant no harm to either her or the herd. When Nimal came to a stop, less than half a metre away from her, she reached out her trunk and touched him gently. Nimal caressed her trunk and then began to walk slowly towards the truck, up the ramp and into it. The matriarch followed him, and so did the rest of the herd – they all wanted to touch the boy.

In an incredibly short time, the entire herd – numbering thirteen in total (nine adults and four infants) – had entered the three trucks, and were munching peacefully at the delicious food laid out for them. Mal-li's presence, along with that of the other elephants, appeared to add to their feeling of safety; on Tswalu's instructions, Mahesika made Mal-li stand beside the entrance to each truck as Nimal led the elephants in – Mal-li trumpeted softly and they trumpeted back. Once they were ready to set off, Nimal returned to the truck which carried the matriarch and sat in the special cabin behind the driver. The matriarch could see and hear him, and she did not panic when the truck began its slow journey, since Nimal continued to talk to her. Tswalu and Modupe, who sat beside Nimal with their TGs ready for action, breathed a sigh of relief – they would not need to use the tranquillizers.

The next stage was easy. The truck reached the NC, and, once they were safely inside, the gates locked and the entrance blocked by more working elephants and a team of twelve staff with tranquillizers, Nimal climbed out. The huge doors of the truck were opened, and Nimal encouraged the elephants to come out, which they were happy to do. Nimal patted each of them, focusing on the matriarch once more, and then climbed into the open Jeep which was waiting to transport him back to the OC. The matriarch, seeing that the boy was going, gave him one last caress with her trunk, and then led her herd into the jungle. The Jeep and the trucks returned to the OC.

Everyone was absolutely thrilled at the success of the plan.

'Man, Nimal! You are amazing! I think you had better come back with me. And Mahesika and Mal-li, too,' said Tswalu, beaming all over his face. 'My relocations would be so much simpler, the elephants would not be traumatized, and we'd save hours of precious time.'

'That was just awesome, yaar,' said Umedh, clapping Nimal on the shoulder. 'I've seen you with small creatures, but this – this was something else!'

'Wish you had seen him with Mal-li – when Mal-li was in a temper,' said the Chief Inspector. 'My eyes nearly fell out of my head.'

Jagith, who had never seen Nimal in action before, was speechless, and just shook hands with him vigorously.

'It's a gift from God,' said Nimal, humbly. 'I'm just glad to have opportunities to use it often.'

'True! It's a real blessing,' said Jim, and the others agreed.

'Actually, having Mal-li and Mahesika standing behind me really helped the elephants to stay calm,' said Nimal.

'You're probably right, Nimal,' said Jack. 'I think we'll be finished in record time. Any suggestions for improving the plan, Tswalu? Anyone else?'

'I cannot think of one,' said Tswalu.

'I can,' said Nimal, with a grin. 'What about your promise?'

They fed him!

'Tswalu, is it too risky or do you think we can take turns to ride on Mal-li with Mahesika,' asked Rohan, who had been having a whispered conversation with Mahesika.

'I'd really like that,' added Mahesika, 'and Mal-li can take four of us at a time.'

'I don't see any harm in it,' said Tswalu slowly, when the others looked at him eagerly. 'The TGs are always ready, and even if the other herds are not as easily managed, I think there would be no danger for whoever is riding on Mal-li. Yes, you can take turns – but I would suggest only three at a time, inclusive of Mahesika.'

'Yippee!' yelled the JEACs.

Naturally, Jagith and the Chief Inspector wanted to be included in everything. It was also agreed that they could go along, in Land Rovers, to the NC and watch the elephants enter their new home.

The entire operation, from the time the elephants had entered the clearing to the time when they disembarked from the trucks in their new home, had taken only five hours.

However, it was still a very long, exhausting day, and although everything went without a hitch, it was 6 p.m. before a tired, dirty group of people arrived back at Lalith's bungalow. Two herds, the ones closest to the clearing, had been relocated.

'I'm bushed,' said Nimal, flopping down on the floor in the drawing room. 'But I have an intense feeling of satisfaction, too. If *I'm* so tired, I hate to think what the rest of you must be feeling, Tswalu.'

'Man, the pure thrill of watching you communicating with the elephants made our job very simple. You, Mahesika and Mal-li, along with the teams who were driving the herds towards us, did the hard work.'

'Definitely,' said Jack. 'It's an amazing team effort. Well done, everyone!'

Mahesika glowed with pleasure. It was the first time she had received such lavish praise, and she was proud to be a part of the team.

'Yes, thanks to Mahesika and Mal-li adopting each other, we've h-had a-a-a w-wonderful e-experience,' said Nimal, valiantly trying to stifle his yawns.

'Early bed for you, son,' said Jim, tousling the boy's hair. 'In fact, an early night for all of you. It's going to be another tiring day tomorrow.'

'I c-could f-fall asleep right now – oooh, excuse moi,' said Nimal, stifling a huge yawn.

'Without food?' asked Anu in a shocked tone. 'Boy, Nimal, the world must be coming to an end!'

'Of c-course not,' said Nimal sitting up hurriedly. 'I'm . . .' he trailed off as the others yelled, 'STARVING!'

The rest of the relocations went very well, too, and there were no major problems at all – except for a small incident while moving the last herd.

'What happened to you?' asked Aunty Matty, looking in horror at Nimal's torn clothes when they returned to the bungalow. 'Was Nimal attacked?'

The group burst out laughing.

'Nimal was adopted by a little rogue, Aunty Matty!' said Anu, with a grin. 'The last herd had only one infant – and she was just a month old. She fell – hook, line and sinker – in love with Nimal and would not let him alone. She followed him wherever he went: clambering up into each truck with him; getting in the way of the other elephants – who, I must say, were very tolerant of her – and, basically, showing him in every way that she adored him.

'She knocked him over a few times with her exuberance and then, after they'd disembarked at the NC, just before she was practically *dragged away* by a couple of others in the herd, she decided she needed a souvenir from her loved one. So, she put her wobbly little trunk into his shirt pocket and pulled. Part of the shirt came away – but was she satisfied? No way!

'Despite the fact that two elephants were in the process of pulling her along, albeit slowly because of her struggles, she managed to wrap her trunk around his left leg, and tugged. Nimal fell over and was dragged a couple of metres along the trail, which happened to be quite gravelly, before Rohan and Umedh, joining in the tug-of-war, managed to disengage the little trunk. She gave a mournful howl as she disappeared into the jungle.'

Aunty Matty looked appalled. 'But he could have been seriously hurt!'

'Oh no, Aunty Matty,' said Rohan. 'If he really was in danger something would have been done immediately. It was a hilarious conclusion to the relocation.'

'And, once you see it on video – yes, they managed to tape that, too – you'll see exactly how funny it was,' said Jim. 'Anu was too busy laughing to take any pictures.'

'*That'll* teach me to be so charming,' said Nimal, grinning widely. 'Now, if only I had the same success with females of my own species . . . ah, well, time for BFB!'

'WHAT?' roared everyone.

'BATH! FOOD! BED!' yelled Nimal cheekily.

CHAPTER 20

Baila Time!

After the relocation, the members of the team were happy to take it easy and relax. Jagith finally went home – he had taken leave from his office so that he could participate in the entire relocation, and he would return for the fundraiser that Saturday. The Chief Inspector, who had stayed on for two days, would also attend the event.

After a day of rest, the JEACs were ready for more. They assisted with the fundraiser; attended youth group meetings at four churches, where they spoke about their group, inviting the young people to join up and attend the fundraiser – which all of them did.

Gina and Mich, after spending a day on their own, came up with a new song for the fundraising event. Gina wrote the words and Mich, with input from Nimal, did the cartoons. Then they ran it past the other JEACs.

'It's superb,' said the teens.

'Let's talk to Neeka about it,' said Umedh.

Neeka was thrilled. 'We'll keep it a secret,' she said. 'We'll involve Jagith – he can sing with you – and Tony will run the slide show. I think you'll only need a few practices with the band and, as they'll be in town on Friday, either Tony or I will take you there to practise for a couple of hours. We'll swear them to secrecy, too.'

Saturday dawned and the fundraiser was a roaring success. It was an open air event, held in the gap between the OC and the NC, and even the weather decided to co-operate by being cool and pleasant instead of hot and humid, or rainy.

The entire town, people from neighbouring areas, and several people from Colombo, attended the event. Aunty Consy, Prithee and her family, and many other family members and friends, turned up and were happy to meet the JEACs and hear about their adventure. Delo

Samaratunge and Jeevana Abeykoon were both there with their families and several other Ministry officials and their families came, too.

Delo was a brilliant speaker and spoke eloquently about the relocation and all the effort that had gone into raising funds for the New Conservation. She congratulated and thanked everyone who had contributed in one way or another. Then she thanked the JEACs, in particular, for the critical part they had played in capturing the rogues who were poaching the elephants.

Jeevana introduced Tswalu, who spoke about the relocation, which was a new experience for the volunteers. They listened avidly to his description of how this particular relocation had worked, and their hopes for the continued improvement of ways in which animals could be relocated, using methods which would cause the least amount of discomfort and stress to the creatures. The video recording of the relocation, projected on the large screen, was watched in an awestruck silence, with thundering applause at the end.

After that, Jeevana asked the JEACs to sing their theme song, while the accompanying cartoons were projected on to the screen. It was encored, and the second time round, the words were also shown on the screen, encouraging everyone to join in. All the children in the crowd clamoured to join the JEACs immediately, and David announced that they would be holding a meeting the following Saturday and everyone was welcome.

Delo concluded the official part of the fundraising event by saying that the New Conservation had a long way to go before everything was set up and ready for visitors. However, with the willing support they had received, she was confident that within three months they would be able to open their gates to the public. She left the stage to the accompaniment of loud cheering.

Neeka, after thanking the crowd for their enthusiastic support, made her speech, which also received lots of applause, and when the crowd had quietened down, she said, 'I would like to present to you, once again, the JEACs and Jagith. Jagith has been of great assistance to us in the past few weeks.'

There was a roar of welcome as the JEACs and Jagith came on stage. The band took their places and Tony turned on the projector.

Neeka lifted her hand for silence and said, 'Friends, we have three more members of our group whom we'd like you to welcome. Mal-li, who is standing just behind the stage – Mahesika, would you go and bring him forward, please?'

Mahesika, blushing slightly, brought Mal-li to the side of the stage. He was applauded vociferously and trumpeted a happy response.

Mahesika left him with Sanjay and the Chief Inspector and rejoined the group on stage.

'Also, please welcome Hunter and Chandi,' said Neeka.

Released by Lalith and Jim, they bounded on to the stage. Hunter, after licking everyone as if he had not seen them in years, sat down sedately. Chandi sat on Nimal's shoulder and whispered into his ear before jumping down to sit on Hunter's back, holding on to him by his collar, while Hunter sat quite still so as not to shake the tiny creature off. The crowd was thrilled and cheered loudly.

Then, to add to everyone's delight, the band began a baila rhythm. The projector was turned on and, as the cartoons drawn by Mich began to appear, the JEACs sang Gina's new composition to the tune of the famous Sinhala song, *Chuda Maani Key*.

> Listen to our song tonight, we know you will agree,
> That our main concern is for the animals to be
> Safe from harm and danger 'cause they need our loving care,
> From the greatest aliya – down to the tiny hare.
>
> Aliyas would break the fence and into danger run,
> Many farmers hated them, they'd shoot them with a gun.
> So the conservationists decided they should find
> A safer living place for them and thus preserve their kind.
>
> All of us are gathered here because we know it's right
> That we move the animals on to a better site.
> We are grateful that the government has lent a hand
> Gave us funds and their support and a great piece of land.
>
> Then we started raising funds, to make our dream come true
> Most of you have contributed and our money grew.
> We have built a wall so strong no aliya can break,
> And the rocky barriers a natural boundary make.
>
> Our kind friends from Africa, they helped us relocate
> Many of the creatures were moved through the northern gate.
> Nimal led the aliyas (and only once he fell),
> Mal-li and Mahesika, and all the teams did well.
>
> This New Conservation will be ready in a while,
> It has lots of trails and campsites that will make you smile.
> And although we know there is a lot of work to do,

It will be a piece of cake with help from all of you!

Also in the OC we've discovered places new,
TOOJ and CH, GOMT and DA, just to name a few.
We are sure that when you visit you will need a map
Don't delay, you're missing out, so make it quite A-sap!

Alighasa Conservation is a jolly place
Anyone who visits it will have a happy face!
We would like to thank you for the work that you have done
Give yourselves a hearty cheer and now let's have some fun!
Oh, give yourselves a hearty cheer and now let's have some fun!
fun! **fun!**

And there we shall leave them, as they were begged, not only to explain all the acronyms in the seventh verse, but to sing their song for the second, third and fourth time, while the large crowd joined in lustily until the whole place rang with music.

See you soon, JEACs – and do tell us – *where will your next adventure be?*

*   *   *

GLOSSARY

Word	Meaning
Acronym	A word formed from the initial letters of other words
Ad-lib	Speak without advance preparation
Albeit	Though
Aliya	Elephant – Sinhala
Amigo mio	Friend of mine – Spanish
Aney	Exclamation – like 'awww' or 'oooh' – Sinhala
APs	Aged Parents – acronym
ASAP	As Soon As Possible – acronym
Aunty/aunties	Nimal uses it on the girls in mock respect
Ayubowan	Respectful Sri Lankan greeting
Binocs	Binoculars – short form
Biscuits	Cookies
Brekker	Breakfast – short form
CH	Crooks' Hideout – acronym
Chin Wag	Have a chat
Confab	An informal private conversation or discussion
CSA	Customer Service Agent
DA	Dense Area – acronym
Dekko	Look – Hindi
Ephalunts	Elephant – fun usage of word
Excuse moi	Excuse me – French
Germ/germs	Gentlemen – fun usage when saying 'ladies and germs'
Hamu	Female employer – Sinhala
Hathi	Elephant – Hindi
Heptad	A group of seven
Hindi	One of the languages of India
Hols	Holidays – short form (vacation)
Homo sapiens	The primate species to which modern humans belong
Jiff/jiffy	A moment – informal usage
Kema hari rassai	The food is very tasty – Sinhala
Kohomade?	How are you? – Sinhala
Lift	Elevator
Lungi/lungis	A length of cloth worn as a skirt in some countries
Machang	Mate/buddy – used most often in Sri Lanka by males
Mahatya	Male employer – Sinhala
Mahout	A person who works with and rides elephants
MAS	Mutual Admiration Society – acronym
Mater	Mother – Latin origin
Mehe ende	Come here – Sinhala

Word	Meaning
Mes amis	My friends – French
Mo	Moment – short form/informal
Mon enfant	My child – French
Moosik	Music – pronounced incorrectly by someone who doesn't speak much English
Namaste	Respectful Indian greeting
Natty/spiffy	Way of saying someone is smart or stylish – informal usage
Nineteen to the dozen	Talks a lot – idiom
No problemo	No problem – fun usage of word 'problem'
Pally	Having a close, friendly relationship
Pater	Father – Latin origin
PC	Politically correct – acronym
Prep	Preparation – short form – used for time everyone does school work
'Q'	Code name for the inventor in the 007 movies
Sari	A garment consisting of six yards of cotton or silk, elaborately draped around the body and traditionally worn by women from the Indian subcontinent
Shukhriar	Thank you – Hindi
Sinhala	One of the languages of Sri Lanka
Sotto voce	In a quiet voice
Stuthi	Thank you – Sinhala
Thambili	King coconut – orange in colour
The BEM	The Brave Exploring Mouse – acronym
The JC	The JEACs' Camp – acronym
TOOJ	Time Out Of Jungle – acronym
Vitamin 'I'	Self-centred person – fun way of saying someone talks about themselves constantly
WC	Wildlife Conservation – acronym
Womyn	Women – an exaggerated way of being politically correct when using the word
WTs	Walkie-talkies – acronym
Yaar	Mate/buddy – most often used in India by males
YCS	Youngsters' Camping Site – acronym

Dear Ms. Lionheart,
I think your book is extremely amazing because it was awesome that these kids could solve and figure out the mystery of the PEACOCK FEATHERS. Every time we stopped reading I was always on the edge about what comes next! I can't wait to read the next book! It won't surprise me if the next book is as OUTSTANDING as this one!!! **From: Brayden – Age 14, Canada.**

Dear Ms. Lionheart,
I loved your book the Peacock Feathers because it includes my two favourite subjects: animals and mystery. I found the story so exciting I did not want to put it down. My favourite character was the dog Hunter, because he played a key part in stopping the poachers. I am looking forward to reading your next book. **From: Alya – Age 12, France.**

Dear Ms. Lionheart,
I like this book because it is fun and exciting. You always want to know what happens next. I'm excited to know what the next book is going to be about. **From: Joshua – Age 11, Canada.**

Dear Ms. Lionheart,
Your book was very good and really interesting. I liked the adventure in it, and how the children planned and caught the poachers. I was sorry for the peacocks when they were caught and left to die, so I was really glad when they got saved. I would like to read another book about the same children solving another animal mystery. **From: Alina – Age 9, France.**

Dear Ms. Lionheart,
My name is Amanda. I am nine years old. I liked your book because it was about saving animals. I especially liked Gina because she wrote good poems. She helped solve the mystery. It was an exciting mystery book. I hope you write another animal book soon. **From: Amanda – Age 9, Canada.**

ABOUT THE AUTHOR

Amelia Lionheart has been writing for many years and is the published author of four books for children. She has a diploma in writing from the Institute of Children's Literature, Connecticut, USA.

Amelia, who has lived and worked in several countries, believes very strongly in the conservation of wildlife and, in particular, the protection of endangered species. She is convinced that awareness of this issue, when imbued in children at an early age, is a vital step towards saving our planet.

As a member of several nature/wildlife preservation organizations, including the Durrell Wildlife Conservation Trust, she invites children and their families to become involved with local zoos and conservation centres and to support their important work, both by creating awareness and fundraising. To encourage this, she created a group called the 'Junior Environmentalists and Conservationists' (the JEACs) in the first book of her JEACs' series, *Peacock Feathers*. In the other books, the JEACs travel to various countries, having adventures while enlarging their group and encouraging local children to start groups of JEACs in their own countries. As of November 2013, Amelia has four *real* groups of JEACs in Canada. The JEACs continue to evolve.

Amelia's other interests include environmental issues, volunteer work and fundraising. She believes that if people from different countries explore the diversity of cultures and learn from one another, they will discover that they have more similarities than dissimilarities. Many of these ideas are included in her books.

Please check out http://www.jeacs.com, Amelia's website for children.